Dog
Soldiers

By Peyton Quinn

Outskirts Press, Inc.
Denver, Colorado

Dog Soldiers MC
By Peyton Quinn

Box 535 Lake George Co 80827

First Printing March 2006

WWW.RMCAT.COM

Outskirts Press
http://www.outskirtspress.com

ISBN is 1-59800-418-2
ISBN13# 9781598004182

Outskirts Press and the "OP" logo are trademarks belonging to Outskirts Press, Inc.
Printed in the United States of America

Dedicated to Melissa,
My wife of nearly 30 years

Peyton and Melissa in 1977.

Peyton and Melissa in 2004.

Dog Soldiers: Prologue

Early morning sunlight illuminated a plume of dust behind the rented sedan as it turned off New Mexico Route 451. The driver slowed the car to a crawl and rolling down the window to study the terrain more closely; the smell of sage and the desert's warm morning air flooded his senses inside the confines of his air-conditioned steel cage.

He checked his odometer reading. Had he missed it, or had he just not gone far enough yet? Outside his car it all looked the same too…just desert, sagebrush, and scrub juniper.

The sedan then came to an abrupt halt.

There it was, the rusted-out 55-gallon oil drum with the yellow splash of paint that he'd been searching for.

To the left of that he could see faint tire marks that had broken the surface of the alkali leaving a discernible trail up the arroyo. The driver cranked the window back up to return to his air-conditioned world and turned the air conditioning up full-blast as he proceeded to follow the tracks into the heat of the New Mexico desert.

He discovered that his breath was now coming a bit more quickly, and he stopped the car for a moment to collect himself and his thoughts. "No need to be uptight. Just relax and go with the flow," he thought.

"Go with the flow," he repeated. Then he realized that he was now speaking to himself out loud.

Three miles later he saw the white Mercedes, and parked beside it was a car he had never seen before. It was a late-model Dodge van conversion. The sliding door of the van was open. Above it an awning protected a man from the desert's harsh morning sun. The man beneath the awning sat at a folding table just outside the open van door.

As the sedan rumbled up to the van, the driver strained to identify the man at the table. As he came a bit closer, he did. It was him all right, no mistaking that.

He was a short, Hispanic man who had a bit of a beer belly. He was about 45 or so, and he wore two large serpentine gold necklaces around his neck. A crucifix was suspended from one of those fine gold chains, and the reflection of desert sunlight occasionally sparkled from it.

A second man then appeared at the door of the van. He dangled his legs outside the big Dodge as he faced the approaching sedan. The driver was now close enough to see that both men were smiling to greet him.

As he emerged from the sedan, he smiled back at them, and raising both his arms with his palms turned toward the man at the table, he spoke.

"Yo! Man, we just got to stop meeting like this," the driver joked.

He wiped the perspiration from his hands onto his jeans and wondered if the strain in his voice had betrayed him as he walked closer to the two men.

"You are so right, my friend," responded the man at the table with a curious tone of sincerity. The man then motioned to the empty chair on the other side of the table from him.

"Sit down, get out of that sun. Let me show you what I got for you."

The driver accepted this invitation and sat under the protection of the awning.

On the table there was a black lacquered box. The Hispanic man opened the box and removed an ornate etched glass plate. He placed it on the table smooth side up. Next, he unscrewed what appeared to be an aluminum cigar tube and tapped out four small lines of white powder onto the glass.

The man screwed the top back onto the metallic cylinder and returned it to the lacquered box. He then withdrew a small, gold-colored metallic straw.

"Perhaps I have even outdone *myself* this time," he exclaimed.

The Hispanic man spoke with a fairly heavy Chicano accent before he placed one end of the tube into his right nostril and the other end to the line of white powder on the glass. An instant later two of the four white lines on the glass disappeared.

The man tossed his head back and made sharp inhalations through his nose before offering the golden tube to the man sitting across the table from him.

"Ah yes!" he continued. "Smooth as a baby's ass, pure as a virgin. It's Star Wars, man!" He inhaled again sharply. "And the Force will be with you!" he declared laughingly.

The driver responded with a wave of his hand to dismiss the offer of the golden tube.

"You know I don't play when I'm doing business, man," the driver declared politely.

The smile slowly drained from the Hispanic man's face. "Hey man, you don't insult me. This is the best shit you've ever seen."

The man emphasized his point by shaking the golden tube at the driver as sunlight reflected off its highly polished surface.

"I'm sure it is," the driver replied calmly. "I don't have to worry about the quality of your product, man. I know that. My only concern is how much? What price? And when?"

"You bet your stinking ass you don't have to worry about the quality of my shit," the Hispanic man responded. "So how much you gonna need?"

"Three kilos for now—if the price is reasonable," the driver said flatly.

"Reasonable?" The Hispanic man tossed up a hand in a gesture of contempt. "Is it reasonable for you to come here and insult my stuff and then not even take a taste like it was some yack shit that they sell down in East L.A.?"

The driver hesitated. His gut told him there was something wrong now.

No, control yourself, he thought. Don't work yourself up into a paranoid sweat. Relax. Go with the flow, he repeated to himself silently, go with the flow.

"Okay," the driver conceded. "You have the best there is, and if it's so damn important to you then I'll take a taste. That make you happy now, man?"

The driver took the gold tube and placed it on the glass to snort the first line.

But as he did he inadvertently exhaled. It was barely a whisper of exhalation, but this blew a good portion of the powder away. Trying to recover from this error, he buried his face into the glass in an attempt to quickly snort up the remaining line and a half.

As he did he heard his host muttering, "You shouldn't have fucked with us like this, man."

The driver raised his face from the glass, and when he did he saw a third man step from the van. He recognized the man even before he saw his face. His eyes dilated in stark terror as he tried to jump from his seat and run.

"No!" the driver screamed as he raised his hands over his face, but his killer had already raised a Ruger Blackhawk .44 Magnum pistol.

Then silence, darkness, oblivion.

With the bullet traveling at 1,420 feet per second, the dead man had never heard the shot that had fired the 200-grain bullet through his brain. Only the living had heard the roar of the pistol and seen a part of the victim's outstretched hand splattered away as the man's head exploded in a pink mist.

The body had fallen over backwards and out of the chair. Now the corpse lay on the sand amidst bits of skull fragments and brain tissue.

"Damn!" the Hispanic man at the table shouted as he turned around to the gunman. "You almost blew my fucking eardrums out!"

The gunman seemed oblivious to this protest.

"Now you listen to me you little monkey!" the gunman yelled. "I told you—you check everybody out with me first! You understand that! Everybody! Otherwise, it's both our fucking asses!"

The Hispanic man at the table was not used to being talked to in this manner and he didn't like it either.

However, glancing at the partially decapitated body before him, he held himself prudently in check. He then spoke clearly and deliberately to the killer. "I understand man. We'll be more careful. We'll do it all just like you say from now on."

The gunman seemed to ignore these words as he pulled a military body bag out of the van and began unfolding a collapsible shovel. Locking out the spade, he carefully scooped up the sand beneath the bits of skull fragments and other tissues and shook them into the body bag. The gunman wore thin, black leather gloves as he rolled the victim's body into the bag.

First he placed the corpse's feet into the bag and then the upper body. Then he zipped the green cocoon shut.

"Remember!" the gunman shouted again, pointing his finger at the man rising from the table, "You clear everybody with me first. Everybody!"

Dog Soldiers: Chapter 1

Captain Shields of the Mountain View Police Department had reached his late 50s, but he'd made a serious effort to keep himself in good physical shape. He exercised daily, and though it was now gray, he still had a full head of hair.

Shields studied the photograph on the first page of the police file on his desk and then looked up to study the man who was now sitting in his office. The man in the picture wore a U.S. Army uniform with the insignia of U.S. First Air Cavalry.

In the photo the soldier looked to be perhaps 20 years old. But from the D.O.B. on the fingerprint card, which was taken in May of 1969, Shields knew that the man sitting before him had recently turned 49. Captain Shields also observed that this man, Savage, had made a successful effort to keep himself in pretty good shape too.

"You seem to have quite a colorful history here, Mr. Savage," the police captain remarked.

"Two tours in Vietnam. Re-enlisted February 1970. Specialist fifth class. Tell me," Shields said casually, "did you find a home for awhile in the army, maybe a job you could really enjoy?" The captain's words were clearly designed to provoke the man.

Savage responded in a tone of moderately frustrated disinterest. "If you're finished playing with yourself, Captain, would you sign the damn permit and let me get my ass out of here?"

Shields continued, but his voice was now just slightly more impatient. "Cambodia in '71, but that would be more than a month after your discharge. That's a bit unusual isn't it? Treated for wounds in Phnom Penh in December of '71. Released from Walter Reed three months later. Whatever were you doing in Cambodia, Mr. Savage? Some free enterprise perhaps? Some mercenary work?"

Savage had never exactly had the captain on his Christmas list, but this time Shields was being a particular irritant. What was the point of this line of questioning? What did this cop have—or think he had—on him this time?

"Mercenary?" Savage echoed with slight exasperation in his voice. "How'd you come up with that one? Got a copy of *Soldier of Fortune* magazine in the bathroom or something? Isn't a mercenary someone who fights for a foreign government exclusively for pay? If so, then I don't think I've ever been any kind of mercenary."

"Well, all that's ancient history now, isn't it?" the captain replied.

"Only if you weren't there," Savage interrupted coldly.

Captain Shields pretended not to hear this last remark as he paced about the room studying the file. "You came into our community about 10 years ago, bought a business which at the time was called Desert Cycle and is now Hog Wild Motorcycles. A couple of misdemeanor assault charges, arrested September 23, 1989 for felony menacing, but no indictment. You are the founder and the first president of the Dog Soldiers Motorcycle Club. You're still a member of that group today, correct?"

Shields knew it was correct. Savage didn't even bother to reply.

"But let's bring this up to date," Shields continued. "You aren't the president anymore, so what's your position in the gang now?"

"First, Captain, it isn't a gang, it's a club," Savage replied casually. "A club is an association of people who share a common interest. You know, like the Elks Club or a bowling league or maybe like a country club for people who like to play golf. It's just that our common interest happens to be an appreciation for riding and building American-made motorcycles."

"Sure," the captain echoed back as he looked through more of the file. "A club, like the Elks or bowling league. And what is your position with the club now?"

11

Somehow Shields managed to make his otherwise flat, dispassionate tone still carry the clear idea that he was mocking Savage's Elks Club analogy.

"I'm road captain," Savage replied. "When the club goes on a run, I decide on routes. I'm supposed to see to it that there aren't any unnecessary hassles with the locals or with any other clubs out there or with you cops. Which brings me back to why I'm here in the first place, Captain. The permit, the parade permit. Is there some reason that I had to come up here to your office to get it rather than just picking it up at the booking desk downstairs?"

A parade permit, Savage thought to himself. Parade permit hell! The city of Mountain View could call it that, but it was really going to be a funeral procession. A funeral for one of the Dog Soldiers' own.

For a moment Savage brought an image into his mind of what that funeral procession would look like to the citizens of Mountain View, Colorado. There would be sixty or so club members on their scooters riding right down the main street of town, and it would sound like rolling thunder.

He then saw how the term "parade," though a bit mild perhaps, nearly fit that mental image he had just conjured up for himself.

Part of a road captain's job was to see to things like getting this permit. Savage would be leading sixty or more Dog Soldiers roaring right through the middle of town, because that was the only route to Pinewood Cemetery for the planting. They needed a parade permit to do that. If they rode through town without one, odds were Shields and his men would pull over the whole procession. The cops would be checking registrations, the serial numbers on motors and frames, running the member's IDs through NCC for wants and warrants, and generally being pig ass dickheads.

Of course, the cop's objective in doing all this would only be to reassure the locals, the "citizens," that the police were still in charge and that there was still law and order in the city of Mountain View, Colorado.

Besides, the club didn't spend $475 a month to keep a lawyer on retainer and then ignore his council. The club's lawyer, Bosworth, had strongly advised Savage to get the permit.

Savage knew that the permit was a good idea although he wasn't real excited about walking into the Cop Shop to get it, and he was now becoming less enthusiastic about that by the minute.

Still, with a parade permit they'd have a police escort all the way to the cemetery. That would be a hoot in itself, Savage thought. With a permit and a police escort, there shouldn't be any hassles from the cops or anyone else. So why didn't the captain just sign the damn thing so he could get his butt out of there?

The captain stared at Savage for a moment, and just as it seemed that Savage might get some insight into this last question, a quick series of rapping sounds were heard on the office door, and then the desk sergeant's head popped into the partially open doorway.

"Captain, Mr. Bosworth's here," the sergeant declared.

"Send him in," Shields replied.

Bosworth? Savage thought. The club's lawyer! He sure as hell wasn't called down here over a goddamn parade permit.

"I contacted your attorney, Mr. Savage," Captain Shields offered. "I've been waiting for him to arrive before we proceeded any further."

"Swell," Savage said cheerfully, trying not to give the captain any clue that he was in the least bit concerned over this new development.

When the lawyer entered the room, Shields extended his hand, and the two men exchanged brisk courtesies.

Bosworth then turned to his client.

"So what's up now, Pete?"

"I think it's like those quiz shows on TV, Boz. You know, where you're supposed to guess."

Bosworth smiled. " I don't think it will be necessary for us to guess, Pete."

The lawyer had always appreciated Savage's off-the-wall, light-hearted sense of humor. But he sensed that his client was now at less than full form in regard to that particular facility.

The lawyer's attention turned to Captain Shields.

"Captain, my client has come down here to secure a parade permit to allow his association to carry out a funeral procession next Sunday morning at Pinewood Cemetery. Has some problem developed regarding the issuance of that permit?"

The captain's next words were voiced in a tone that suggested that he had made this short speech many times before. It was almost as if he were reading a prisoner his rights off a Miranda card.

"Mr. Bosworth, we are conducting a special investigation at present, the nature and objective of which I cannot fully share with you at this time. But we have reason to believe that your client has key information that would assist us in that investigation."

"Then you are asking for my client's voluntary cooperation?" Bosworth clarified.

"That's correct," Shields admitted grudgingly.

"Captain, if my client is a potential suspect in this investigation, then I need to know that *now*, and I have a right to know that now." Bosworth wondered why he needed to state the obvious to Shields.

"Further," he continued, "why is it that I assume we are dealing here with some sort of felony investigation?"

"Maybe Mr. Savage can respond to that," Shields replied.

"I'm afraid my client is not going to respond to any questions at all unless you first give me some information so that I can give him proper council," the lawyer declared flatly. "But, given such cooperation, we stand prepared to assist you in any reasonable way we can." The attorney spoke calmly, trying to avoid unnecessarily provoking the captain while clearly being firm in his demand.

"Now, first I need to know what you anticipate might be the nature of the charge or charges that you think may develop from this investigation."

Shields looked directly into Savage's face as he spoke.

"The principal charge will be capital murder."

Bosworth's face did not betray it, but he had been caught completely off guard on this one. He immediately turned to his client.

"Pete, you don't have to answer any questions. In fact, I think we need to confer in private before you say anything here under these circumstances."

Savage smiled. "Well hell, Boz. I haven't killed anybody all week, so let's hear what the Captain's after. Then maybe I can get him off my back and he'll sign that permit."

"I wouldn't concern myself with that permit at the moment, Pete. I'll handle that. Again, I most strongly advise you not to say anything here until we can have a chance to confer."

"So who was greased, Captain, and when?" Savage asked.

Captain Shields' face momentarily contorted as he attempted to subdue a silent rage building up within him over Savage's remark.

"Very well, Captain," Bosworth declared. "As my client has rather indelicately put it, can you tell us who was killed and when?"

Captain Shields responded to the question by yanking out an 8 x 10 photo from another file folder. He abruptly stuck the photo in front of Savage's face.

"Recognize anybody here, Mr. Savage?" he demanded.

Pete studied the photo, as did his attorney. The picture was apparently taken at some Dog Soldiers party at some unknown time. Savage could clearly identify the faces of Speed and Shotgun. It also looked like the Mouse was in the background standing with a few non-members. Sitting on his Harley in the center of the photo was Pete himself.

"Well, I'd say that handsome bastard on that magnificent Shovelhead was none other than yours truly, Captain. Say, you don't happen to have a few wallet-size copies of this pic, do ya? I—"

15

"Just cool it, Pete," his attorney cautioned. "Is there something in this photograph that should concern myself or my client, Captain?"

Shields produced a second color photograph that was a little less sharp than the first. Bosworth then realized that it was a blowup of a portion of the first photo.

It showed a man standing with two other men who were wearing Dog Soldier colors. The photo was dominated by the face of a shorter man who was wearing some sort of gold necklace with a crucifix. The man with the gold necklace seemed somewhat older than the two bikers he was standing with.

"Do you recognize this man?" Captain Shields demanded as he pointed to the man in the photo wearing the crucifix.

"He's not a member of the club. Guess you'd have to find the guy that invited him," Savage responded.

Shields was far from satisfied with this reply and pushed Savage further.

"Maybe I can help you out a little on this one then. He drives a real nice car sometimes. Have you ever seen this car before?" With that the captain produced yet a third photo.

Pete Savage looked at the photo of the car. It was a late model white Mercedes that probably cost $85,000 or more.

"We do a lot of riding and we see a lot of cars on the road, Cap', but a car like that kinda sticks in your mind, I guess. Yeah, I think maybe I have seen that car before, or one like it."

Shields quickly interrupted.

"You know something, Mr. Savage. I think that car sticks in your mind real well. In fact, I'll bet you know the man who owns it." The Captain's tone made his statement more of an accusation than speculation. "When was the last time you saw this car?"

"I can't say," Savage responded.

"You mean you won't say," Shields snapped back.

Savage was becoming more irritated with Shields, and the tone of his response to the Captain reflected it.

"What the fuck I'm saying, Captain, is that I remember seeing a car like that, but I don't remember exactly when or where.

I just . . . I just think I recall having seen a white Mercedes like that around town here somewhere. But fuck, I can't remember exactly when or where."

Captain Shield's voice now betrayed his anger with Savage even more clearly.

"You sure as hell are going to remember, Mr. Savage or—"

"I think that's enough, Captain," Savage's attorney interrupted sharply.

"I believe the best thing for both of us, Captain, is for me to speak with the District Attorney about this case and for me to confer with my client. Then we'll be happy to come back and answer whatever questions we can. My client is not under arrest is he, Captain?"

Shields remained silent.

Bosworth simply raised himself from his seat and gestured to his client that they were leaving.

"Mr. Savage will remain available. He has a business and a home in this community. You can call my office at any time after I talk with the DA. Then, if you want I'll bring my client back in and we can continue with this."

"Hold on, Law Dog," Savage interjected. "What about the damn parade permit?"

Bosworth was slightly embarrassed. His mind had been racing ahead to determine what these rather surprising and quite disturbing events might portend for his client, and he was quite anxious to get Savage out of the captain's office as fast as he could. Hence, the parade permit had been completely displaced from his mind. Still, the permit was a concern for his client and no reason had been put forth to deny its issuance.

"Captain Shields, could we have your signature on the permit, sir?"

The lawyer's question was polite and relaxed as if none of the previous hostility and thinly veiled accusations had ever happened.

The captain bore down with the long pen he plucked from his desk set, but he used far more pressure than was needed to sign the document. He scribbled out his signature so hastily that when he raised the pen, it dragged across the paper and a small piece of the lower corner was torn away.

Shields immediately shoved the document toward Bosworth, and the lawyer snapped it up just as quickly and popped it into his attaché case.

Captain Shields leaned forward over his desk and looked Savage directly in the eye. He pointed the end of his long pen at the biker as he spoke slowly and deliberately.

"It doesn't end here. This is just where it begins. Nobody's going to let this thing go. You think about that."

Savage stared directly back into the captain's eyes, but he said nothing as his attorney pulled him out of the office and into the hallway.

The attorney and his client both remained mute until they stepped into an empty elevator and the doors closed.

Abruptly, Bosworth pulled out the stop button on the descending elevator, and it immediately jolted to a stop between floors. He turned to face his client in the small confines of the iron cage work of the aging elevator.

"Pete, I don't know for sure what's going on here or what you may have been up to lately, but I have been practicing criminal law in this community for over 12 years now, and in all that time I have never seen that man up there act like that."

Likewise, Savage thought. He had also never seen his attorney act or speak to him like this before either.

Bosworth continued, " He's going to nail somebody's ass to the wall, and it sounds like he wants to make that for life."

The attorney was speechless for a moment as he searched for the words that he hoped would communicate the urgency of his concern to his client.

"That man is after blood for sure, Pete, and I think any-body—*anybody*—who gets in his way is in for some serious problems. Am I getting through here?"

The lawyer raised both his hands as if he were gently pushing on an invisible and very delicate glass wall between him and his client.

"You heard him yourself. He's going to have you under the microscope now. So if anything is going down, then you had better tell me about it real soon, but for now you had better just cool it and lay very low. We are going to have to talk, but outside of that you don't mention any of this to anyone."

Savage punched the stop button back into the panel, and the elevator jolted as it resumed its decent.

"I wouldn't fret too much about that, Counselor," Savage replied. "I mean, if I had blown somebody's brains out," Savage said as he smiled at his lawyer, "well, you can bet I'd be pretty closed lipped about it now, wouldn't you?"

Dog Soldiers: Chapter 2

Poor people stay poor people and they never get to see, someone's got to win in the human race and if it isn't you then it has to be me, so smile while you're taking it, laugh while your making it...and nobody's going to know.

Allan Price

Pete Savage sat alone in his Jeep parked at the third turnout on Lookout Road. Below him he could see most of the two-lane blacktop road that snaked up the mountain. As he looked out over the plains, he saw the lights of Denver some 26 miles away.

Although he was less than 1,500 feet above the city of Boulder, he was now above the pollution cloud. Savage recalled that 25 years ago when he'd first arrived in Colorado, there had been no pollution this far out from Denver.

Unfastening the large-handled screws that locked the jeep's windshield, he folded it down over the hood for a clearer view. He could see jets rising up from Denver International Airport and the lights of cars appearing and disappearing as they traversed the small hills between Boulder and Denver on Highway 36. The sky was clear, the evening air clean and cool and lightly scented by the mountain pines.

He drew that air deeply into his lungs. He was thankful that he was there and that the city was far away and far below him. Savage didn't go into Denver much. He didn't go into any city if he could help it. Cities were all about the same as he figured it. Some were just a lot worse than others.

But, for those people who had condemned themselves to expending their lives in places like New York or Los Angles, Savage imagined that they might not even see Boulder or Denver as being "real cities."

The motorcycle that Savage now heard coming up Lookout Road was ridden by a man who had originally come from one of those mega cities back East.

Like Savage himself, the man on the bike had made his escape out West decades ago. But in this man's case there was still just a little too much city left in his blood, and he just couldn't completely cut it loose. Savage figured that was part of why the man lived in Denver.

As the sound of the bike came closer there was no mistaking it, not for someone who knew. Savage tipped his head back against the high top of the Jeep seat and listened carefully. He heard the rich blast from the straight pipes on the old Panhead as it got the R's and pulled up the straight-aways. He heard the machine downshifting before the turns followed by the sound of the bike accelerating hard "out of the pocket" as it negotiated the curves.

Closing his eyes for a moment, Savage felt as if he were driving the machine himself. He felt the pull of the scooter and even found himself leaning just a bit in the seat of his Jeep as he heard the bike blasting out of the turns.

Just when Savage knew it would, the sound of the bike disappeared for a moment as it dropped behind the last hill before the final turn. Then, turning his head, he saw the bike's headlight. He thought he heard a slight backfire as the machine decelerated just before it pulled in alongside his jeep.

The full-coverage helmet made the rider's face invisible. For some reason or another he nearly always wore that skull bucket, Savage thought. When he pulled the helmet off white teeth sparkled from an ebony face and the man spit through a large space between his front teeth before he spoke.

"So what's the deal now, white boy?" the man asked.

"I got a note here, it says, 'Send the nigger another mile,'" Savage responded.

The black man's grin broadened at the worn-out joke. It referred to a fable from the slave days of the old South where a master sends an illiterate slave to the next plantation with a note and instructions to deliver it personally to the master of the neighboring plantation. All the note says is, "Send the nigger another mile."

The black man swung down the kickstand of his Harley, dismounted, and slid into the passenger side of the Jeep.

"Nice view," he remarked. "But then, you always was the nature boy type. " The rider then pulled a joint out of the top pocket of his leathers and pushed in the cigarette lighter on Savage's Jeep.

"Had a real interesting talk with Captain Shields this morning," Savage offered.

"So I hear," replied the black man.

When the lighter popped out, Luther Brown plucked it from the dashboard and lit the joint. He took a long, slow drag on the splif and held the smoke in his lungs before letting it out and resuming speech.

"Before we get into your rap with Captain Shields, what you say we get our regular business done first?" Brown suggested.

The "regular business" between Luther Brown, the President of the Denver chapter of the Wheels of Soul, and Pete Savage, now Road Captain of the Dog Soldiers, had begun a bit more than 11 years earlier when Savage had first organized the Dog Soldiers.

Brown was an ex-jarhead Marine who had taken a couple of AK rounds through his left shoulder and hip in Vietnam. One of the bullets had fractured that hip, providing him with a medical discharge in 1970 along with a modest disability benefit. He still walked with a bit of a limp, but only if you were looking for it, and he was still definitely not somebody you'd want to scrap with.

It was to avoid pointless confrontations between the two clubs that Brown and Savage had first begun these periodic series of secret meetings. It just wouldn't do for Brown's "darkies" to know he'd been "making deals" with "whitey." Likewise there were members in Savage's group who wouldn't understand this thing either, especially some of the younger guys. The younger guys tended to be the hotheads in both groups, and each club had an ample share of them.

So like Brown had suggested, it would be the regular business first.

"Right," responded the Savage. "The Dog Soldiers will begin forming up maybe about 10 in the morning at Kermit's Bar. I figure everybody who's going to be there will be there by about 11:30 or so. Then we take 119 through Boulder. The mortuary expects us around noon. We follow the hearse to Pine View Cemetery, and so we will be riding right through the main street of town in Mountain View."

Savage's face then showed a strange smile of all but impish satisfaction.

"Complete with police escort, mind you," he added gleefully. "After we get our boy into the ground, most of us will head back up the canyon to Harper's ranch. We'll camp there for the night, with the usual festivities, I'm sure." He spoke this last remark with a small note of anticipation in his voice.

Savage shook a hand in front of himself to emphasize his next point. "OK, you know that road up to Harper's ranch? It goes right past that titty bar, what's it called?"

"The Bus Stop," Brown replied.

"Yeah, that's the one, the Bus Stop. I'm sure a good number of our boys will stop off there for a few cool ones." Savage paused a moment as he drew on the joint Brown had passed to him and exhaled before continuing.

"The funeral's an official function, so we'll all be wearing the colors. I already set it all up with the manager at Kermit's, so we won't have any problems about the colors, but obviously you got to see that none of the Souls happen to show up at the Bus Stop next Saturday to watch the white gals' titties bounce," Savage pointed out.

"Yeah, I can arrange that," Brown replied.

This is how the relationship had first begun. Years earlier it had started out simply as a truce, but it had developed into something much more than that. The two leaders secretly informed each other of runs and routes so that 50 or 60 Dog Soldiers didn't happen to arrive for a party where a like number of the Wheels of Soul happened to be doing exactly the same thing. Such an encounter would almost certainly mean trouble, and for what? With a little cooperation, some trust and communication, it was all so easy to avoid in the first place.

As both men saw it, keeping their members out of such senseless conflict and "looking after the troops," so to speak—well, that was exactly what being a real leader was all about.

Savage wasn't president of the Dog Soldiers anymore, and he didn't want to be. But as Road Captain he still called the shots on routes and times for runs, so he was still able to keep things working secretly with Brown.

He sometimes felt that the club he had created had gotten away from him somehow. Pete still enjoyed the runs, for sure, and all of his best friends wore the colors. But now there were younger guys in the club, some he just barely knew. The whole deal had just gotten a little bigger than he had ever expected or wanted.

As the years passed and the membership grew, the Dog Soldiers Motorcycle Club had sort of taken on a larger life of its own. At the same time, Savage was always scrupulously honest with himself regarding his true motives for doing things, even the darker things.

Maybe, even especially the darker things.

He seldom tried to isolate himself from his true emotions and feelings. After all, "true emotions" and "feelings" were something that time and bitter experience had already partially drained out of him . . . and that was precisely what made such feelings even more precious to him.

Savage would miss "Gas Chamber" for sure, but for the moment that thought was displaced from his mind as he visualized himself riding his Hog at the point of the funeral procession. There would be 60-odd members behind him. They would all be roaring through the mountain tunnels, sometimes causing the citizens in their cages to pull off the road just to get the club past them.

These and some of the other simple pleasures of playing "motorcycle outlaw" still gave Savage a real kick. It made him feel younger than he was, and besides, there were few men who just truly enjoyed having a good time like Savage did.

But Savage knew that money made having a good time a lot easier on this squalid little planet. With the "regular business" taken care of between him and Mr. Brown, his thoughts now returned to that hard reality.

"It's a very dangerous game we are playing here, buddy, and you are sitting smack in the middle of it," Savage told Brown.

"No shit," the black man responded.

Savage turned and looked directly at Brown.

"All I'm saying is to keep your common sense about you. If it looks too wild, just say the word and we scrub the whole mission. We can afford to take our time on this thing. Next month, hell, even six months from now, it don't matter. We just need to be there and be ready when things come together. We just need to know when and where and then be prepared to make our move right then," Savage declared.

"When the time is right, seize the time!" Brown shouted back in a tone of mock heroics.

Savage shook his head. "Jesus Christ on a bicycle. I'm a white boy from Georgia with a black partner who thinks he's some sort of Malcolm X, and we are talking about a deal that could get us both shot down like dogs.

"Let's see, what else? Oh yeah, of course. Today I discover that the cops seem to want to fry my ass over some murder." Savage paused to think a moment. "And oh yeah, we're both mentally unstable delayed-stress cases. Did I leave anything out?" Savage asked innocently.

"You can bet your pink-white ass on that!" Brown replied.

Savage reached back into a small cooler behind his seat and after some fumbling and the sound of ice and water splashing, he produced two cold beers and passed one to his companion.

"I'll drink to that," Pete replied. Both men popped their cans almost simultaneously.

"So what did fucking Shields have to say? I hear he was plenty hot."

Savage turned his head to face his companion directly.

25

"All this shit went down with Captain Shields about six hours ago," Savage said as he glanced at his watch, "and not only do you already know about it, but now you tell me Shields was plenty hot. Maybe you can tell me more about this shit than I can tell you?"

"Maybe I could, bro, but right now I'm asking you to tell me," Brown replied.

"OK, I was there to get the permit for the funeral so we could have the cops escort, you know, trying to avoid hassles with the Man. Next thing I know, fucking Shields has me brought into his office and shows me some pictures. And guess what?" Savage spoke with mock sarcasm. "One of the people in those pictures was our very own Mr. Gold Chains himself, and would you believe it?" Savage asked innocently, "I think he was trying to tie me in with Gold Chains and with some other dude's murder."

"Did he tell who it was that got greased?"

"No, he was real tight-lip about that. He showed me a picture of the Mercedes. They got it tied into this thing somehow. But shit, who knows what they really know?"

Savage's tone suggested that just perhaps Brown did know something more.

Brown rolled the cool can of beer between his palms as he thought.

"The guy who got wasted, he must have been working for the cops, maybe even was a cop. The Man is so damn hot over this . . . I mean real hot. As a general rule they just don't get that whacked-out over a killing unless the guy killed was a cop too. So let's just cut right to it. How you figure all this shit affects our deal?"

"I'd say it turns the heat up about a thousand degrees." Savage tossed his head back and looked straight ahead into the night sky.

"We definitely have to think about this some more before we do anything. Suppose Gold Chains is working with the DEA?" Savage pondered that possibility further before he continued.

"But then if he was working with the DEA, how could he be involved in this murder? I mean like, especially if you're right and the dead guy was a cop, shit, you'd think killing a cop would be going too far even for the fucking DEA."

Even as these words left Pete's mouth, he began to partially doubt them.

"Yeah, I thought about that, too. Maybe Gold Chains wasn't even there at the killing, or maybe he just got caught up in something when it happened to go down. It could even be that he's just been seen with somebody else—somebody that the cops want to talk too."

Brown looked pensive, leaned his head out of the Jeep, and spat through the space between his front teeth.

"Even if our Gold Chains boy was working for the feds and he was there when the killing went down, what could the Feds do about it now? If that how it was, then what could they do but just play their string out with him to see where it took them? I mean, shit, they already know this dude's as slimy of a rat ass weasel as the planet's ever seen anyway."

Pete laughed out loud at Brown's last remark. "That's a fact for sure," he agreed. "But, we can't know for sure that he's working with the DEA, can we?" Savage asked.

"Yeah, maybe not. Then again, it might just be wishful thinking for us to think he isn't working with them."

Brown's face took on a cognizance as if he were trying to mentally assemble a jigsaw puzzle.

"We are going to be safer to just assume that Gold Chains is working hand-in-glove with the DEA, so if we're going to pull this thing off, maybe it's going to have to be right under their federal DEA noses."

Savage chuckled and shook his head.

"Listen, every DEA man isn't stupid or crooked any more than every cop is on the take. What is for sure is that we need some more intel' on this thing. I'll be working my end for that, and you work yours. Of course it would be real nice if you could find out how Shields figures he's got me tied into this killing."

"Yeah, I figured you'd be curious about that," Brown replied dryly. "I'll see what I can turn up for you."

"Solid!" Savage declared with satisfaction as he slapped the outstretched black palm.

The large black man slid out of the seat of the Jeep, got on his bike, and began to slip on his helmet. He gave the scooter a priming kick without turning on the ignition. Then he tapped down gently on the kicker with his boot to get the gears meshed before dropping his full body weight on the kick starter.

"Yo, man!" Savage called from the Jeep. "Didn't I hear that thing backfire on the way in here?"

"Shee-it," Brown replied with mock disgust.

"It's a damn Bendix, it's supposed to do that!" he declared as he flipped on his ignition switch and dropped his weight sharply down on the kicker.

The bike spit blue flame in the darkness as it instantly roared back to life. For a moment it sounded something like a big American V-8 that was missing on six cylinders. Then Brown gave it a bit more juice and the mill smoothed out nicely.

He rolled the bike backwards to clear the Jeep. Then, with a wave of a gloved hand and a twist on the throttle, the man was gone. Only the sound of his engine lingered, growing fainter as Brown cruised down the mountain on his way back to Denver.

After a few moments Savage stepped out of his Jeep to bring himself a little closer to the overlook. From there he could follow the bike's headlight blasting down the mountain road. Pete didn't have quite as far to go as Brown, but he'd still be late getting home. He knew his old lady wouldn't like that, but all in all it had been a pretty full day.

Savage started up the six banger in his old CJ-7 and started down the mountain for home.

Home for Pete Savage was also his place of business, the Hog Wild Cycle Shop. The shop was about eight miles outside of Mountain View on Highway 287, set back about half a mile from the pavement. It was out on the plains, but his bedroom window had a nice view of the mountains. He was also in the county there and not within the actual city limits. That made things a lot easier with zoning, taxes, and just about everything else.

At the shop, Pete had about 35 grand worth of machine tools, including a used Bridgeport mill and a Turret lathe, and it was all jigged up to work exclusively on Harley Davidson motors, transmissions and frames.

There wasn't much you could do or repair on a scooter that Savage couldn't do in his own shop. He owned all the tools outright now, but he still had to lease the property. Pete didn't like that too much, but the old man who owned it wasn't about to sell the land for anything affordable.

Dog Soldiers: Chapter 3

Then one day I met a pretty ballerina with hair so pretty that it hurt my eyes. And when I asked her if she'd come with me, was I surprised, was I surprised...

The Left Bank

When Savage arrived home after his meeting with Brown, he saw that the lights were off in the upstairs bedroom. That meant Sharon had already gone to bed. Not good, he thought.

He hit the button on the radio control unit in his jacket, and the garage door opener that he had converted to operate the heavy iron gate across his driveway opened. But as the gate swung open, the motion detectors tripped on the mercury vapor lights he had installed. Suddenly the whole countryside was fully illuminated.

'Shit,' Savage thought as he pulled up to the keypad on the pedestal post and entered his disarm code. All the lights went off except for the ones just outside the shop.

'So, the little woman's trying to tell me something by setting the alarm lights on,' Pete thought.

Then the possibility occurred to him, remote as it might be, that someone *else* had set those lights to trigger. The Jeep engine continued to run as he unlocked the console box between the two seats. From inside the box Savage withdrew a Smith & Wesson Model 586 revolver. He knew the gun was loaded with six 125-grain jacketed hollowpoint bullets. Even so he pushed the cylinder catch forward with his thumb and swung out the cylinder to check that the weapon was loaded.

He deliberately parked the Jeep by the side of the shop instead of in his usual spot and then came into the house through the shop entrance.

Savage removed a monster Abacus lock from the second steel gate and entered the shop yard. He inserted his key into the alarm lock, a small green LED came on, and the heavy steel door to the shop itself unlocked and opened. He moved inside quickly and to the opposite side of the room to enter the disarm code on the second motion detector. Otherwise, when the 8-second delay was expended, the alarm would sound off and wake up half of Boulder County.

The first thing he saw in the shop was his own bike, the Silver Serpent. Passing the weapon to his left hand, he caressed the hemisphere of the five-gallon fat bob tanks like they were a young girl's bottom.

"Hey baby," he whispered. "Did you miss me? We're going for a little cruise in the morning, ya know."

At this point Savage was convinced that he and his woman were alone in the house. He placed his pistol under his belt in the small of his back before going upstairs.

He could see the bedroom lights come on from under the bedroom door as he came up the stairs. She was awake now.

Sharon raised herself from a light sleep and watched Savage coming up the stairs on the small, flickering black-and-white TV monitor in their bedroom. She pushed the intercom's "talk" button.

"It's 12:45, honey," she said with acidic sarcasm.

"I should have never taught you how to tell time," Pete replied. He sat on the bed and dropped his boots on the floor. Removing his socks, he prepared to toss them across the room.

"Don't toss your clothes all over the floor, you creep. Put them in the hamper," she commanded.

"Yes, mommy," Savage said as he complied.

He studied his woman as she held the sheet to her chest. Damn! She truly was a fine-looking woman, he thought.

At 32, Sharon was a nearly 15 years younger than Savage. She worked as a real estate agent and had also managed to get a few local modeling gigs. She and Pete had been together going on five years now.

Savage pulled the gun from his belt before unbuckling his jeans and placed the weapon on the nightstand.

"What are you carrying that thing for?" Sharon asked. Before she had met Pete she had never even seen a real gun.

Pete chuckled. "Your little trick with the floodlights had me going for awhile," he admitted.

"You are a paranoid. But I won't do it again," she added.

"Paranoid, sweetie?" he mocked as he approached the bed.

Savage assumed the exaggerated tone and heavy breathing sounds like an obscene phone caller. "But there are so many evil people in this big, wide and so very wicked world, my dear. And you know, they'd all like to have their way with you," he explained as he pulled the sheet from her hands.

Displaying herself proudly, Sharon responded defiantly, "Would they now?"

Pete continued the exaggerated breathing as he admired her body. "Yes, yes. And they would even perform unnatural acts upon your person too."

"Ummm," she purred. "Unnatural acts you say?"

"Yes," Pete declared flatly as he flopped into the bed. Lying on his back he seemed to stare wistfully at the ceiling, and his tone returned to something closer to someone else's idea of normality.

"But now you are safe from such degenerate rabble, my love, for I am here, and my strength is that of ten because my heart is pure."

"Oh," she laughed as she crawled on top of him, her breasts hanging pendulous over his face for a moment. "Your heart is pure, is it?" she echoed.

The two lovers laughed aloud as they kissed and turned over in the bed like playful children.

"You know I got to lead the boys at the funeral tomorrow. You want to come?"

"I'm not sure I want to go." Sharon had learned long ago to always respond directly and honestly when talking to Savage.

"Besides that, I can't. Saturday is my best sales day, and I've got a good prospect for the Jordan property in Bow Mountain."

Sharon's face reflected another more emotionally engaging concern than her real estate showing.

"I'm sorry he's dead, but I'm not even sure if I ever even met him. I just can't understand how someone could do that, take their own life. Why did he do it?" she asked in a bewildered voice.

"I can't say," Savage replied solemnly. "I guess he just felt that he'd come to the end of his run. I guess he decided he just didn't want to or couldn't go on with it anymore."

Sharon was lying on her back as if looking into blank space. "I just can't imagine why anyone would do something like that no matter what their problems were. There's always got to be some hope, some other way."

Savage placed two fingers over her lips. "I know, sweetie. That's part of why I love you. You can think like that."

"Are you coming back after the funeral, or do you have to stay with them up there at Harper's ranch?" she asked.

"Ah, so you know about the get down at the ranch, huh?"

"Shotgun came by looking for you, and he asked if I was coming with you."

"I think I will have to stay over, sweetie. I mean, fuck, I am the Road Captain. But I'll just have to see what's going on—what's going to be necessary at the time. But yeah, I figure I'll have to stay up there that night."

Sharon made a face at this reply. "I don't like you spending the night up there. I've seen those women who tag along for those kind of parties. They're mostly just tramps and whores."

"My, my," Savage responded. "Such harsh language from such a sweet, pretty young girl." He kissed her lips lightly. "I guess the only thing for you to do then is to see that the old man is just too tired out to be interested in those women, huh?"

"Yeah," she replied as she ran her tongue over her lips, "that's just what I was thinking."

Dog Soldiers: Chapter 4

The chrome plating gleamed off the 67 custom Harleys parked outside Kermit's Bar while a dozen or so Dog Soldiers wandered around the parking lot studying each other's scooters. Each bike had its own particular features and modifications, which reflected a lot more than just the individual owner's finances.

A man's bike was a material representation of his spirit, his own personal blend of both style and functionality.

There was hardly a bike there that wouldn't cost at least $10,000 to build, and many would cost three times that much or more. Yet, many of their owners lived in $375-a-month apartments or trailers, and some were even on food stamps.

To their owners their machines were beyond any price. Many of them had the name of the original manufacturer tattooed into their very flesh: HARLEY DAVIDSON.

All four generations of the basic engine design were represented among the bikes whose dates of manufacture ranged from 1947 to the present.

It was the shape of the engine's valve covers that immediately identified any Harley motor. Motors from the fifties and early sixties had valve covers that were round like inverted cooking pans and were called "Panheads."

In the later seventies and early eighties the engines had narrow wedge-like valve covers that resembled shovels. Thus their moniker became "Shovelheads." Savage's own Silver Serpent was an early model Shovelhead.

Finally, there was the latest version of the Milwaukee legend. This was the engine that had saved the company from possible extinction from Japanese competition. It was an evolutionary refinement of the basic 50-year-old design, and that's just what the factory called it, too: the "Evolution."

But the Evolution bikes still had the basic lines and feel of all the classic V-twin monsters. Without doubt, some bright boys at the factory knew they had to look that way or they would surely risk losing the faithful. The new motor had also rescued the company from near bankruptcy after a short but very dark period of ownership by AMF, the bowling ball people.

The new company owners—among them Willie G. Davidson, great grandson of the co-founder of the firm—had realized that they had to retain the basic lines, the look and feel of the classic Harleys if they were to succeed and get the company back in the black.

Hence, the external appearance of the V-twin motor, the very icon of Harley itself, had to remain basically the same even while some very fundamental changes were made inside. They were evolutionary changes, all right, and thus the official factory designation, the Evolution motor. Yet the lines, frames, and sheet metal of these new bikes were styled in a way that actually made them look more like the Harleys of 30 years earlier.

But the true acolytes of this American iron horse had given their own name to these new engines. The valve covers were squared off like blocks, thus so they dubbed this latest creation the "Blockhead."

No one seriously questioned that it was the smoothest, most reliable and maintenance-free motor the factory had ever built, because it was. The Blockheads were highly prized, and at a low of $18,000 for a bone-stock machine off the showroom floor, the Blockheads were also the most expensive bikes that Harley Davidson had ever sold. About half of the Dog Soldiers rode Blockheads.

From the cool darkness inside Kermit's barroom, Savage watched a family in one of those "prestige" Japanese luxury cars slow down and survey the spectacle of the scores of bikes and the dozen or so bikers outside. The car slowed down a moment. Faces of the occupants were seen looking out from behind its lightly tinted windows, and then the car continued on it way.

Pete wondered: Had they slowed down to admire the scooters? Or was the whole spectacle merely a strange curiosity to them? Maybe something to be studied a moment simply to confirm that they had really seen it?

On the other hand, perhaps they had originally intended to stop and eat at Kermit's, but seeing the small army of bikers they'd changed their minds and drove on. If it had been this last possibility, Savage knew it didn't matter much to the owner of Kermit's.

Max had owned and operated the bar since the early seventies. He knew that a group of bikers like this together with their old ladies would swill down more beer and eat more food in two hours than he'd ordinarily sell in a good weekend. Besides, the Road Captain had contacted him several days earlier about the run, and Savage had been real polite just like he always was. He'd also offered to leave a "good faith" deposit to cover any tabs for beer or burgers that some of his people might neglect to pay for.

Max said that wasn't necessary. He had dealt with Savage and the Dog Soldiers long enough to know that he'd get his money and that there wouldn't be any trouble or damage either.

Max was 72 years old now, and he had lived out West all his life. To have his bar filled with these Dog Soldiers and to watch their unrestrained laughter and partying made him feel good inside even more than the money did. Just having them in his place made him feel like he'd recovered something that at times the old man was afraid he might have lost.

Pete glanced at his watch and surveyed the spectacle about him. He then gave a nod to the Sergeant at Arms, who pulled up on the chain around his neck to retrieve a silver whistle dangling under his black T-shirt. A shrill blast from the whistle caused a nearby brother to slap his hands over his ears in an attempt to escape the overpowering decibels that the man was able to achieve with this instrument. When the biker pulled his hands away from his ears, he heard the Sergeant at Arm's commanding voice.

"OK! That's it, troops!" Momentarily, the din of raucous laughter, conversations, and clanking plates and bottles came to a halt.

"Get on your bikes, get 'em started, and let's get on the road!"

Getting on the road was an effort that required a little time and a bit of ritual too. Some of the members had camshafts in their scooters that were ground quite radically. That meant that starting their machines required that a few of the boys push them across the parking to get their high performance motors to fire up. Yet there was no need for communication or instruction from the bikers who needed this help. They got it automatically from whichever club member happened to be standing nearby.

They pushed the bikes down the parking lot with some expenditure of muscular effort, and when the rider popped his clutch and second gear engaged, the bike most often fired up. In a matter of minutes, a half dozen bikes were roaring up and down the parking lot.

Sometimes a bike had to be pushed a few extra times across the lot to get it to fire up. Until this task was accomplished and the most radical bikes were started, most of the rest of the members didn't even bother to mount and start their own bikes.

Attention was next drawn to the bikes that generally started up without any problems but which had decided not to do so on this particular morning. Repeatedly the starter pedals were kicked but to no effect. Their owners then frequently and imaginatively cursed their beloved mechanical marvels.

"You piece of shit, start you mother fucker!" one member shouted as he kicked the pedal repeatedly until he was nearly exhausted. His companions spontaneously began to surround him as they all hooted and jeered at his plight.

Ultimately, those jeering the loudest would push the bikes to get them running even over the objections of their riders. "Wait, wait, man. She'll start, she'll start!" protested one rider as a group took his machine off its stand and began pushing it across the lot. This left the man with no choice but to hold onto the bars just to stay up on his ride. Once a little momentum was achieved, he slammed it into second and popped the clutch, and it roared to life amidst the collective cheers of the multitude.

Finally, only a handful of bikes remained to be started. But these were the bikers who had chosen to "let technology do most of the work." By simply pressing the magic buttons of their electric starters, their motors roared dutifully to life. The thunder of the collective engines was now nearly deafening.

Savage primed the Serpent, turned on the ignition, and with a single kick he was running. He brought his bike to the far end of the lot and drove up to the edge of the pavement, which was well elevated over the parking lot. This placed him in clear view of the other riders and at the same time allowed him to survey the canyon road. He could see more than a few hundred yards in either direction, and there was no traffic in sight. Savage signaled with a wind up of his arm and then pulled onto the road. The whole pack poured onto the open highway behind him.

Once all 67 riders were up on the highway, the Road Captain raised his left arm into the air and gave two exaggerated pulls of the limb, and the pack quickly organized itself into two long columns. Savage had established a laid-back cruising speed of just about 50 miles an hour.

He glanced into his twin mirrors to see sunlight dancing off the sea of chrome on the hogs that flowed behind him. Savage smiled and enjoyed the familiar music which now played in his head. It was a concert of wind, vibration and low-end torque that the Serpent sang to him each time he mounted her.

"I love this bike!" he shouted aloud, though no one could possibly hear him over the collective roar of the motors.

"I love this bike," he repeated.

The 20-minute cruise down the canyon was pleasant and uneventful. But as the group pulled into the outskirts of Mountain View, Savage spotted the two city police cars parked on opposite sides of the road. One car pulled out to lead the pack through town while the other waited for the last bike to pass before taking its position at the rear of the column.

The Dog Soldiers now had their police escort.

In town, the police had established traffic control by simply closing off Turner Street, which led from the mortuary to Main Street. The deputy in the lead patrol car radioed the officer ahead as the bikes approached Main.

The hearse containing the body of William R. McFadden, otherwise known as Gas Chamber, was then led onto the road to Pine View Cemetery.

A half a dozen bikes flowed around the hearse as Savage, the President of the club, the Sergeant at Arms, and three of Gas Chamber's closer friends took their positions at the head of the procession. Their iron horses thundered down the main street of Mountain View. They rode rather slowly, but even so their collective numbers shook the glass in the small office buildings.

Savage dropped back alongside the President of the club and motioned to identify a cop on the roof of the city/county building.

The lens Captain Shields had screwed onto the camera looked to be about two feet long, and the cop's vantage point was ideal.

Savage smiled broadly as he waved to the camera. Then he thought how nice it would be to have one of those 8 x 10 glossies of himself leading the pack.

When the Road Captain waved to the police cameraman on the roof, the rest of the pack's attention was immediately drawn to the officers and their camera equipment. Spontaneously a bit more than 60 hands went up extending their "fuck you" middle fingers to the camera lens. It was a spontaneous and yet almost obligatory show of defiance for them.

The glittering sea of scooters rolled on to discover a second tripod on the far corner of the police station roof. Savage identified it as a Betacam video camera.

The officer panned the group slowly as it passed by the station as one of Gas Chamber's buddies pulled his bike alongside Savage and yelled toward his ear.

"Shit, man! Look! Fucking videos! Maybe we'll see ourselves on the fucking six o'clock news, baby!"

Savage laughed as he shook his head from side to side. Maybe, he thought to himself. But those pictures and tapes were being taken so Captain Shields could identify each member of the club who had shown up for the funeral. He'd probably add them to some big organizational chart he no doubt kept in the station house.

Pete's mind imagined what that chart might look like.

There would be a picture of Macahan, the Pres, at the top, then maybe a little black line leading to a photo of himself. On the same level as that, Bulldog, the sergeant at arms, and The Doc, the Vice Pres, would be shown too.

Who knows? Maybe Shields would even have frame grab stills taken from the video. If so, the still photos would certainly be cropped and enlarged to show the riders' faces more clearly. Savage imagined all those images on the detective's wall showing the members in attendance at Gas Chamber's funeral and maybe even portions of their bikes. There would be names and notes grease-penciled below most of the photos.

Damn, Pete fantasized. What a magnificent piece of Dog Soldier memorabilia that would be for the clubhouse to have! A broad smile fell over Savage at this thought while another camera's shutter tripped to record the Dog Soldier's Road Captain smiling contently.

Some of the town's citizens stared with a combination of wonder, fear, disgust and for some even envy as the bikers passed through town. A few smiled and waved. There were even some who flashed the "peace sign" to the riders.

Shortly thereafter the group arrived at Pine View Memorial Gardens. The actual planting was a relatively brief and conventional affair. A guy in black with a turned around white collar said some nice things about someone he'd never met. Then there was some mention of Jesus and God Almighty before a simple pine box was lowered into a hole in the ground.

The Dog Soldiers stood respectfully, and a few called out their last farewells to the Gas Chamber as he was lowered into the pit.

A bugler from the local VFW prepared for Taps while a flag was brought forth. This caused every Dog Soldier present to assume a stance closely resembling attention before each saluted the flag.

Gas Chamber had been a member of local VFW Post 459, and seven members of their honor guard now raised their blank-firing, chrome-plated, M-14 rifles and fired a volley simultaneously.

Savage noticed that the blank charge in one rifle wasn't quite sufficient to cycle the action, but it's operator deftly and instinctively worked the slide by hand to eject the spent cartridge and feed a fresh round into the breech. He had accomplished all this in time to fire in sequence with the next volley. Only the very observant would have even noticed the problem.

After the last rounds were fired, the bugler stepped forward and cut loose with a clear and surprisingly decent version of Taps.

Gas Chamber didn't have any family outside the Dog Soldiers themselves, so the honor guard officer pivoted smartly, and using crisp right-angle turns, he presented the President of the club with the flag.

In his precise and polished uniform, the soldier looked into the eyes of Macahan but with no hint of emotion. He showed no sign of disdain, approval, or any other sort of personal judgment whatsoever. As far as he was concerned, the deceased had earned his right to this ceremony, and as a member of their post he was damn well going to get it, regardless of how he died, how he'd lived, or anything else.

The President of the Dog Soldiers somehow found himself on the threshold of perceiving these thoughts in the man, which made him hesitate for a split second as he extended his hands to receive the flag. He then caught himself and gathered his words for the Honor Guard.

"Thanks. Damn decent of you men to see to it that Bill got a proper funeral. Thanks."

The President turned to face the club members. He silently surveyed every face for a moment. Then he shouted, "What are you?"

The reply came immediately, loudly and in unison.

"Dog Soldiers!" they thundered.

"Damn right!" Macahan shouted back after a short pause.

Immediately came a collection of deafening hoots and howls from the entire pack, but it abated at once when the President raised his hand and continued.

"Bulldog, front and center," he commanded. Dutifully, Bulldog came forth.

"And what is a Dog Soldier?" the President asked him.

"A Dog Soldier is a survivor," Bulldog roared back.

"And how does a Dog Soldier survive?" Macahan asked.

"Dog Soldiers survive as a team and as a unit!" Bulldog shouted back with genuine pride.

"And what does a unit need to survive?" the President asked.

"A unit survives on leadership, preparedness and discipline," Bulldog roared back again.

"Damn right!" Macahan shouted back to the members, and again came the thunderous shouts of affirmation from the multitude. These words were the official litany and part of the creed of the Dog Soldiers MC.

The President then pointed to the hole in the ground that contained Gas Chamber's coffin.

"Well, Gas Chamber didn't survive, so I want you all to take a few moments and think about that. I want you to ask yourselves if there was anything you or maybe a fellow bro' might have done to keep his ass out of that box today."

The Dog Soldiers listened to the Pres in silence.

"Maybe there was nothing any of us could have done. I don't know. I'm just asking you to think about it, because he was one of us. He was one of the original 12 guys in the club, too.

"We're Dog Soldiers, and that makes us survivors, but we got to do that by looking out for each other. We have got to do that as best we can, too. We have to think about that. We have to think of our bros. Each of you has to realize it's the only way the club will survive, each soldier watching every other soldier's back. It isn't just another man that can get you from behind, either. It can be drinking too much booze every day, it can be doing too much of the wrong drugs, it can be a lot of things, bros. We just got to watch each other's back in that way too.

"OK, so we're getting ready to head out to the party at Harper's ranch and I guess that's why some of you are mostly here anyway for the party afterwards. Well, goddamn it, that's just fine, too, cause I know Gas Chamber wouldn't have wanted it any other way!"

With these closing words from their President, the silence of the club members immediately exploded into an even greater roar. "Damn right, Pres!" was somehow heard over the den of howls.

With their man in the ground, the long string of bikers began to flow out of the cemetery, and once again the police cars took up their escort duties.

This time Savage's objective was to lead the pack out of the fair community of Mountain View and back on to Route 119 out of town. Once on Canyon Road, the run to Harper's ranch would only take them about 20 minutes.

Dog Soldiers: Chapter 5

Life is a party, so let's get out and strut!
Mick Jagger

Savage led the group of 67 Dog Soldiers off the dirt road and onto the grass of the lower meadow of Harper's ranch. Three pickup trucks and a van were already waiting to greet the entourage. The four-wheeled cages carried some of the members' women. But also inside were several kegs of beer, a freshly butchered side of beef, institutional-sized cans of refried beans, tortillas, hot dogs, chicken, hot mustard, sauerkraut, several huge plastic bags of potato chips, and gallon-sized cans of hot salsa.

A few of the roaring iron horses circled about the pasture like ancient outriders on a long-ago cattle drive while the bulk of the scooters rolled out onto a large outcropping of sandstone. The sandstone would support their bikes on their kickstands better than the meadow's soft soil.

A handful of the more forward-looking members pulled their bikes closer to the beer and food, which was now being deployed on folding tables next to the vehicles. From inside their leathers, these riders pulled out small flats of plywood or sheet plastic and placed them on the soft dirt beneath their kickstands. The plywood or plastic flats distributed the weight of their scooters more evenly, allowing the softer soil to support the kick stands securely. The reward for this advanced planning was that they would be the first to reach the beer and eats.

A pit approximately six feet long and three and a half feet across glowed with burning coals in preparation for roasting the side of beef. The fire pit had been constructed and lit the day before so the heat of the coals was just about right now.

"Ever think what the club might be like ten years from now?" the President asked. "I mean we are all at least pushing 50. Hell, some us are past 50. In ten years maybe there'll be only two, three, maybe five at most of the original guys left. Shit, maybe there won't be any of the original guys left. Hell, maybe there won't be any Dog Soldiers M.C. left in 10 years."

The very instant these last words passed his lips, he wished he hadn't said them.

"Bullshit!" Bulldog snapped back. "Dog Soldiers are survivors. They can nuke this fucking planet till it glows, and the Dog Soldiers will still be here! They'll still be a unit, too." He tipped his beer to Macahan. "They'll still have leadership, and they'll still be riding!" he responded defiantly.

Macahan smiled. "Maybe so, Bulldog, but only if we make it so, buddy."

"Right," the Bulldog responded. "And besides, if every one of us got his ass greased, the Dog Soldiers would just regroup in hell!"

Savage had heard enough of this kind of talk. "Come on, let's get off this death shit. Like you said, we're still here, we're still alive. Now let's act like it!"

"I though that's what we was doing," Bulldog replied somewhat confused.

As these words were spoken, the trio observed two of the younger members walking up the hill toward their position under the tree. The pair passed a bottle of whiskey back and forth between them as they made the ascent.

"It's Goforit and his pal, Bright Eyes," Bulldog declared, as if these brothers needed to be identified to his companions.

"Swell," replied Savage somewhat unenthusiastically. In a few moments the two members stood before the three club officers swaying slightly with inebriation.

"So, what you old farts doing? Sitting under the tree telling your war stories?" Goforit inquired.

Insolence was the prerogative of every Dog Soldier, but always at his own risk.

"Yeah," responded Savage. "I was telling the Pres here how me and Bulldog captured old Ho Chi Minh and a whole NVA division while him and the Doc was back in Saigon running whores in tandem."

"Right," Bulldog added with a broad smile. "Yeah, there we was, ankle deep in grenade pins."

Goforit had just taken another pull on the bottle, but he nearly spit out the whiskey with laughter at Bulldog's remark. When his bloodshot eyes refocused on the trio of club officers, it became more apparent that these two were well on their way to a full-on, fall-down, whiskey drunk.

"I hope you boys brought your sleeping bags, cause neither one of you is leaving this camp tonight," Macahan declared calmly.

These words caused Bulldog to smile broadly at the pair as it would now be his duty as Sergeant at Arms to see to it that neither of them tried to start their bikes and leave camp before morning.

"We know the rules, Pres," Goforit responded. "Fact is we come here on official club business."

"Official club business," Bright Eyes echoed drunkenly.

These guys are truly precious, Macahan thought to himself.

"And what, pray tell, on thy drunken and demented minds, dost thy have?" Savage joked, twisting his head so that he looked directly into Goforit's eyes as if playing the part of some hunchback from a late-night television horror classic.

Goforit straightened himself up and threw his shoulders back as if to impart some level of seriousness or dignity to his next words.

"Got a new prospect to pledge up."

Jesus, Savage thought. Just what the Dog Soldiers needed—another depraved psycho such as he imagined that these two might try to recruit.

Fortunately, the Dog Soldier by-laws were clear on this point. Only members of five years or more could sponsor a pledge, and that left out both Goforit and Bright Eyes until about sixteen more months. They would thus have to convince some qualified member to sponsor their candidate.

This caused Savage to wonder a bit. Surely both these dudes knew that neither he, Macahan, or Bulldog were at all likely to sponsor any of the sort of trash they'd likely come up with. Fact was, they weren't often too keen on bringing any new members into the club, period. So what was their angle?

Savage got right to the point.

"What makes you think we might sponsor any sort of derelict you sleazebags might come up with?" he asked.

"Well, ain't you the high and mighty one," Bright Eyes returned, displaying a surprising simulation of semi-sobriety. "He ain't quite the old fart like you three are, but he whipped ten times his weight in rag heads over in Kuwait. "

"Saved our asses over at the B-70 Club," Bright Eyes added quickly and rather loudly.

"He's got a sweet Panhead and he knows that fancy slant-eye fighting like you, Savage. Hell, maybe even better 'an you, old man!"

Goforit taunted Savage as he slowly drew out the final words 'old man' in an exaggerated fashion. He also returned Savage's direct eye contact.

"You boys are beginning to wear a little thin," Savage cautioned politely.

The President chose to redirect the subject.

" You cretins got into some kinda trouble over at the B-70 Club in Westminster?" The Pres asked.

"Now that's just the point, Pres," Goforit responded quickly. "Me and Bright Eyes was just there having a drink and watching them fine titties bouncing."

"Minding our own business," Bright Eyes interrupted again. The two drunken bikers looked at each other and nodded as if to confirm their own story to one another.

"Get on with it, you drunken fucks!" Bulldog demanded. "What went down at the B-70?"

"Three Sundowners comes over to us, and they tells us we better get our asses outta there, and like right away. Says we oughta tell the rest of our 'wimp ass gang' to stay outta there too on a count of the bar's Sundowner turf now," Goforit declared.

"How do you know they were Sundowners?" the President asked. "Were they wearing colors?"

"No, but shit, the dude had it tattooed right on his arm there, 'Sundowners M.C. Denver.' So when he runs that shit on us we know it's gonna be a battle, us against all three of um' too, and they was all bigger. But we was ready to scrap," he declared proudly.

"Right!" Bright Eyes echoed, turning to face his friend once again as if seeking some sort of a mutual confirmation. "We was ready to tangle alright."

"Only I'll bet somehow it didn't come to that, huh?" Savage remarked.

Their two squirrelly minds were taken slightly back by Savage's statement, as if his words required some sort of clairvoyance on Savage's part.

"Well no, it didn't 'cause as soon as they were about to move on us we got some help from the guy who works there, a bouncer."

"He's the guy you want one of us to sponsor, no doubt," Macahan said.

"Yeah! You shoulda seen this guy!" Goforit seemed somewhat excited now. "He tells 'em to chill out and sit down, real polite like, too," He said in tone of curiosity. But then bammo! The three Sundowners go right for him! He drops the first guy hard and like, well I didn't even see what he hit him with. Next thing, the second guy's rolling around on the floor and hell, that was it! The third guy didn't want to fight no more."

"Did these guys leave the place under their own power? I mean, were they able to walk out of the place?" Savage asked.

"Well sure," Goforit responded. "The one guy was limping a little maybe, but they wasn't like busted up real bad. He sure put it to them, though. Eighty-sixed them from the B-70, too, like it was really something to see, ya know?"

"How did this idea come up about him joining the Dog Soldiers?" the President asked. "Was it your idea or his?"

Goforit looked at Bright Eyes as if he wasn't sure of the correct answer to this question.

"Don't remember, exactly. We talked to him a little, you know. He asked us what caused the beef, and we told him who we were and who they were. He said he'd heard of the Dog Soldiers and asked us a few things about the club."

"What kind of things did he ask about the club?" Savage interrupted.

"How it got started, who began the club, how many members we had, stuff like that," Goforit replied. "But we didn't tell him too much about any of that, of course. Just asked him if he'd like to meet some of the guys, maybe become a prospect."

"So it was your idea. You brought it up first?" the Pres asked.

"Yeah, yeah," he repeated with a bit more confidence. "Look, what are we gonna do about Sundowners at the B-70 trying to push us out? I mean, is it the policy now to just let anybody—"

"Whatever the policy's going to be," Macahan interupted, "I'll be the one that makes it."

"Yeah, we got that straight, Pres," Goforit replied.

"Now here's the deal," the President continued. "You guys just keep quiet about your little problems over in Westminster for now. I don't want you running your mouth off about it and stirring up any of the members into some half-ass show of force over there. If that happens, I'll know you two are responsible. Think about that," the President warned. "Now, I'll have this looked into, and if I don't hear any stories being kicked around about this thing, then we'll take a look at this guy you want to pledge. What's his name?"

"Mark. He's a bouncer over there," Goforit said.

"Well, I'll have somebody check him out. I'm not saying that we'll prospect him, understand? I'm saying somebody will talk to him. We'll just see how he vibes out."

Macahan glanced at Savage and Bulldog a moment before continuing. "Remember, you don't talk about these Sundowners giving you shit at the B-70, and both of you stay here in camp tonight."

"We ain't stupid. You don't gotta tell us shit twice," Goforit complained.

"Nothing's gonna be said neither," Bright Eyes added. "Only I don't see this as such a big fucking deal anyways. Just wanted to bring somebody into the club that might be a real plus for us, and now I gotta catch all this shit for it?"

Macahan realized he'd hurt the man's pride a little.

"Listen, Goforit. I know you and Bright Eyes are good soldiers; otherwise I wouldn't have your raggedy asses in the club, understand?"

Goforit and Bright Eyes both nodded their heads.

The President continued. "And that's why we will always win, because we are a unit, not just a mob like the Sundowners. We use our heads and we look ahead, and we always look after each other."

"And we have good leadership," Savage added coolly. "Something every unit has to have to survive, bros."

"Savage is right, and we got to have some discipline too," Bulldog added.

Macahan rose and extended his hand to the two men.

Despite the alcohol, Goforit and Bright Eyes clasped hands with the President, and their faces reflected that their feathers had been smoothed out a bit.

The drunker of the two, Bright Eyes, flashed his penetrating yet beady little eyes, for which he had gotten his club name. Then, looking into the face of each of the three club officers, he spoke in a slow and deliberate fashion.

"What are we?" he roared.

"Dog Soldiers!" came the simultaneous shout from all present.

"Damn right!" Bright Eyes said. Then he and his companion turned and staggered back down the hill.

Bulldog popped another beer as the trio watched the two stumble away.

"So you worried about this?" Bulldog asked Macahan.

"No, not right now anyway. But we gotta stay on top of this kinda shit right from square one," he declared with authority.

"Otherwise one thing leads to another, it escalates, and then we're at war with somebody. Only that's not going to happen, because we are all going to stay on top of things and never let it get started in the first place."

"You know, Goforit has a point about not letting them get away with this kinda stuff. It could just encourage um' to go further," Bulldog cautioned.

"Maybe so, Bulldog, but look. We don't know what really happened. Those guys could have been as drunk then as they are now. They could have started the fight for all we know. We don't even know for sure those other guys were Sundowners. Besides, even if they were Sundowners, they weren't wearing colors, so it can't be considered any sort of official move. Probably just individual members throwing their weight around because there were three of them, not necessarily any sort organized movement to expand their turf."

"Most likely true," Savage agreed. "But if the Sundowners did have that in mind, this might be just how they would go about it. Send in a few guys with no colors and then see what happens when they muscled out a few of ours."

"That's occurred to me too," Macahan responded. "And that's why I'd like you to go over there in the next few days and check it out. If you see a bunch of the Sundowners' bikes outside, then don't even stop. Otherwise, have a drink, maybe talk to this bouncer, and try and get some facts for us."

"OK," Savage replied. "I'll get over there and have a look see.

"So what do you guys think of old Captain Shields taking those pictures and videos today?" he asked.

"Target of opportunity," Bulldog said. "I mean, how many chances does he get to photo practically the whole club all at once like that?"

"He sure took advantage of that opportunity today," Savage replied.

"You think Shields is something we should concern ourselves with?" Macahan asked.

"You know what happened when I went in there to get the permit. He's definitely bent out of shape about that killing, and there can't be much doubt he figures the club's involved somehow."

"The club," Machahan asked, "or just you pal?"

"Gee, thanks for the fucking support, Pres," Savage said. "Actually, I don't think he's got clue one on that score. He tried to rattle me because I was there, but he must think he has something to tie us into that thing. The pictures he took of the club today should convince you of that. I mean, he's got pictures of me already."

"You're saying he might try to throw down some harassment busts on the members, try and get a hold of somebody he hopes might know something, try and put the screws to somebody to turn over?" Macahan asked.

"Not to put too fine an edge on it, Pres, but yes," Savage replied. "I think he's gonna try something. You should have seen the old Cap', I mean he was totally bonkers."

"OK, I guess you got a point. I don't have a whole lot of confidence it'll do much good, but we'll apprise the membership to expect some extra heat and harassment stops. Maybe some of 'em will listen."

"Say, look. Both you guys are staying here tonight, right?" Savage asked, "and when everybody leaves tomorrow, they'll be going back to their own cribs on their own, not wearing the colors I mean."

"You want to go home and see your old lady?" Macahan declared, "Then get after it buddy. We'll look after the store."

"Damn," Savage replied as he looked into the faces of the two men. "I guess my whole life's just an open book to you guys, huh?"

Dog Soldiers: Chapter 6

Seymour Horowitz turned a dial on the Tektronix scope and the squiggly green line of light on the screen transformed itself into a wave of perfectly spaced peaks and valleys.

"There it is, right on the money," he said with satisfaction.

Without looking up, Seymour's hand found a small syringe of epoxy, which he brought down into his work area.

To Savage the man's electronics shop had always looked like a rat's nest of wires, cables, and computer screens with tools seemingly scattered everywhere. But for Seymour, everything was right in its place.

"Now, we make sure that it stays that way," Seymour announced as he carefully squeezed a small drop of the epoxy onto the variable trim pot capacitor he had been adjusting. Having completed this task, he slipped the cover back over the cellular phone, and after sliding his swivel chair back from the bench, he spun around to face Savage.

"So, maybe we run over how all this works again."

Savage smiled. "Maybe it would be better if I tried to explain it to you. That way you can see if I got it down right."

"Shoot," Seymour replied cheerfully.

"OK, the electronic serial numbers you programmed into the phones are actual paying customers in some other city somewhere."

"New York and Miami," Seymour added.

"Both those people have the full roamer service, so these phones will work just about anywhere in the country that has cellular service. When these phones are turned on, those serial numbers are broadcast to the local cellular switching computer, they come up legit so they go on the air and talk," Savage recited.

Seymour raised a finger and pointed it at Savage. "Correct." he said.

"But since we are using their electronic serial numbers, the guys back in New York and Miami will get the bill. It takes a month for the bills to come in, so until then nobody has any way of knowing any calls have even been made. Even then, nobody is the wiser unless the subscriber reads his bills real carefully and they notice the extra calls, like from cities they weren't even in. So maybe then they complain to the cellular carrier. If that happens and just a few calls were made, the carrier will likely just drop the charges from the guy's bill. Anyway, all the heat's got is basically the name of the city the calls were made from and nothing else to trace the calls back to anybody," Pete explained.

"Right!" Seymour congratulated. "Only in this case, I hacked the carrier's accounting computer for people who had heavy traffic on their phones, more than a 600 calls per billing cycle, so any bogus calls will most likely go unnoticed anyway. OK so far, scooter boy, go on," the technician encouraged.

Savage had come to like this little computer nerd's spunk. So now he was "scooter boy." Savage continued with his explanation of the workings of the phone system.

"As long as these two phones can only call each other and they can't originate or receive any other calls from anyone else, the carrier has no way to track them down. Again, the carrier will just have two ESNs and the cops will only have the name of the city, but no names, no address, nothing else to go on."

"ESNs huh?" Seymour smiled. "Picking up the old cellular lingo, I see."

"Explain the coding and computer part again," Savage asked. "I need to feel good about that. I mean, that part's got to be foolproof."

Seymour opened his hands toward Savage.

"Really very straightforward from a user's point of view. Just pick up the phone, push the send button, and talk. Keep in mind that the calls from these phones are broadcast by microwave. Cellular communications is just a conventional radio transmission that's relayed from one tower site to the next as you move. This means the authorities could intercept the voices and listen and record the conversation. So could anyone who tunes in the proper frequency. So, if the transmission were not scrambled, then anyone could still hear and understand everything said if they were on a RF receiver that was tuned in."

Seymour stared at the two units on the bench for a moment before continuing.

"They could also make audio tapes of the calls, and those might show up later as evidence in some courtroom. Voice identification is getting close to an exact science, you know."

"Now tell me again why we aren't worried about that, Seymour," Savage asked quietly.

"Because we are running the audio from the voice transmission of the phone into an analog-to-digital converter. Once in digital form, we reprocess the voice with the computer that's in the case with the phone. In effect, the voice is disassembled into thousands of different parts every second. This is called 'digital sampling.' These parts are then put into a new sequence before they are transmitted, like shuffling a deck of cards."

Savage knew that Seymour enjoyed giving these little lectures. He had long ago observed how so many people had their personal self-image, their very identity, that is, 'who they were,' inexorably tied into some particular skill they had. That skill might be playing a guitar, or even being a welder or carpenter. Sometimes it could be selling real estate, or being a "scooter boy" too.

In Seymour's case it was his superior understanding of electronic and computer technology and, more particularly, using that knowledge to "beat the system." He really didn't see himself as any sort of a criminal since he didn't see any real crime in what he was doing. He didn't see any crime, because he didn't see any victim.

The only "victim" he saw was maybe a multibillion dollar communications conglomerate, and that didn't disturb him too much. It just sort of added to the fun, and that's just what it all was for Seymour, fun. For him it was like playing some kind of giant video spy game.

Only Seymour knew that this particular game *was* for real, and he had discovered that this was the ultimate kick of all. Pete Savage was also the most "real person" he had ever met too.

Seymour's description of the system continued. "The program that scrambles the voice also transmits a decoding key. However, there are actually 4,096—that is, 64 squared—encryption algorithms. Each of these is a cipher demanding a translation table that exists only in these two programs. Since no single encoding cipher is engaged for more than a few hundredths of a second before the next cipher is called up, there is no practical method, no basis whatever really, upon which to employ code-breaking techniques. The communication is secure between the two units. If intercepted and recorded, it sounds a little like Teletype noise, just humming and static. Not something that would be very useful for identifying anybody."

A fresh smile came to Seymour's face. "As originally conceived, what's the one way somebody might track down the units?" He posed the question like a child putting a riddle to a playmate.

Pete was surprised by the question but took up the challenge.

"If either of the two units received or made calls to any other phone, other than the other phone in the set, then the billing computer would make a record of the number called and the number of the caller, since both are billed."

Savage paused a moment to think it through while Seymour encouraged him by making motions with his hands as if he were trying to physically pull the answer from the biker.

"Come on, come on, you got it. Finish it up. How would they match it all up?" Seymour prodded.

"Since the guy's actually getting the bills, the guys who have those ESNs legitimately might be squawking to the carrier. I guess the carrier would be searching for any billing statements involving those other numbers and have the computer flag them.

"But as long as the two sets only call each other, that doesn't do them any good. But if either phone calls or receives a call from someone else, then that number shows up and ties back to a real person. Then they have a person's name and address to go asking questions to, right?"

"Go to the head of the class," Seymour replied. "Which is why I made more changes so that can't happen. The two phones are now set up so they can't send out any other phone number to call except the number for the other set. It was pretty easy," he said with a prideful casualness.

"You can enter anybody's number you want, but when you hit 'send,' the computer checks it against the number stored in the set. If it doesn't match, the cancel line is tripped and no call goes out. Likewise, each set sends a preamble code when the gain goes up on audio preamp stage. When a call comes in, if that code isn't there, the unit breaks the line, simple. They can't send or receive calls from anyone but each other."

"Outstanding," Savage declared. "When that phone rings, you know it can only be the guy with the other unit at the other end."

"Exactly, but there is one more modification I made," Seymour added. "Limited life span."

"What the hell is that?"

"Once the units send or receive their tenth call, a timing circuit begins to decrement, and after three months it trips a relay that discharges a capacitor into a coil and, zappo! The ESN chip is fried. The unit won't operate anymore until it's reprogrammed by installing a new chip and, of course, a new ESN."

Working with Seymour was always a bit amusing, Savage thought, as he contemplated the full significance of this additional feature.

"Got it. So no matter what else happens to the units, the carrier has just three months, that is three normal billing cycles, to try to figure it all out or find out who it is, which they have no way of doing anyway." Savage's words reflected his genuine admiration for the man's work.

"Pretty sweet, Seymour, pretty sweet. So how much you need now for creating these little gems of your diabolical genius for me?"

"I had a figure in mind until you had me put this little hummer together," Seymour pulled an aluminum Anvil case from under his workbench. He opened the latches on the container, which was a bit larger than the attaché cases that housed the other two phones. The contents of the case were set into a block of Styrofoam that had been carefully cut out by hand for each component.

Inside the case was a cassette tape recorder and a notebook-size computer like the ones in the other two phones cases. There was a cellular phone antenna, but there was no phone inside the box.

"You tested it, right? It works?" Savage asked with some small urgency in his voice.

"Getting a little excited, huh?" Seymour teased. "Just like a kid at Christmas. Let's give her a spin. Get on the other unit."

Savage flipped open the case that housed one of the cellular phones while Seymour did the same with its mate. When Savage hit the talk button the phone automatically chirped out the dialing sequence for the other unit and Seymour's phone rang. When Seymour picked it up, the cassette deck in the Anvil case started recording.

"Is that you, buddy?" Savage spoke into the phone as he looked at Seymour.

"Level Seven," Seymour replied. "This is the Wizard speaking."

"Play it back, play it back," Savage asked somewhat anxiously.

Seymour complied, and the two heard their voices on the tape with crystal clarity. The de-scramble unit in the recording box unit functioned perfectly.

"I think I'm gonna shit," Savage crowed.

"You realize that this will only work when all three units are in a cellular service area," Seymour cautioned.

"Yeah, but that would be like, well, the whole Front Range, a lot of New Mexico and a lot more, right?"

"Yeah, as far north as Cheyenne and all the way down to Albuquerque. Maybe further, I guess. Not much good in some of the mountain areas, though."

"You did a good job here, Seymour. Now what do I owe you?"

"I guess there's not much point in my asking how you're going to use these things, is there?" Seymour asked.

"No, I guess there isn't," Savage responded with a smile.

"Well you know, at first when you had me put together the phones, I thought maybe we might be dealing with an ongoing thing here with black-market cell phones or something like that. But that's not what you're up to at all, is it? The third unit makes at least a part of your plan pretty clear, so what are the stakes? How big is the payoff?"

Savage glanced back at Seymour as he packed up the phones and recorder units.

"The stakes could be life and death pal, so you don't even want to know what the game is. But, I figured you'd get around to this at some point, being such a bright lad and all."

"OK, Savage, I don't need to know anything more about this. I know the value of the payoff must be in proportion to the risks that you plan on running, so with stakes being 'life and death,' you can have the phones and your magic box for nothing now, and later on, you can just cut me back a percentage of the score."

It was kind of funny, Savage thought. He actually liked this little weasel with the soldering iron, and it amused him to see the guy step out of his element. Seymour was trying to paint himself into some cross between a James Bond film and some old Humphrey Bogart movie he'd seen on late night TV. "A percentage of the score." Where did he think up that line?

Yet none of this was really too unexpected. Savage had come to know a bit about how Seymour thought, and the kid did a lot of thinking.

Savage decided to try to wrap the negotiations up quickly.

"OK, what would you otherwise need for the equipment? Maybe four or five grand?" Savage asked.

"Maybe about that, maybe a little more," Seymour replied.

"You realize there might not be any score at all. If so, then you will likely lose the equipment and get nothing. Otherwise I'll cut you back seven percent of the take and you will just have to trust me. Seven percent should be a lot more than five grand, too. What do you say?"

"Done," Seymour replied, extending his hand to seal the bargain.

Savage smiled, and shaking hands with the man, he realized that it was the first time in their relationship that he'd done so.

The bargain made, Savage's attention turned to the three cases he had packed up on the workbench. As he ran his fingers over the top of one of the cases, his smile developed into a chuckle, and then Savage broke into song.

"Danny boy, Danny boy, the pipes, the pipes are calling," Savage sang fully as he packed up the gear.

Dog Soldiers: Chapter 7

Savage wasn't much of a fan of the B-70 Club. He didn't like spending much time in dark, smoky barrooms in general. But he had told the Pres he'd check the place out, and that made it club business. Something of a recognizance mission.

Remembering Macahan's directive, Pete observed that there were only two bikes parked outside. Both were Jap café racers, and even a Sundowner wouldn't be low enough to be seen on that kind of shit.

He turned his bike around and rolled it back into the parking space. Savage had not come there looking for any sort of trouble, but he'd barely shut off his motor before trouble found him.

Two rather salty dudes on chopped hogs arrived and rolled their bikes in on either side of him.

"Definitively a nice Shovelhead," the first biker observed. "Too bad it's got that sack of dog shit on it."

Pete realized that fate was dealing the hand and that these two guys were arriving at the bar by chance. It was clear enough from their appearance that these two dudes were legitimate scooter trash, but were they Sundowners?

Savage looked straight into the face of the man who'd spoken. "Oh my," he said calmly, "you do look so fierce."

The remark was so off the wall that the biker's limited faculties left him at a loss for a moment as to how to respond. This, of course, was precisely Savage's intent. But the other man took up the slack up for his companion.

"Wasn't that your momma I saw whoring down on East Colfax?" he offered.

"Right," the other man added. "She was being butt fucked by them two niggers down there. I guess you're here looking for some queers to bunghole too, huh?"

Savage appeared undisturbed by these remarks.

"Well, you gentlemen seem to be pretty up on your anal antics," he replied with a confident smile. "Try not to drool too much around my scooter if you can help it."

Savage maneuvered around his bike in a manner that avoided moving into the striking range of either man and then stepped toward the door. Once on the sidewalk he turned his back to the door and stood smiling at the two men in the street.

He wasn't about to go inside and leave the Serpent with these mongoloids still out there. He hoped they would just get on their bikes and go or follow him into the bar.

Somehow, though, he knew it wasn't going to be that easy.

The larger of the two made a sound like he was clearing his throat, leaned over Savage's bike and spat on the gas tank. His eyes then turned up to meet Savage's as a demented smile broke across his face.

Though on the inside a cold rage was now swelling up inside him, Savage made an attempt to control himself. He spoke clearly and calmly.

"Now listen carefully, you fucking little toads. You can spare yourself a lot of pain by just getting on your bikes right now and leaving."

The man who'd spat on the gas tank whipped open his combat folder knife in one fluid motion. While looking Savage straight in the eye, and all the time smiling, he turned to place the point of the knife to the front tire of the Serpent.

The man's companion was standing between Pete and the man with the knife. Savage knew he had only a split second to act.

The guttural scream that Savage let out as he attacked captured both of his enemy's minds for an instant and momentarily distracted the one with the knife.

Pete had closed the distance before either man could react. When the edge of his boot smashed into the first man's ribs, it carried his full bodyweight. The man was knocked backward as if a small car at low speed had struck him. He crashed forcefully into the man with the knife. The impact sent both men to the pavement.

Savage had felt the guy's ribs crack nicely under his boot. He knew that guy wasn't getting back up and into the fight any time soon.

He moved behind the biker with the knife so quickly that when the man got up, he was still looking for his enemy in front of him.

"Put down the knife, Bozo, or it could be the biggest mistake of your short life," Savage warned.

As he spoke these words, Pete immediately regretted not seizing the opportunity to finish the knifer before he'd recovered. He knew only too well how instantly and deadly knives could be, even in the hands of an amateur. Savage knew he wasn't getting any younger either.

He knew he shouldn't have played with this guy and let it go this far. Instinctively he moved to interpose one of their scooters between him and the knifer.

As the knifer closed, he held his blade low and very close to his body where it was hardly visible at his farside hip and dropped into a moderately low crouch. The man said nothing as he moved for position on his intended victim.

Pete didn't like this at all. He was hoping he'd see a threatening and flashy display of the knife accompanied by some verbal threats and insults while the blade was held high and visible. Those were the marks of an amateur.

It was now disturbingly clear to Pete that he was not facing an amateur. Psychologically he prepared himself to be cut, but also to survive and drop this fucker hard. It was now a fight for his life, and one way or the other he knew that once the guy closed, the battle would be over in seconds or less.

Savage tried to relax his mind and settled his gaze on the center of the knifer's body mass.

Mentally he attached his consciousness to the enemy's body, to every movement the man made and yet to no one movement. He kept the distance open by mirroring the knifer's movements, keeping the bike interposed as the man tried to move around the bike to close the distance into striking range.

The attack would be an instantaneous charge with a razor-sharp blade that was in the hands of a man who'd almost certainly used it before and used it successfully. He would not lead with his weapon hand or try to slash out at his intended victim from a distance. Instead he would first engage the victim's defense with some other movement or his other hand to create the opening to close chest to chest. Only then would he use his blade. It would not be a single thrust of the weapon, either.

Once the blade struck home, there would be a quick series of pumping motions with the knife in and out of the victim while the killer held the victim's body as close to him as he could. This would all happen in the space of a second and a half. The thrusts would be short, but they would penetrate to the hilt, and the knife would be retracted as quickly as it was thrust out, and then it would be sunk again and again into the victim.

Savage knew that this was the way the knife was used for real and not like what was seen in movies. He also somehow knew that the man he was now facing had likely learned to handle the blade in prison.

"Say yo!" a loud voice called out suddenly and loudly.

The voice distracted the knifer's attention for the blink of an eye, but Savage's focus was not. There was then not the slightest hesitation between Savage's intentions and his actions.

With a sliding up side kick, he blasted the side of the gas tank on the bike between him and the knifer, and then 460 pounds of steel fell to the pavement. As the bike fell, it hit the knifer's leg and took him down. The iron monster crushed the bones in his foot between the anvil of steel and the hard pavement.

The biker screamed out from the unbearable pain, but both his conscious suffering and his screams were cut short when Savage unleashed a kick to his head that knocked him cold.

Savage observed that the first man was now trying to get up from the asphalt. He was lying on his belly and had just placed the flat of his palms on the street to raise himself up. Savage quickly entered and struck him in the face with a powerful, rising knee that partially lifted the man's body off the ground.

"OK, OK," the voice called out calmly and clearly but with authority. "Let's not run this thing into the ground, pal. I think they're pretty well done now."

When Savage looked over to where the voice was coming from, he realized it was the same man whose first words had provided him that fleeting instant of distraction that had allowed him to go on the offensive with the knifer. Pete also began to realize that his entire body was now trembling with adrenaline.

"Well, maybe not the cleanest technique I've ever seen, dude, but clearly effective," the stranger commented as he casually walked over to the two bodies lying prostrate and bleeding in the street.

"Now help me get this sled off this guy," the man told Savage in a tone of moderate annoyance. Savage obliged by helping him lift the bike back on it's stand and off the man trapped beneath it.

The stranger rolled the knifer over, and using his thumb, he peeled back one of the man's eyelids to examine his pupils. He produced a small silver penlight form his pocket and shined it into the man's eyes. He waved the light back and forth and watched the man's iris expand and contract.

A penlight, Savage thought. Why would the man carry a penlight like that? To check IDs in the dark, of course. The answer had come from some other region of his still adrenalized mind—he must work at the bar.

"Well, you didn't croak him," the man said. After briefly placing an ear to the man's chest, he declared, "Yep, this dude's still breathing. But I figure he'll have that foot in cast for sometime. Might not ever do the 'cha cha' again either," he concluded.

The second man lying on the ground was clearly in better shape and received an even more cursory examination from the stranger.

Pete watched all this like it was some sort of a hallucination. He could hear himself breathing hard, and his body felt a little cool and clammy.

"You aren't cut up, are you, pal?" the stranger asked Savage. "Looks to me like you might be in shock."

As the man said this, a second person stepped outside the bar and immediately thereafter, a third.

"Mark, what the hell is going on out here?" one of the men called out to the stranger. The man's face reflected his astonishment at the sight of the two blood-splattered men lying on the ground. "Shit! You didn't kill those guys, did you?"

Mark smiled while looking into Savage's face as he gave his reply. "No, but it was definitely touch and go there for a minute."

Still facing Savage, he continued. "Say, Ron, I think it would be best if I took the rest of the night off. But give me a minute or two before calling the cops and ambulance." Mark glanced around for a moment. "And the story is when you came outside, you just found these guys like this. I wasn't here of course, left about a half hour earlier. You didn't see anybody else out here either. Got it?"

"Sure, sure, got it. No problem, Mark. See you on tomorrow night's shift then."

"Not likely, Ron. Tomorrow is Thursday—my night off," Mark responded happily.

Mark turned to Savage and then to his bike. "Magnificent scooter," he said sincerely. "Very well done. Quite tasteful. I suggest you get on it now and call it a night, pal."

"Appreciate the thought," Savage replied, trying to make his voice seem as calm and natural as he could. He began to feel himself calming down a bit now, and when he heard himself speak, his confidence increased. "This shit's sorta got me a little wired," he admitted.

"Yeah, you kind of looked that way," Mark observed.

"Is this a regular deal here or what, man?" Savage said spontaneously.

"Well hell," Mark shot back flippantly. "You should see what it's like once you get inside the place."

Savage found his own sense of humor a little strained, and this guy Mark was something else entirely. He seemed to remember the Pres saying something about checking this guy out. Now seemed as good a time as any.

"I could definitely use a drink. I'd like to buy you one too if you're up for it."

"Why not?" Mark responded. "Now let's stop beating our gums out here and get moving before the cops do show up. My ride's around back. I lock it up inside that big walk-in cooler. It's safe there, but it makes the engine cold so she takes a few kicks to get running sometimes. Meet you out back," he declared as he disappeared around the corner of the building.

This guy locked his bike up in the beer cooler? Pete tried to consider what kind of a dude he was dealing with here. He tried to assign some logic to such a thing, but all he could come up with was that the cooler was the only place to secure the bike from vandalism. Considering the guy was a bouncer, he certainly couldn't afford to leave his bike outside the bar.

The Serpent puttered back to the rear of the bar as Mark rolled his rigid-frame Panhead out of the cooler. The cold atmosphere of the refrigerator condensed when it met the outside air, and an eerie white cloud surrounded the scooter for a moment as it appeared from the cooler. Mark prime-kicked the old mill a few times before flipping on the ignition, but his repeated kicks failed to fire it up.

"I guess that motor's a little cold," Savage noted.

Both men now heard police car sirens, and they were getting louder.

"Yeah, that's one of the handicaps of this deal," Mark admitted.

After a few more kicks the bike rumbled to life. But Mark just sat on it and let it idle.

"Say, buddy," Savage said, "I know you want to warm that motor up a bit before we hit it, but like you said, maybe we should be rolling out'a here." He glanced about casually to see if he could spot any flashing police lights yet.

"Most all real motor wear occurs in the first few minutes of operation, you know. Can't be working a cold mill too hard, especially an old Panhead like this," he replied.

"All right. We'll take it slow until it has a chance to warm up, OK?" Savage shouted over the roar of the engines. "Now let's get it in the wind, man!"

A slight note of urgency was creeping into Savage's voice as he worked the throttle of the Serpent back and forth and the motor roared obediently.

"Sure," Mark replied. He was almost laughing as he snapped his bike into first and let out the clutch to take the lead.

When the two riders had cruised about a mile down the road, two police cars flew past them at pursuit speed. Their lights flashed and their sirens screamed as they headed in the opposite direction of the two bikers.

Dog Soldiers: Chapter 8

I'm running down the dream, working on a mystery, as far as I can see, working on a mystery.

Tom Petty

Danny Mapes sat at a table next to the windows at the Eagle Lodge In Aspen, Colorado. Glancing at his watch, he observed that he had now been waiting there for over an hour and a half.

During that time he had counted seven Mercedes and one stretched-out Cadillac limo arrive and depart in front of the Snowmass Condominiums.

That German luxury car was a popular make in this ski resort community where the average home sold for about two and a half million bucks and most for lot more than that. He remembered reading somewhere that more than half of those homes were vacant most of the year, too, being only vacation retreats for their owners during the ski season.

As his mind wandered from boredom, he began to think what it would be like having a zillion dollars like that. A zillion bucks is about what you needed to live in this town.

If you had to work for a living, you couldn't afford to live in Aspen. The bulk of the people in Aspen who did work—mostly waiting on tables, pumping gasoline, or working on the ski slopes—made a daily commute of either 38 or 75 miles each way, depending on whether they were coming from Glenwood Springs or Leadville. Those were the nearest towns where working people could afford housing.

In sharp contrast, the people who could afford to live here could afford a lot of other things, too, like Rolls Royces, private jets, and, in a few cases, small Middle Eastern sheikdoms.

Danny's thoughts were pulled from these fantasies of fabulous wealth by the sudden entrance of a white Mercedes into the outside parking lot. When the car arrived outside the lobby doors, Danny was already standing outside on the sidewalk. He placed his face against the tinted glass to peer inside at the man sitting alone in the back of the car.

The electric lock popped up. Danny opened the door and slid in. He found the short, somewhat portly man in the back fumbling at the crucifix suspended around his neck by gold chains.

"You haven't been waiting too long, *ese*," the man asked.

"No, no, not too long," Danny replied quickly.

"That's good. Time—it's the thing we can't ever get back, eh?" Gold Chains remarked.

"Right," Danny said.

"You bet, 'cause none of us really know how much time we got left, no?" Gold Chains continued.

The man wearing the gold chains and crucifix was Ralph Gutierrez. He was born outside Barstow, California, but his speech still carried the heavy accent of an East LA Chicano which, is exactly what his father had been.

Ralph was a second-generation speed cooker who had learned the trade from his old man, and he was now carrying on the proud family tradition. It was a tradition that included the manufacture of almost pharmaceutical quality methamphetamine, otherwise known as "crank" or "speed."

Eighteen years ago his father had been shot dead by a rival speed producer as he'd stepped outside their trailer on his way to the liquor store in Yermo, California. At nineteen years of age Ralph had held his father in his arms while the man died before his eyes. Ralph had been too young to remember his mother.

All the old man had left Ralph was an old aluminum Travel All trailer, the '71 GMC pickup that towed it, and, of course, his speed cooking equipment.

Materially speaking Ralph Gutierrez had done a bit better than his father. He had managed to turn the small family business into an operation that afforded him such luxuries as the

$75,000 Mercedes he was now riding in as well as the salary of the man who drove it.

He also owned a luxury motor home into which he had invested about twice the amount of cash he had in the Mercedes. Mobility was important to Ralph.

"So, you bring me some toys, Danny?" Ralph asked as he picked up one of the two attaché cases that Danny Mapes had carried with him into the car. Ralph popped open the latches and admired the contents.

"You understand, like they only work with each other. I mean you can't call anyone else with 'em or even get any calls from anybody else except the person you give the other phone to."

Danny's voice reflected his anxiety to somehow get this information out as quickly as he could. Like it was something real important he had to say, but somehow he was afraid he'd forget or not get the chance to fully explain it.

"Yeah, Danny, I'm not stupid. I remember things, you know? I remember what you told me about how these fuckers work. Now let's see 'em work. How you work it, Danny?" As he said this Ralph found the sliding switch marked ON and pushed it into that position.

"So just press SEND," Danny instructed. "It will dial my set on its own."

A series of seven quick telephone tones were heard when Ralph hit the SEND button, and the telephone set that Danny held began to emit a beeping tone.

"Heh, heh! I like this, Danny. This is a good thing!"

Danny was encouraged, and he was quite eager to show off all the bells and whistles for the man. "Okay, now watch this." Danny pulled out a Radio Shack portable radio scanner and turned it on.

"Have your man up front make a call to somebody on his cell phone," Danny said as he reached over and turned off Ralph's portable phone as well as the one he carried.

Ralph held down the button that lowered the dark glass screen between him and his driver.

"Julio! Call somebody on the phone up there."

"Quien?" the driver asked. "Who am I supposed to call?"

"Anybody, man! Call anybody. Call your old lady or something man'o! We're testing this shit out back here. *Entiendes ese?*" Ralph shot back impatiently.

"OK, OK!" Julio responded.

Julio picked the cellular phone set from the pedestal mount and hit an auto-dial key. When the call went through there were five rings before a voice from an answering machine came on the line. "This is Roberta. I'm out now. You can leave a message when you hear the beep."

Danny's small radio echoed this recorded greeting from Roberta's answering machine. After the beep, Julio's voice was heard. *"Hola Angelina! Que undes mujer? Que lastima que usted no esta aqui. Pero, Yo veo usted manyana, Entonces, creo que yo veo todo, no?"*

Julio's maniacal laughter crackled over the receiver that Danny held as well as inside the Mercedes itself.

"You see?" Danny said as he shook the scanner in his hand to underscore his point. "On your regular cell phone anybody with one of these scanners can hear every word, on both sides too, no problem, and so could the Man."

"So you gotta a fix for that, eh Danny? You show me."

"Watch," Danny replied.

Danny hit the SEND button on his phone set and Ralph's phone rang in it's attaché case. Ralph picked up the phone and heard Danny's voice. "Hello. You can understand me fine, right?"

"Yeah, it's like long distance, Danny," Ralph answered as he looked at Danny sitting right next to him.

"Now listen to what anybody else would hear." Danny passed the portable radio scanner to Ralph.

Ralph put the radio to his ear as he spoke to Danny through the phone. When he spoke, the portable receiver crackled in time with his voice but none of his words were intelligible. All that could be heard was randomly modulated static.

"We got some James Bond shit here, eh *ese*?" Ralph crowed.

"You can depend on it," Danny replied.

"That's real good. You can hear it's us talking on the radio, but you can't understand nothing." Ralph's voice reflected both clear satisfaction and wonder at his new toy as his thoughts raced ahead to its near limitless applications for him in his special line of work.

"It's scrambled, and nobody can unscramble it, either. Not the feds, not the DEA guys, not any kinda cops," Danny assured.

"OK, it's a good deal, Danny, but you still owe me nine Gs, due two weeks from now, *ese*. But still, I give you five grand for the phones now like we talked about before."

Ralph pulled a wad of hundred dollar bills from his pocket. The money was pre-counted and there was a rubber band around the bankroll.

Somewhere in the back of his mind Danny had hoped that Ralph's enthusiasm for his new toy might have displaced his immediate awareness of the outstanding debt. No such luck, he realized.

But Danny Mapes had things on his mind other than just getting the five grand for the phones. He had more business to conduct with Mr. Gutierrez, and potentially the most profitable business of all. Danny knew it wasn't going to be something Ralph would be anxious to discuss, either.

It was the same old problem. Danny was on the outside looking in. He was always forced to make deals with the big dogs like Ralph. Without guys like Ralph to supply the drugs, Danny would be out of business. The bottom line was, Danny needed Ralph a hell of a lot more than Ralph would ever need guys like Danny. That simple fact determined the true nature of the entire relationship between the two men.

Danny tried to speak as coolly and calmly as he could. "My people were real impressed with the stuff you gave me, but I gotta show 'em, I mean, I gotta show 'em I can deliver the weight, you know? They need to know that they can rely on that kind of quality every time, and that I can deliver some weight for them, you know?"

Danny was anxious and Ralph knew it.

"I don't know, Danny. Why do I need to do business with new people? Besides . . . I don't know . . . you tell me about these people, but I don't know them," Ralph repeated.

It was the same old game, Danny thought, and everyone knew their part.

"Look. These guys move a lot of weight in blow, man. Your stuff is so fucking clean they can use it to cut their shit, man, and they got the bucks to pay for it. I tell you, man, they could give their sneeze a 20 percent cut with your stuff and still sell the load to these rich fucks right here in Aspen as primo shit. And I mean for top dollar too!"

"Yeah, you make it sound real good Danny, and so you gonna want me to front you the weight." Ralph's words were an observation rather than a question.

"But what you got on the line, man?" Ralph asked. "We gonna be friends, Danny, but you know, you take my stuff and I don't see the cake, maybe we aren't friends no more, you understand? Maybe it's better we just keep our business like it is and we both stay friends, huh *ese*?"

"Two keys—that's all I need to make it work. Just to get the flow going, man." Danny sensed even greater opposition to his new enterprise than he'd expected.

But Danny Mapes was tired of reasons why he couldn't make the deals that would pay him the real bucks and eventually give him a share of the real money, and that also meant the real power.

This time he'd be the one who'd have to make it work himself. Whatever that took, that's what he'd have to deliver. Somehow he was going to persuade Ralph to front him the stuff. He knew it was his only ticket to move up from being a mid-level dealer to making real money.

Danny reached over, took Ralph's hand, and slapped the five grand back into it.

"It's all I got, man. Two keys; two keys and then it's flying, man, two keys, man."

"Ha! You got the real hots for this one, *ese*! How you figure these fuckers gonna cut their blow with my shit that heavy and move weight?"

Here was the fundamental question. It was kind of funny, Danny thought. Ralph was so into the quality of his "speed" product and yet he was completely out of touch with what was currently selling on the streets and in the executive boardrooms and bathrooms as "cocaine."

The fact was that if the score was less than a ounce, and a lot of times even if it was, what people bought that was supposed to be cocaine was actually mostly a decent grade of speed, with maybe 3 to 18 percent coke in it, if that.

On more than a few occasions Danny had made some small sales of Ralph's speed as cocaine and at primo coke prices. There had been no complaints either, mostly just repeat customers.

The people Danny had on the line now moved five or six kilos a month of primo quality blow that could easily stand a 20 percent cut of Ralph's meth with no sweat. That meant much more than a 20 percent increase in their profits, which were already enormous. Danny wouldn't have any trouble with them. Ralph was the man he had to convince.

Danny tried not to show just how anxious he was to make the deal, and so he spoke as calmly and assuredly as he could.

"I can do it, man. I know how to move the weight," he declared.

"OK, *ese*," Ralph agreed. "We see what you come back with and how long it takes. We give you your two keys. I don't got to say nothing to you about what happens if you mess up, *mano*, but you know, we won't be friends no more, eh?"

"Right," Danny replied with clear satisfaction. "I understand. We won't be friends no more."

Dog Soldiers Chapter 9

Mommas don't let your babies grow up to be cowboys.
Willie Nelson

The white line spit beneath Savage's wheels as he was drenched in the warmth of Colorado sunshine. A slight twist on the Serpent's throttle and the broken white line became all but a solid white blur.

Experienced ears took in every note of music that his engine made. Lifters, valves, primary chain whine—it all spelled celestial harmony to the Savage. He had been on the road nearly an hour, and that had brought him about 35 miles northeast of Denver. The highway was straight, flat, and deserted.

This was prairie country, and these plains stretched eastward for hundreds of miles into Kansas.

A bit more than a century ago these plains offered the last great obstacle to settlers in Conestoga wagons before they reached the Rocky Mountains. Those wagons had carried countless families with their entire worldly possessions west.

Hostile Indians, the great tribes of the plains—the Kiowas and Comanches and others—had made life interesting for those pioneer folks. Several of the small towns that dotted these plains still bore names from the languages of those proud warrior tribes.

But those poor red bastards must have felt the world turn beneath their feet when the white man came, Savage thought. This was a thing that wasn't so terribly difficult for him to imagine, either. Not only was he an imaginative man, but in the nearly fifty years he had been on the planet, he'd seen plenty of surrealistic changes in the world himself.

Not the least of those changes was the war that he had participated in becoming little more than a cancelled television series while barely making a paragraph in the high school history books. Savage had been a teenager during the early sixties, the Golden Age of American materialism and power. He had survived to see the United States become the greatest debtor nation in the world. Still, it was also the last remaining superpower.

A world in changes, still going through, he thought. Perhaps a bit like those Indians long ago, the world had turned beneath Savage's feet more than a few times too. The soundtrack of his life was now the "oldies" station on the radio. Worse yet, the music played and written in his youth—music that maybe meant something to him—would all too often turn up on his TV as the background tune for a shampoo or car commercial.

The Savage did a lot of thinking when he rode the Serpent. For one thing, only a small part of his mind, almost the subconscious part, was needed to pilot the machine. It was sort of like the involuntary nervous system—you don't have to consciously think for your heart to pump blood, and as a rule you do not have to remember to breathe. It all just takes care of itself naturally on it's own. That's what it was like for Savage riding the bike, too.

On the other hand, if a car pulled out from a side road or some slime ball in a steel cage tried the old "left turn in front of him" trick, the involuntary nervous system acted before the conscious mind was even aware of it.

As he dialed the throttle back to a more comfortable 55, another part Savage's mind began to kick in. It was the part of his brain that was concerned exclusively with one thing—survival—and it was now hearing gunshots somewhere off the highway.

The exit sign he was waiting for was now in view. As he looked off to his left, he spotted the familiar 1971 Dodge Charger parked about 150 yards off the service road. Next to the big Dodge he could make out the figure of a large black man with a pistol in his hand.

The President of the Wheels of Soul was playing cowboy again.

Brown turned around and holstered his gun when he heard the sound of the big V-twin exiting the highway. He watched the sunlight dance off the Serpent as the bike turned onto the service road. He could hear Savage drop a few gears before leaving the blacktop and bouncing across the dry prairie grass toward him.

As the bike came to a stop, he observed Savage reach inside the leather bag attached to his handlebars and toss out a small, round piece of plywood and drop it on the ground near his bike. When he popped out his kickstand, it landed nearly dead center on the wooden disk.

"Be prepared," the black man commented.

"That's the Boy Scout motto, pal," Savage responded as he swung his leg over the Serpent and dismounted.

Brown was engaged in the task of individually ejecting the spent shells out of the big, single-action, .44 Magnum pistol. He collected the empty brass in his left hand and tossed them into a plastic bucket on the hood of his classic 71 Charger.

After reloading the weapon, he ran the cylinder over his left arm, spinning it to make sure it would not bind upon firing. The six-shooter then went back into the quick draw holster so smoothly that it appeared to be a reflex action.

"Shit!" Savage said mockingly, "a regular Deadwood Dick."

Brown's face showed genuine surprise at the remark.

"What the fuck do you know about Deadwood Dick, white boy?"

"Well pardon me all to hell for being the educated man that I am. Now where's the brews, Darkie?

"In the trunk," Brown snapped and tossed Savage the keys.

A broad smile broke across Savage's face as he popped the trunk open and saw the large cooler of iced beer. He quickly extracted two cans from the cooler, tossing one to Brown and popping the other almost simultaneously as the black man caught his.

"Would you like me to show you how to handle that iron, partner?" Savage challenged.

"How much money you got on you?" Brown replied.

Savage laughed aloud and picked up an empty beer can. He funneled a handful of sand into the can for weight and then held it above his head.

"Ready?" Savage asked.

"Toss it."

Savage tossed the can over Brown's head. When it hit the ground, Brown drew his gun and the air exploded with the roar of the magnum pistol. The black man had fanned off three quick shots that bounced the can three times, depositing it behind a scrub oak bush.

"Hold your lead, partner," Savage shouted before he ran up and retrieved the can.

"An impressive display, pal, but check it out. No holes in the can; just close hits blasting sand!"

"You know what the difference is between shooting a can and shooting a man is?" Brown asked coldly.

Receiving no immediate response, Brown answered his own question.

"Generally," he said, "a man's a little bigger."

"That's a fact," Savage agreed, "but I believe there's three slugs left in that iron, so pass it over."

Savage turned the can around and around in his hand as he inspected it closely.

"I guess we can use this can again," he taunted, "seeing's how it's still fresh, what with no bullet holes in it or anything."

"Eat shit and die," Brown responded. "Ready?"

"I was born fucking ready. Toss it."

Brown threw the can hard and far and with a high arc. When it hit the ground, there was a half of a second of delay before Savage's first shot bounced the can back into the air. Clearly a solid hit. Each time it landed, Savage took an extra small fraction of a second to flash-aim his front sight shot, and each time he fired the can was struck.

"The race does not always go to the swift, my friend," Savage offered as he began ejecting the empty shells.

"Let's get down to business," Brown suggested with a tone somewhere between exasperation and genuine but mild irritation with his companion.

"OK. So what did you find out?" Savage asked.

"The dead man was definitely some kind of cop," Brown replied. "Not a fed, though, maybe CBI, maybe even a county mounty. I don't know. But some kind of undercover cop, and they ain't even found no corpse yet."

"Damn! Pretty much like we figured from square one," Savage replied.

"And our boy with the fancy jewelry and big Mercedes—well, he's the number one guy they wanna talk to," Brown continued.

"So how come they haven't brought him in?"

"Don't know. Maybe they can't find him. Maybe they're waiting on something else—you know, more evidence, something like that—before they make their collar. Who knows?"

"We got to know," Savage said flatly.

"This is a strange one, man. People don't seem to want to talk. I mean, people just don't want to talk," Brown repeated.

"What people, man? Who?" As soon as the words had passed his lips, Savage knew he had asked too much.

"I don't give you their names, partner, just like I wouldn't give them yours, understand?" Brown turned and looked directly into Savage's face as he spoke.

"I understand, pal, and you better understand this. Never trust a fucking cop." Savage's warning was stern and sincere.

"Yeah, yeah. My daddy told me that too, white, but you know what? You want to do business, then you got to do business with the Man sometimes too."

"No, I don't understand," Savage responded. "I do business with people I can trust and that doesn't include any fucking cop. Think about it, man. A fucking pig's sworn to uphold the law, and he sells it to you for some money on the side. Well, what the fuck is he going to sell next, huh? I'll tell you, fucker. When the time comes, when the price is right, he'll sell your black ass too . . . and that's a sale that might be final."

"Lighten up, man," Brown returned. "We gonna go ahead with this plan or what?"

"We play it as it lies. We don't make a move til the opportunity presents itself and all our ducks are in row and all quacking for us. But now we stand a real good chance of knowing exactly when and where that will be, partner."

With that, Savage casually tossed his empty beer away. But, the instant it hit the ground the black man snapped the pistol from his holster and blasted away at it.

The can was only about 12 feet away and the roar of the muzzle blast was deafening to the Savage.

"Jesus Christ, you fucking asshole. How about letting me know before you do shit like that. Jesus!"

"Target of opportunity, man," Brown laughed. "Gotta move when the mark presents itself." He had enjoyed making the Savage jump.

Savage shook his head. "Like you said: let's get down to business. The greaser's got the phones now. He's playing with them already, too. I've listened to some of the tapes and—"

Savage was cut short by his companion.

"Hallelujah and thank ya, Jesus!" Brown shouted as he bounced his now empty beer can off the big Dodge. His mood had now suddenly changed to outright elation.

"Don't get your pee so hot just yet, pal. So far, all the shit I've heard is in some sort of gutter Spanish, weird-ass slang. I can't figure a lot of it out just yet."

"But you will, brother, you will," Brown encouraged. "Then it's gonna be high tide and green grass, fuck me with a stick!" he shouted. "We got the main line to the mother lode now!" Brown was barely able to contain his enthusiasm.

Savage looked at his partner with a touch of amusement but also with more than a little concern. The disturbing thought was dawning on him that despite the more than eight months of planning and secret meetings they had conducted together over this heist, it was perhaps only now that Brown was beginning to take the operation seriously.

"Look, buddy," Savage continued, "we have a plan and we are executing it one stage at a time." Again Savage was interrupted.

Brown held the pistol to his ear as he spun the cylinder. His speech came in a quick, excited staccato.

"Come on, man, I mean we're gonna know now! The time, the place, everything we need to know to be there, baby! I mean it's always gonna be someplace out of the way, and the cash and the stash will be right there . . . and so will we, baby. All we gotta do is take it, mama!"

"Are you high or what, man?" Savage asked. "Now I'm going to repeat the obvious for you. We can rip these guys off for all the cash and you can sell the fucking drugs, but if we have to kill anybody or there is any gunplay at all, we'll just be buying ourselves a ticket to fucking prison. You got that? We gotta work it so we just take the money, the meth, and any blow, and no shooting. Then who are they gonna complain to? The cops? That's what makes it work, but if the cops get involved, then we're just working our way into the slammer and for a real long stretch, man."

Savage saw the hunger in his companion's eyes, and so he reinforced his point. "You better get that straight, partner, because if you don't, I'm out. I don't plan on going to any fucking prison for 20 years because you're so fucking hot to trot you can't stick with the plan."

"I can stay with the plan, brother," Brown said defensively.

He was now making a conscious effort to restrain his display of enthusiasm. But restraint had never been the man's strong suit. "Fucking relax, man. I'm just excited because . . . well, shit . . . I mean, getting the phones in there, that's the whole key to this deal. I mean we can really make this thing work now."

"If I didn't think we could make it work, I wouldn't have gone to all this trouble in the first place." Savage felt his patience strangely tested with Brown.

"Listen to me, man. What we can't afford to do is to let those dollar signs fill our eyes and lead us into moving before things are just right. I'm telling you, the stakes are big on both sides, partner. We make it and we're damn near set for life. But if we fuck it up, we might lose our lives. That, or shit, it'll be hard fucking prison time."

Brown knew when Savage was trying to be serious, and he seldom let him get away with it.

"Yeah, you trying to tell me you haven't already spent that money in your own mind, maybe a dozen times, maybe a dozen ways too. Maybe it's *you* that needs to ease up a bit, huh? Cause' I already got the message."

"Maybe so," Savage conceded, "but if we want to get that money and be around to spend it, then we have to measure every fucking move we make before we make it. That's all I'm saying."

Brown popped another beer and handed it to the Savage as he wrestled a second brew from the cooler for himself. He rolled himself out onto the hood of his big Dodge and leaned back against the windshield. He stared into the crystal blue sky as he sipped his brew, and he spoke his next words with deliberation.

"So how do you plan on spending your share?" he asked.

Savage decided to indulge himself in that speculation. Besides, he thought it might relieve some of the tension between them.

"First off, I'm going to build myself a righteous crib up in the mountains. You're gonna need a four wheel to get there, and if you come," Savage's smile returned to his face, "you had better have been fucking invited."

"What about your shop?"

"I'll pay somebody to run it for me most of the time. Got to have a place to put together those righteous, super high priced sleds I'll be building, you know, for the folks with more money than brains."

Savage raised his beer can and pointed it at Brown. "And what about you? Maybe a big pink 'pimp mobile' and a stable full of hard working mamas?" he joked.

Brown responded as if he had not heard Savage's remark.

"My little girl, Kisha, she's graduating from CU next September." Brown leaned over the fender and spit between his front teeth. "Working in that damn cafeteria slopping down shit for that rich, white trash. She's got good grades, man, and I'm gonna see to it that she has everything she needs to go to that law school. She ain't gonna have to work no damn side job while she's doing it, either. She's gonna be somebody," he declared. "Time's gonna come and my girl's gonna be somebody. You hear that, white boy?"

"I hear," Savage responded.

Dog Soldiers: Chapter 10

Before Sharon had met Pete Savage, all she knew about "bikers" was what she had gotten from TV and the few biker films her high school boyfriend had dragged her to as a teenager.

From time to time any one of the four men who now sat at her kitchen table might easily, at least by their outward appearance, be mistaken for the fiction of those same celluloid images.

But after five years of living with Pete Savage, there was no possibility of doubt in her mind. For better or worse the four persons sitting in her kitchen were the genuine article—certified scooter trash.

They were at once both dangerous children and yet at the same time some of the most substantive men she had ever encountered.

Their word meant something to them, and they never gave it lightly. Friendship and loyalty were at the core of their whole association, yet they all were basically loners, even misfits of one sort or another.

They just didn't fit into mainstream society. They did not want to, either. They had created their own society, and they ran it by their own rules. It all seemed to work for them, too, most of the time.

Sharon knew they weren't too reliable for things like holding down a nine-to-five job or even taking out the garbage, but there were other tasks for which they could be completely relied on. But it wasn't easy for her to figure out exactly what those things were going to be.

Experience had shown her that it did include things like getting out of bed in the middle of the night and driving more than a hundred miles to bring a primary chain to some member whose bike had broken down on the road. Likewise she knew that if she needed help, she could call any one of 60 or so Dog Soldiers. All she had to do was get them on the phone and ask, and they would be right there, anytime, anyplace, for any job.

Sharon had made that call once, too.

Savage had been out of town buying Harley parts in Los Angeles. It was a Friday night, and she was driving home from the real estate office. She had nearly crashed her car into a dune buggy containing three teenaged boys. The kids had obviously gotten an early start on the weekend's beer drinking.

Sharon figured their drinking was likely why she had nearly collided with them. But it all happen so fast she wasn't really sure whose fault it had been.

In any case the trio in the dune buggy elected to pursue her all the way home to the shop. She had used the remote control to close the driveway gate behind her, but when she got out of the car and looked back, they were still in the driveway just outside the gate.

One of them stood up in the open-air buggy yelling loudly at her. She couldn't make out what he was saying, but it wasn't too hard to guess at. Receiving no reply, they all began tossing their empty beer cans against the iron gate.

Just kids, really, playing at juvenile delinquent, she thought.

Still, the shop was out in the country, and the nearest neighbors were more than three mile away. She didn't know how far their act was going to go, and she didn't want to find out. But most of all she wanted to make sure these kids never came back to her house.

Still, it never even occurred to her to call the police.

She called the President of the Dog Soldiers, Macahan, and a short time thereafter the teenagers outside her gate realized their worst collective nightmare as two dozen grizzly looking outlaw bikers roared up and surrounded them.

The way all the bikers smiled at them and especially the polite way the leader asked them what they were doing there only amplified the teenagers' unchecked speculations as to what horror might become their possible fate.

Sharon had thought that perhaps these kids had seen some of the same old biker flicks she had.

Once Macahan and the others arrived, it all seemed sort of funny to Sharon. She could see that the kids were nearly in a state of shock, but she also knew that nobody was going to hurt them.

In the end all Macahan did was make the kids pick up their empty beer cans and promise not to come back. It was enough. For those kids it had all been much more than enough.

Sharon's thoughts were snapped back into the present in her kitchen as she saw Bright Eyes cocking his arm in preparation to toss his empty beer can into the trash.

"Don't throw it! Walk over there and put it in the can!" she snapped.

"Busted!" Goforit jeered.

Bright Eyes shuffled truculently over to the trash can and deposited the empty. On the return trip he knocked open the refrigerator door, snatched out a brew, then snapped the door shut with a thud.

Bright Eyes used only one hand for this maneuver because the other was busy tossing a handful of unshelled peanuts down his throat. These were all washed down with the freshly popped brew. Yet somehow, through all of this activity, his speech continued unabated.

"You guy's are just gettin' where you don't wanna do shit! No fucking run to Mesa Verde this year, like now that's too fucking far for the shit, and now it's what? No fucking new pledges? What the shit? I mean it's like—"

"Stop your fucking whining, you dickless piece of shit," Savage interrupted, "and let's listen to the what the Pres has to say."

"There's no rule against new pledges, Bright Eyes," Macahan said. "Just a rule about who can sponsor one and right now that ain't you. Not quite yet anyways."

The President of the Dog Soldiers continued, "Bright Eyes and Goforit want this guy to pledge. There's some other members who want him, too. So maybe why not? Why not see if he works out? That's what a prospect is—somebody who is being evaluated as a prospective member. We get a chance to know them and they get a chance to know us."

Savage was more than a little surprised with Macahan, especially since it seemed this little speech was aimed directly at him.

"You want me to sponsor this guy?" Savage asked incredulously.

"That's got to be for you to decide, man. If you want to, that's fine. If you don't, well that's fine too. But first off, I have to ask if you got something against this dude. I mean something we should know, like if he's selling skag or some shit like that."

"No, man," Savage replied at once, "I got nothing against him. Shit, he's an OK guy as far as I'm concerned. Fuck," Savage hesitated a moment. "I guess I just don't want the responsibility for a damn prospect right now."

"Seems like maybe that's becoming a trend with you, man, not wanting club responsibilities," Macahan responded.

"But taking some fucking responsibility is what leadership demands. You're first officer in this outfit. That means something to me. What's it mean to you?"

"Well Jesus!" Savage complained as he began the journey for a fresh brew. "Rag on my ass over this shit, why don't ya."

"I'm saying you've been getting a little too much distance lately, man," the Pres said. "Maybe you need to start making some better decisions."

Savage smiled at Macahan as he popped the brew. Making some better decisions, he thought. That's just what he'd been doing alright. He'd made a decision, and that decision was that he was going to be free. He was going to tap that big score on Gold Chains and come away with more cash money than he could make in 30 years.

Freedom was what it was all about alright, and freedom never came cheap. It never came without risks either. Since the Savage needed a lot of freedom, he'd been taking a lot of risks of late.

Still, Macahan was a good president. He looked after things, and not much got by him, even the subtle shit. And besides, Savage knew he was right. He had been distancing himself a bit from the club.

He figured that with his plans with Gold Chains being what they were, it was better for everyone that way. Better for him and better for the members. Only now, old Macahan was calling him out on it.

The Pres couldn't have any real idea what was going down, of course, but Savage suspected that he had some suspicions that he was up to something outside the club.

What the Savage needed at the moment was a graceful way out of taking on this new pledge. He gurgled his brew and smiled as the sparkling solution came to him. The beer and the weed were working on him a bit, but he knew exactly what he was doing.

"Big decision, people," Savage announced to his comrades, as he looked each of them directly in their eyes. "So we have to ask, what do the runes say?"

A shallow but collective groan arose from the others.

"Oh man! We gonna go through this mumbo jumbo again." Goforit's complaint was spontaneous but was quickly cut short by Savage.

"My house, brother, my rules," Savage cautioned. "Bring us the runes, honey."

"Why of course, right away, your scumship," Sharon mocked as she left the room to retrieve the bag of runes from their bedroom.

Her response brought on a cackle of jeers and taunts from Bright Eyes and Goforit.

The runes. A bit more than a thousand years ago shaman holy men among the tribal Vikings had used this collection of stones to divine the future, to decipher the meaning of omens, and to see into the very hearts of men. The runes consisted of 25 flat stones each with its own inscription in the ancient Nordic alphabet. The individual stones were drawn at random and represented such archetype concepts as strength, self,

90

partnership, defense, warrior, protection, growth, movement, flow, gateway, and others. These were all guideposts and icons for the spiritual warrior.

Indeed, when the Savage created the colors for the Dog Soldiers, he had selected three of the runes—Teiwaz, Raido, and Dagaz—meaning Warrior, Journey, and Breakthrough. On sanctioned runs each Dog Soldier wore those colors on their backs, and some had them tattooed into their very flesh.

Sharon returned with the worn leather bag that for two decades had contained Savage's set of runes. She placed them reverently on the table and was silent. She was content only to watch.

Savage shook the bag, and the clatter of the stones within was heard clearly against the silence. "Draw three stones," Savage told Sharon. Once again, he turned his gaze directly into each of the eyes of his brothers.

"Here comes the spooky shit again," Goforit commented.

"You got it pal, the spooky shit," Savage responded in calm earnest.

Sharon reached into the bag and felt the cuts in the ceramic pieces to determine the sides that bore the runic characters and the sides that were blank. She chose one and placed the stone on the table face down so its symbol could not be seen. It was just like dealing a card in a game of poker. The second and third rune were drawn and placed beside the first, all face down.

Savage gave the signal, and Sharon began to turn the runes from right to left.

The symbol upon the first rune was Teiwaz.

"Teiwaz, the Warrior!" shouted Bright Eyes.

Sharon smiled to herself. Playful and superstitious children, she thought, but reasonably happy children. She turned the second rune.

"Raido!" Bright Eyes' voice betrayed his own shock, but he elected to move boldly.

"Odin!" Bright Eyes shouted. He stood, raised his arms, and looked up at the ceiling.

"Is there any need, brother?" he challenged Savage. "Two of the three runes of the colors, just as they appear here." His eyes dilated with satisfaction as he thrust out his tattooed arm, which bore those same runic symbols indelibly etched into his flesh.

"No need," Savage conceded.

The game he had devised to avoid the commitment of sponsorship had, against all odds, turned against him.

But the Savage knew the runes for what they were—not a fortune telling device so much as an oracle. An oracle does not reveal the future but directs one's attention to the real substance of the matter at hand by illuminating one's own preconscious thoughts and fears. The runes were not a window showing what waited outside the door; they were more of a window offering a view of what, though obscured by shadow, lay inside oneself.

Savage swept the runes from the table in a single motion and returned them to the bag.

What was the final rune? Savage would leave that unknown.

Was it Dagaz, the Breakthrough, the final rune of the colors? It did not matter, for the Savage had recognized his own breakthrough. For him, the signs were clear.

He dropped the third, unturned rune into the change pocket of his jeans, leaving it unseen and unknown both to himself and to his companions.

"So what you figure now?" Savage asked directly of Bright Eyes.

"We move! We go! If this dude's gonna be a Dog Soldier, he'll be ready to make his run right now, tonight!" Bright Eyes declared.

It was a requirement that every Dog Soldier pledge complete a run of at least 500 miles round trip on his own scooter and accompanied by at least one club officer. After that, his pledge status was elevated to prospect.

Savage had instituted this tradition in the early days for one very pragmatic reason: to establish that the pledge had a reliable, roadworthy scooter since it would be Savage who generally ended up servicing the members' bikes.

"Fine," Savage responded.

Sharon looked at Savage with indulgent exasperation. Her voice was somehow still pleasant even though exaggeratedly sarcastic.

"Does this mean you are going to ride off into the sunset again, leaving me here alone for two or three days?"

"Well, sweetie, great heroes have been known to do that sort of thing from time to time," Savage responded.

"We're gonna ride over to this guy's crib. If he's there and he's willing, I'll be gone three days, maybe four. I'll be coming back here to get my road gear in any case, so I'll see you again before I leave, if I even end up making this run at all. The guy may not even be home or able to go. That's what we're going to find out tonight. Anyhow, you won't be left alone. If I'm on the road, Goforit and Bright Eyes will come back with me and stay here and look after the shop while I'm on official club business, right Pres?"

"Right as rain, man," Macahan declared. He directed his next words to Bright Eyes and Goforit.

"If this guy Mark's ready to ride, then those are the orders. You come back here and watch things till Pete gets back, understood?"

"Got it, Pres," Bright Eyes replied and Goforit nodded his assent.

Savage was grateful for Bright Eyes's enthusiasm. He had resigned himself to what had been an unchallengeable interpretation of the runes.

But now, Bright Eyes's daring condition that the prospect be ready to make his run that very same night gave him a final chance to be honorably excused from the duty of sponsoring the new guy.

The Savage smiled despite himself as he felt the face of the third unseen rune through the fabric of his jeans.

Dog Soldiers: Chapter 11

Mark O'Shey tossed the firearms magazine he'd been reading onto the desk and snapped off his desk lamp.

The one-room ground floor cabin that he'd called home for the last ten weeks had the slight smell of gasoline about it since his motorcycle was parked inside.

Besides the small desk, the bike, and a refrigerator, the only other furnishing in the room was a foam rubber pad on the floor that served for a bed. Despite its sparseness, the room was curiously neat and clean.

Mark had been ready to flop out on the foam rubber pad when he heard the sound of Harleys arriving outside. A second later he was sure that this was exactly what he heard as the big V-twins roared outside his door for a moment. He then heard the bikes shut down one after another.

He tossed a copy of the *Denver Post* over the Colt Detective Special revolver that lay on the desk and snapped the lamp back on. As expected, he heard loud pounding on his door. He recognized the voice of Bright Eyes yelling outside.

"Open up, man! We got important business with you!"

"Important to who?" Mark responded as he opened the door to admit his unexpected guests.

"Welcome all to my humble abode," he greeted them. He noticed immediately that in addition to his pals Goforit and Bright Eyes, Savage and another biker were there.

"Important to *you*, man," Bright Eyes said with as much seriousness as he was capable.

"Man, you got a gas leak on that Pan," Goforit remarked as he knelt down by the bike and looked up at the float bowl of the old Model M carburetor.

"Check it out, bro," Mark responded, thus giving the man permission to touch his bike.

"Yeah, fucking wasted float bowl seal. Could try to torque down the bowl nut, but a new seal is what you really need here."

"Check that shit out later," Bright Eyes protested. "We didn't come here to wrench on the dude's bike."

"Just why did you guys come here?" Mark asked.

Bright Eyes turned to Macahan. "I reckon that's for the Pres to say."

"Hi," Macahan said, offering his hand. "I'm John Macahan, President of the Dog Soldiers Motorcycle Club."

"A pleasure," Mark responded as he shook Macahn's hand.

Macahan gestured to Bright Eyes and Goforit.

"These dudes led me to believe that you might want to see about joining our club. Is that right?"

"Shit, it makes me feel real good that you'd even ask," Mark replied. "Yeah, I sure would like to ride with you guys."

"Well, here's the deal, Mark. Here's how it works. We have to know that we can depend on you. By the time we have a good feeling about that, you'll know that you can depend on us. We got a process to do all that, to find out if you can fit in with us, and I hope you can, man."

"I figured I'd have to earn it," Mark replied.

"Your kinda short on places to sit, pal," Savage observed. "Got any brews in that fridge?"

"Yeah, help yourself. I think there are a few left in there."

"Indeed there are," Savage said as he snatched the last three brews from the refrigerator. "You know, a Dog Soldier's always willing to share with his bros. It's an important part of the association, right Pres?"

"Correct," Macahan responded. "But first, Mark needs to know what a Dog Soldier is . . . and what is a Dog Soldier?" With this began the recitation of the litany among the patch holders.

"A Dog Soldier is a survivor," Savage responded.

"And how does a Dog Soldier survive?" Macahan asked.

"A Dog Soldier survives as a unit," Goforit replied.

"And what must a unit have to survive?" Macahan asked.

That night Mark and Savage packed their bikes and headed for New Mexico.

Dog Soldiers: Chapter 12

Savage had let the campfire burn down to nearly coals as he lay on his back on top of his sleeping bag and studied a clear, moonless desert sky.

"Thousands of 'em, man. Thousands and thousands," Savage declared.

"You mean stars?" Mark responded, instantly feeling a little stupid the moment he uttered the words.

"Yeah, stars. Ever wonder what's out there, man?"

"Sure, I guess just about everybody has. You can sure see a lot of 'em out here though . . . once you get out of the city, I mean."

"You have to get out of the city to see a lot of things," Savage offered. "So what do you think's out there?"

"Who knows? I think there has to be someone out there, though. Space is so vast. There has to be somebody out there," Mark repeated. "Fuck, maybe something better too, man, maybe somewhere out there, somewhere, maybe there could be something better."

"Maybe so, pal, but there could also be something a lot worse."

"I guess that's true too. Never really thought about that," Mark confided with moderate amusement.

Savage studied the thousands of lights in the clear desert sky. A satellite passed overhead and he pointed it out to Mark.

"That's a satellite, man. See it?"

"Yeah. Never saw one before. Damn it moves fast!"

"Something else out there," Savage echoed. "Yeah, maybe there is, and ya know what? Maybe if we really knew what was out there we'd shut off all our radio and television transmissions and pray that our little planet was never discovered."

"Well, you're just full of bright and cheery thoughts tonight, pal," Mark declared. "But if that were the case, then who would it be that we'd pray to?"

The question took Savage off guard for a moment. "Well, now, that's the real question, I suppose. Is there anyone to pray to? And if there was, would they give a fuck to listen anyway?"

The previous evening the President of the Dog Soldiers had explained to Mark the purpose of the run that he was now making with Savage, the number of miles required, and everything else he needed to know. It was also made clear that Savage would call all the shots.

But what had not been explained was their exact destination except that it was somewhere near Taos, New Mexico.

Where specifically was Savage taking him?

"So what's the deal here, Road Captain? Is it supposed to be some mystery?" Mark tossed another small branch into the campfire. "I mean, is like that part of the setup? Or can you tell me where we're going?"

Savage reached into the coin pocket of his jeans and withdrew the single rune he had placed there earlier that last night.

He held it in the firelight a moment so Mark could see that the object was in his hands during the brief flare-up of the campfire. He then tossed it to him.

Mark deftly snatched the rune from the air and studied it. He drew his thumb over both its surfaces, turning it over in his hand and examining both sides carefully.

"What's this, man? A flat, blank white stone. What's it mean?"

"Odin!" Savage replied. "The blank rune stands for the unknowable, the void. It is the rune of destiny."

Mark was silent for a few moments. He didn't quite know how to handle this mystic stuff, and he didn't want to do or say anything that the Savage might take offense to.

Savage had not felt it necessary to explain that the blank rune also represented both the beginning and the end. In this sense it could mean death. But most often this was just a symbolic death—the abandonment of one way of life for another; transition, life's forces in motion.

"Does this mean you can't tell me where we are going?" Mark asked, tossing the rune back into Savage's hand.

"There are no destinations, brother, only the journey," Savage remarked. He noticed Mark's face wince slightly in amusement at this response, but he continued. "Our present journey is to Taos, then Mescalero, New Mexico."

Mescalero? Mark had no idea where that was, but he did recall the name from some western movie he'd seen as a kid. Mescalero was the name of an Indian tribe. They were Apaches, if he recalled correctly.

"That's an Indian name, right?" Mark asked.

"Apache Indians," Savage responded, "and that's where we're ultimately headed. To see an Apache."

"Then what?"

"Then whatever fucking happens, happens, man," Savage responded. "You got to learn to relax, roll with things. It's a real nice ride down that way, too. We'll pass through Taos tomorrow, stop, get some eats, then take 14 out of Santa Fe down to 54 and hit Carizozo. Maybe we'll have a drink there at the Torro Del Oro."

"Torro Del Oro?" Mark echoed.

"Filthiest desert rat hole of a low-life bar I know of, least ways between here and Juarez. It's got character. You'll like it."

Mark laughed to himself at the absurdity of the situation he had so suddenly found himself in. Then standing up, he paused a moment to stare once again at the brilliance of the heavens on his way to his bike.

"There's a jillion and half of 'em alright," he said.

Savage observed Mark rummaging briefly through his saddlebag before extracting a half pint of Jack Daniel's.

"A touch of the demon?" Mark asked.

"Why not?" Savage assented.

"You go first, Road Captain," Mark replied as he tossed the bottle to the Savage.

Savage caught the fragile glass bottle smoothly.

"Whoa man! Can't risk smashing the precious juice," he scolded.

"You seem to be quick enough," Mark observed. "So who's this Indian we're going to see?"

Savage twisted off the cap of a fresh bottle of fine whiskey and took a long sip.

"Billy Laughing Dog," Savage responded as he passed the whiskey back to his companion.

"Laughing Dog? How do they get names like that?" Mark thought a moment. "Is this guy a member? A Dog Soldier?"

"Only in spirit, pal," Savage replied. "I met him in 'Nam in '69. Haven't seen him since the Red River Run two years ago. Fuck, I guess it's three years ago."

"What does he ride?" Mark's question carried with it the unspoken assumption that any such friend of the Savage must ride a bike.

"Strange you should ask. Take a guess—what might suit an Apache?"

Mark passed the bottle back to Savage and pondered the riddle as his companion swallowed the bourbon.

"No!" Mark exclaimed. "You can't mean this dude's got an old Indian! Nobody's got an Indian like that anymore."

"Billy Laughing Dog does," Savage responded.

The Indian had been the only other American-manufactured motorcycle besides the Harley Davidson. Both machines shared the V-twin design and had similar profiles and displacement. But Harley Davidson had survived; Indian had not.

The Indian factory closed down in 1953. Anyone fortunate to have an Indian motorcycle had a rare treasure, but it demanded a dedicated owner to keep the machine running and roadworthy, some being more than 50 years old.

Unlike for most any year of Harley, Indian parts were quite scarce. It was the only bike besides a Harley that any Dog Soldier would consider riding if he could. It was also the only bike besides a Harley that the Dog Soldier by-laws would allow him to ride.

"Not only that he's got a 1955 Indian Chief, Black Hawk. Bet your wondering how?" Savage entreated.

"Seeing as how the factory shut down in '53, yeah," Mark acknowledged. "Seems more than a little curious."

"Bingo!" Savage agreed. "Factory shut down in '53 alright. Damn, it's good to know that I'm riding with a properly educated man."

Savage tossed a pinecone on the coals. As the fire flared up again, he examined the amount of whiskey remaining in the bottle.

"So how does this Apache pal of yours have a '55?" Mark asked.

"Seems the New York City police department loved the bikes so much that in 1955 they wrote a bid specification for an order of 200, but they wrote it up so only an Indian could qualify. The factory had been shut down for two years, but the order was filled by assembling 80-inch Blackhawks from parts still remaining on the shelf. There were only 200 ever made, and ol' Laughing Dog's got one. One hit left, pal," Savage observed as he passed the bottle.

"Damn, and all this time I've just been happily living in ignorance about Indians," Mark commented. The Savage immediately broke out laughing.

"Yeah, well they say ignorance is bliss." This guy Mark had a sophisticated sense a humor and Savage liked that.

"I gotta call the bar and let then know I won't be in Friday night," Mark declared.

"Thought you weren't on till Saturday evening? Well, tomorrow's only Wednesday. We should be back by Friday evening. But you better call 'em up tomorrow when we get to Taos."

Dog Soldiers: Chapter 13

The Mescalero County deputy unsnapped his holster, withdrew his Glock 9 mm pistol, and placed it in the lock box. Having thus secured his weapon, he unlocked the cellblock door, and he and the trustee entered with the morning food cart.

There were only six cells in the county holding center, but only one of those cells was currently occupied. As soon as the deputy stepped inside the cellblock, he heard the chanting coming from that cell.

He figured that the Indian had been at it all night long again.

The deputy lifted the round aluminum cover over the food tray and examined its contents.

"Now listen, Laughing Dog. Are you going to chant or are you going to eat?"

The Indian continued to chant. He sat in the center of the cell, his body rocking in cadence with his song.

"You got two nice sausages here, scrambled eggs and a piece a toast, some coffee. I'm not saying it's like the Holiday Inn up in Ruidoso, Billy, but it's decent grub and you gotta eat something. You didn't eat anything yesterday, so how long do you plan to keep this up?"

The Indian continued his chanting as if Deputy Martinez wasn't even there.

"I'm responsible for you while you are in here, Billy, and if you don't eat something today, rules say that I have to call Dr. Sanchez to come over here. They might decide that they have to feed you, maybe through some tubes in your arm. Now I don't want to see that, Billy. Just eat something, anything, so I won't have to make that call."

Abruptly Billy Laughing Dog stopped his chant and turned to deputy Martinez.

"I am fasting. My body must be purified before the second full moon."

The deputy was gratified that his directness had now given him the chance to at least communicate with the prisoner. He decided to continue with equal frankness.

"Well, Billy, that's going to be Monday, and Judge Saperstien won't be hearing your case till that morning. My guess is you'll be going right back here Monday night, and I don't think all the chanting in the world is going to change that. So I'm asking you again: just eat something. You don't have to eat it all. Just something to—"

"You are wrong," Laughing Dog declared flatly and confidently. "The second moon will not find me here."

"I hope you're right, Billy." Deputy Martinez's words came with a mix of exasperation and sincerity.

Billy Laughing Dog turned and faced the deputy for the first time as he spoke.

"You are a decent man, Deputy Martinez. Maybe you will pray to your Jesus for me."

The deputy was taken off guard by the remark. His hand found itself fingering the small silver crucifix he wore around his neck.

"OK, Billy, I'll pray for you. I'll pray to Jesus for you."

As Deputy Martinez left the cellblock, his ears were once again visited by the Indian's chanting.

Dog Soldiers Chapter 14

Bright Eyes looked up from the scooter he was working on in Savage's shop and saw a late-model blue sedan pull up in front of the gate.

"What's that look like to you?"

"Cop. Detective, I'd say, likely Denver Metro division," Goforit responded confidently.

"Definitely some kind a cop," Bright Eyes agreed. As the words left his mouth a Colorado State highway patrol car pulled up directly behind the sedan.

"Definitely some kinda cops," Goforit repeated.

"I'd better see to it." Bright Eyes quickly glanced about the shop. "Nothing too wild in plain sight that I see."

As he looked back at the police cars he saw a large black man in a business suit exit the blue sedan and reach around the back of the control box to open the electric gate. The man had some sort of small tool in his hand.

"That guy's gotta be Denver Metro," Goforit declared. A moment later the electric gate began to swing open and the black man got back into his car.

"Jesus! How the fuck did he do that?" Goforit asked with astonishment.

"Shit, fuck. They are coming right on in. Shit!"

Bright Eyes jumped on his bike and kicked over the engine.

"I'll go out an' stall 'em. Be casual, man. But you know, look around here. Just see that nothing wild is in plain sight."

Nothing wild might mean a small bag of pot, a roach from an old spliff or maybe a pipe.

"Got it," Goforit replied as his companion jumped on his bike and roared out the few hundred yards to the gate entrance.

The two police cars were passing through the gate, but when their occupants saw the cycle coming toward them, the man in the business suit stopped his car, blocking the gate. The man stepped from the car with his gun drawn.

Concealed carry, thought Bright Eyes. A fucking detective for sure, and it looked like he had an attitude, too.

Bright Eyes locked the rear tire of the big Harley and brought the bike to a sliding stop on the grass. Jumping off the bike he dropped the kickstand all in one motion.

"You are fucking trespassing on private property! Who the fuck are you and what's your goddamned business here!" Bright Eyes shouted defiantly at the black man with the pistol.

"You better just hope that you don't become my business," the detective replied.

At that moment, the two uniformed highway patrol officers exited their car. One came between the man in the business suit and Bright Eyes while the other remained next to the open door of his patrol car.

"Fuck you!" Bright Eyes shouted.

The black man instantly holstered his gun to free his right hand. He pushed the highway patrolman aside and snatched Bright Eyes up by the lapels of his cutoff denim jacket and tossed him solidly against the sedan.

"You trash!" he screamed into Bright Eye's ear as he bounced the biker's head against the roof of his car.

"Now that's enough, Detective Sloan!" the highway patrolman shouted with authority. State Trooper Sander's voice carried the command presence of a Marine drill sergeant, which is just what he had been 23 years ago. He began to pry Bright Eyes away from the detective's grasp.

"These bastards always carry weapons and drugs," the detective declared, "and I'm searching this prisoner, trooper!" Sloan shot back at the patrolman.

"Prisoner?" the patrolman responded. "I don't recall any arrest being made. Are you arresting this man, detective?"

Detective Sergeant Sloan was seething with anger as he tossed the diminutive biker into the hands of the patrolman.

"You search him then, goddamn it!"

After a brief but professional pat down, Patrolman Sanders took his hands off Bright Eyes and displayed his open palms toward the man in a gesture of reconciliation.

"Now son, we seem to have gotten off on the wrong foot here."

The patrolman turned to Sloan. "Detective, if you will let me have the warrant, then with your help, Trooper Styles and I will see that it's executed. But I will not allow any abuses here, detective. And I hope you understand that I mean just what I say. Remember, myself and Trooper Styles will have to write a report just the same as you will."

Detective Sloan jammed his hand into his inside jacket pocket, produced the warrant, and slapped it into Patrolman Sander's hand.

"Thank you, detective. Now what's your name?" the patrolman asked Bright Eyes.

"Harold Jenkins," Bright Eyes replied.

"Can I see your driver's license, Mr. Jenkins?" the trooper asked.

Bright Eyes extracted his license from his wallet and handed it to the officer, who examined it and passed it to Detective Sloan.

"Then you don't live here?" Sanders asked.

"No, we're just here watching the shop while Pete's gone."

"Where is Pete Savage?" Detective Sloan demanded.

"He ain't here," Bright Eyes replied.

"Where did he go?" The Detective's tone was more than insistent.

"Like I said, he ain't here now," Bright Eyes repeated flatly.

Trooper Sanders could see that the detective was working himself up for another outburst, so he cut Sloan's next question short by asking one of his own.

"Well, Mr. Jenkins, we have a warrant here to search the shop for stolen motorcycle parts and narcotics, so I'm going to ask you to get in the car with us, and we'll drive up there and look things over."

"I can ride my bike," Bright Eyes replied.

"Go ahead, you little monkey," Detective Sloan threatened. "Try to ride out that gate. That would suit me right down to the ground."

The look of exasperated disgust passed over Trooper Sander's face once again as he turned to the detective.

"Detective Sloan, your attitude is all wrong here, and frankly I don't give a damn why either. It's unprofessional and it's unproductive. I want you to get in your car and follow us over to the shop there. My partner and I will search the inside; you look around and see what you can find outside." The trooper then turned to Bright Eyes.

"Now Mr. Jenkins, are you planning on trying to get out of here on that bike, or will you ride it over to the shop there?"

"I got nothing to hide and I got no fucking reason to run."

"Very well then. You get on your motorcycle and ride over there right now." The biker complied and was followed shortly by the two police cars.

Bright Eyes arrived a moment before the lawmen. He had dealt with this "good cop, bad cop" shit before, of course. Only this time he felt like that it wasn't that simple. The state trooper just seemed to genuinely be a straight-up lawman to Bright Eyes.

"They got a warrant to search the shop," Bright Eyes informed Goforit with a tone of resignation. "Watch out for the nigger. He's got a fucking attitude and a half. The big highway patrol guy seems, well, straight, OK."

Bright Eyes' last statement carried a tone of grudging resignation of the facts at hand.

"Straight" was about the only decent thing Bright Eyes was capable of calling a cop, and he'd had pitifully few occasions to ever use it. None of this escaped his pal Goforit's attention.

The two highway patrolmen copied down serial numbers off Harley engine blocks and opened and closed dozens of metal tool drawers in Savage's shop for the better part of an hour. Detective Sloan searched the outside perimeter of the property.

Savage's Jeep was parked outside, and the black detective smiled as he approached it. He inserted a slender metal pick into the lock of the center console of the Jeep and had it sprung open in seconds. The smile broadened across the detective's face exposing his mouthful of perfect white teeth as he withdrew the heavy frame pistol from inside the console.

Sloan placed a pencil in the barrel of the gun and then inserted the pistol into a plastic bag that he withdrew from his suit jacket pocket. He returned to the shop, where the two state troopers were just about finished with their search.

"What do you have?" Sloan asked.

"Nothing. None of these serial numbers match any on the stolen list," Sander's younger partner replied. "How about you, detective?"

"Nothing," Sloan echoed. "I didn't find anything either."

Dog Soldiers: Chapter 15

Pleased to meet you, hope you guess my name. Confusing that's the nature of my game.

Mick Jagger

Savage's eyes adjusted from the brilliance of the sun-drenched desert highway to the cool darkness of the Torro Del Oro barroom. His eyes weren't getting any younger, and this task of adjusting to the darkness wasn't getting any easier.

Complicating this visual adjustment was the glare of neon lights radiating from behind the bar, which illuminated the glasses and liquor bottles as if they were some kind of garish religious shrine.

This particular bar might otherwise not have been the Savage's first choice of a place to down a few cold brews before making camp again. But it was there and it was open . . . and besides, he wanted to see how Mark would handle himself in this type of place. There were a lot of tables right up against the large storefront-type windows. That would allow them to drink their beer and keep an eye on their bikes.

It was from one of those tables that Pete Savage now looked outside to the street and admired his motorcycle.

"Truly an elegant study," Savage said to Mark, "and remarkably tastefully executed as well."

"Yeah, I notice you bring up the subject a lot."

"A masterful study in," Savage searched for the words, "understated elegance, and yet purely functional beauty."

"Yeah. You got a nice bike, Savage. I can see how you might have difficulty finding words to describe it an' all," Mark acknowledged before offering his own tribute to his own machine.

"But while there is the functional, semi-modern beauty of your very clean Shovelhead," Mark raised both his hands as if in prayer, then turned his open hands towards his own motorcycle, "there's also the very essence of the heritage itself, the classic grandeur of the Panhead engine, such as you see there." He reached for his coffee.

"Yeah, you got a sweet pan, not too many on the road these days either."

Both men saw that the discussion could only lead to an endless, mutual escalation with each of them discoursing on the particular and unique virtues of their individual motorcycles.

That's exactly how it ought to be, too, Savage thought as he glanced back out the window at his bike. When he did he also observed a tall, thin man on the street coming up the steps to the door of the bar. Something in the man's face told Savage to keep an eye on this guy.

The man came inside and walked directly to a table at the far rear of the bar where two men and two women were sitting. Mark and Savage could hear the man shouting something at one of the women at the table, but neither of the two bikers could understand what he was yelling.

The woman stood up and screamed back at the man. Her loud voice was perfectly clear to everyone in the establishment.

"You? Why should I come home with you? You haven't gotten it up in three years!" she shouted.

The tall man glowered like a blast furnace at the woman, and the man sitting next to her became visibly uncomfortable. "You're my wife, and if you ain't with me, you ain't gonna be with nobody!" the tall man shouted back. His body and his lips in particular were trembling with rage.

He turned and stormed back out the front door to the street. As he did he passed the table where Savage and Mark were seated.

"A serious domestic conflict, wouldn't you say? " Mark asked Savage just as the man left the bar. He had put this question to the Savage like he was requesting confirmation on his identification of some rare bird species.

"Yeah, sounds like a real stormy romance alright," Savage replied.

Both the bikers smiled and laughed mildly with each other over the incident. But suddenly Savage bolted from his chair, making a quick pace to the front door. Mark's head snapped around to look out the large window, but he saw nothing.

An instant later, the door was violently thrown open. The tall man had returned, and Mark saw the large-frame revolver in his hands.

"Gun!" he shouted to warn his partner, and then he saw Savage strike the man hard on the side of his neck using the edge of his open right hand. The man's knees buckled slightly while Savage's left hand controlled the man's gun hand.

"I'm going to kill you, bitch!" the man screamed as he struggled with Savage.

The roar of the gunshot was deafening within the confines of the barroom.

Savage felt the sharp recoil in his hand and felt the sting of a shower of tiny hot metal shavings burning into his hand as the revolver's .44 caliber slug blasted itself out of the cylinder and into the forcing cone of the barrel. Savage had managed to keep the muzzle of the gun down. The slug's impact raised splinters of wood as it exploded into the barroom floor. He now controlled the weapon's direction. He had both of his hands on the gunman's weapon hand.

Raising the gunman's hand straight up above him, Savage brought the gun down hard and struck the man in the face with it. This was accomplished while the weapon was still in the man's own hand. Savage then snapped a brutal wristlock onto the dazed gunman's weapon hand and used the unyielding metal edge of the revolver to enforce the Sankyo technique.

The next thing Mark saw was the gunman suddenly raising himself up on his toes and screaming out loudly with pain. His hair seemed to stand on end, and his scream seemed almost as deafening as the previous pistol shot.

"God awful painful, isn't it?" Savage asked the man as he re-applied torque to the radial nerves.

111

"But you know? It can get even worse . . . well, like this." Savage twisted his body while sticking the man's inverted wrist against his own chest. The man screamed again.

In the next instant the man's feet left the floor as he apparently tried to launch himself up to the ceiling from his toe tips. At that instant, Savage allowed the gun to fall from the man's hands onto the floor.

Mark snatched the pistol up.

"I got the gun," Mark shouted, even though he and the Savage were only three feet apart.

"Good, buddy. Just hold onto it for now. And would you step away from that window, please?" Savage's tone sounded like he was asking someone to pass the mustard at the dinner table.

His voice remained strangely relaxed and calm as he continued to hold the gunman, who still involuntarily strained to stay on his toes to help relive the terrible pain from the wrist lock.

Mark was confused for a moment but then stepped quickly out of the way as Savage took three large steps backwards with the gunman hopping on his toes behind him quite desperately. The pain bolted through the tall man's brain like white lightening each time he let his weight come even slightly off his toes.

Savage then yanked down on the wrist, bringing it to just above his belt buckle. The gunman's head whipped down, allowing Savage to speak directly to the man's face. He was brief.

"Airtime!" Savage announced.

He then ran the man forward across the length of the floor toward the windows. Just before they both collided with the tables, he cut straight down with his arms as if he were wielding a Samurai's blade rather than the gunman's wrist and arm.

The gunman's feet were ripped out off the floor, and his body hurled, head first, through space, easily clearing the table. There was an explosion of glass as the shooter's body blasted through the window and projected into the street below.

Savage and Mark looked at each other for a blank second, then directed their attention to the street, where they observed the man regaining consciousness. He was attempting to raise himself up from the pavement, but his right wrist buckled as he set weight on it. He collapsed to the asphalt as he issued yet another scream that could have waked the dead.

"Damn, where's the video camera when you need it?" Savage asked coolly.

"Shit!" Mark exclaimed, still a bit rattled.

He glanced around the bar at the terrified patrons. Some of them were only now getting up from the floor or out from behind the bar, where they had taken refuge at the roaring sound of the .44 Magnum.

Not to be outdone, Mark searched for words that would match Savage's obvious show of coolness under pressure.

"Well," he uttered, "I noticed you threw the bastard a bit to the left so if you missed he'd hit my bike and not yours."

A burly man quickly came from behind the bar. He was wiping his hands on a white bar apron as he stood next to Mark and looked at the man outside in the street.

"The cops are on their way," he shouted nervously. "Don't worry, they're on their way now."

"This is *his* gun," Mark said as he gestured toward the street. "He came in with it, he tried to use it, and my partner stopped him."

Mark dumped the shells out of the revolver into an empty water glass on the table.

"Let those be," Mark cautioned. "The police will want to take prints off the shell cases."

"Hell, I saw it. I saw it all," the bartender said anxiously.

He turned toward the remainder of the patrons in the bar. "Everybody here saw it. If you hadn't stopped him, he'd a shot somebody for sure. He's crazy. He was trying to kill somebody," The bartender repeated nervously.

Turning toward Savage, the bartender asked, "That was some kind of martial arts thing you used there, wasn't it?"

"Yeah, some kind of martial arts thing," Savage echoed back.

"Well, don't worry. The police will be here. Randy's called 'em, and they'll be here any minute," he repeated excitedly.

Mark observed two sheriff's cars pull up in front of the bar, their lights blinking. When the two deputies jumped out, their weapons were already drawn.

"Actually, the police are here now," Savage calmly announced to the barkeep.

Dog Soldiers: Chapter 16

If dogs run free, then why not we? Across this swamp of time. My ears hear a symphony, two mules in harmony with the cosmic sea. For what must be, must be, and that is all, if dogs run free.

Bob Dylan: Dogs Run Free

Deputy Martinez handed the driver's licenses to the Sheriff, who glanced at them momentarily before he smiled and looked across the barroom at Savage and Mark. He glanced back out the window at their scooters.

The bikers sat quietly enjoying their meal of cheeseburgers and onion rings, which prudence now told them to wash down with coffee instead of a brew. They wondered how long all this police paperwork was going to take.

Neither of the men was too worried about the legal fall-out from Savage's pitching the gunman through the window. There had been plenty of witnesses, and the deputy had made it clear to the sheriff that their statements backed up the motorcyclists' version of events.

Still, dealing with cops was never something the Savage looked forward too.

Savage smiled back as the sheriff of Mescalero County, Arizona pulled out a chair at their table and sat down.

"Evening men. Well, it seems I have you two to thank for stopping a killing here. Have either of you ever met Mr. Simms before?" Sheriff Ryder asked.

"Is that the guy who had the gun?" Savage replied.

"Yes," the Sheriff responded.

"Never laid eyes on him before."

"Me neither," Mark added.

"I see. Fact is this isn't the first time we have had to take Mr. Simms into custody, but this time I think the state of Arizona is going to see to it that we won't have to deal with him again for some time to come."

Even though this guy Simms had been a total dickhead and might have killed him or anyone else in that bar, a part of the Savage still couldn't wish prison on even his worst enemy.

"Too bad. It was just a plain stupid thing to do. Should have learned to control himself better. Once it goes to guns, though—." The Savage was at a momentary loss to finish his sentence.

"You did exactly the right thing, man," Mark said.

The sheriff's attention returned to the motorcycles parked outside in the street.

"Those are certainly some real fine Harleys you put together. Is that your work? Custom motorcycles?" The sheriff inquired.

"Yeah, I got a shop back in Colorado," Savage replied.

"I was a motor officer once, back in Phoenix, '69 thru '72. Department had us on the Flatheads then, police specials of course. Then in '73 they sold them and went to Hondas. Hell, that's when I quit."

At this remark both Mark and the Savage glanced at one another momentarily and then simultaneously broke out into laughter.

"All right!" Savage declared approvingly.

"So what brings you men down here to Mescalero County?" The sheriff asked.

The Savage smiled, but in one portion of his mind a voice said to him, 'Seems like a decent cop, but still a cop, so watch yourself.'

"Sort of a vacation, and I thought I'd look up some old friends while I was down this way," Savage offered.

"Maybe I can help you find them."

The sheriff's tone was easy and friendly. "Who were you coming to see?"

The Savage continued to smile pleasantly, but both men knew exactly what was going on, and Savage knew it was best that he appear not to be hiding anything.

"An Army buddy of mine, haven't seen him in I guess two, maybe three years."

"And what would his name be?"

The sheriff maintained his easy tone as if there were no badge pinned to his chest or gun on his hip.

"Billy Laughing Dog. He's an Apache," Savage conceded.

Sheriff Ryder's face reflected surprise as he turned momentarily to Deputy Martinez before he returned his eyes to the two bikers.

"Well, I guess you men are in luck. Hell, sort of, anyway," the sheriff explained.

"How's that?" Savage asked between a bite on his burger.

"Because I can tell you exactly where you can find Billy. He's in one of the holding cells, right here in our county jail."

Mark said nothing, and the Savage was momentarily mute as well.

"It's a simple assault charge," the sheriff declared. Then he turned to his deputy. "When does he come up for his hearing, Deputy?"

Deputy Martinez fingered the crucifix at his neck.

"He has his hearing 9:00 AM Monday morning, Sheriff."

"Well, would you men like to go see him?" Sheriff Ryder asked.

"Yeah, I would," Savage replied.

"Fine then. The deputy can drive you over to the jail and bring you right back here. We'll see nobody bothers those motorcycles either. I'll bet Billy will be real glad to see an old friend right now. Does that sound all right to you men?" the sheriff asked pleasantly.

'Just swell,' Savage thought. 'So now we get to ride in the police car to the county jail. Swell,' he thought, 'Just swell.'

It was, however, one of those rare times that the Savage thought it best not to speak his mind plainly.

"I suppose that would work, Sheriff. I'll tell you I'm a bit distressed to hear he's in jail, but I came down here to see him, so that's what I'm going to do. Maybe it's timely after all."

Savage had relaxed his mind and resigned himself to events as they unfolded.

Deputy Martinez smiled as he hooked his thumbs under his duty belt and hoisted the rig higher on his ample waist.

"You might be right, Mr. Savage. Your coming to see Billy might just be real timely now—real timely," the deputy repeated. "And would you please ask him to eat something when you see him? He isn't eating, and if he doesn't eat, then it's my duty to report it."

Dog Soldiers: Chapter 17

Billy Laughing Dog was sitting perfectly still on the cold concrete of his cell when the sound of the turnkey placed into the cellblock door distracted him from his meditations.

Deputy Martinez entered the cellblock. This, of course, was no surprise, but the sheriff accompanying him was, and of far greater surprise, and brighter still, was the appearance of his old friend, Pete Savage, walking with the sheriff.

Deputy Martinez inserted the key into Billy's cell. As he opened the door, he spoke.

"Well, Billy, somehow it looks like you were right. This man here has paid your bail."

"You OK, Injun?" Savage asked.

"I'm just fine now, my friend," Billy replied. "I could use a bite to eat, though."

Billy Laughing Dog then looked directly at Deputy Martinez and the silver crucifix that hung around is neck.

"It seems your Jesus is strong, Deputy."

Dog Soldiers: Chapter 18

Sometimes I think this whole world is just one big prison yard, some of us are prisoners and the rest of us are guards.

Bob Dylan

Mark and the Savage sat on their bikes in the back parking lot of the Mescalero County Courthouse and waited.

From time to time they glanced over at the windowless steel door that read:

PRISONER DISCHARGE: AUTHORIZED
PERSONNEL ONLY

Billy Laughing Dog's court appearance that morning had resulted in a not guilty plea and a preliminary trial date set five weeks later. Bail had been set at $10,000.

Savage had $1,000 wired to him, which was now in the hands of Tri-County Bonding Services. Now it was just a matter of waiting for the Indian to be processed, and then he'd be coming through that steel door to freedom.

"A thousand bucks, man. This dude must be some real friend, huh?" Mark declared.

"Yeah, I guess," Savage responded somewhat impatiently.

"Fuck, I do hate waiting on people," Savage complained as he spun himself around in the saddle of his bike. He rested his head on his sleeping bag and propped his feet up on the handlebars.

"You call out when you see him," Savage instructed the pledge.

"He'd be kinda hard to miss. The fucker's as big as a house. I thought Apaches were smaller and—"

"I'd be careful not to bring that kinda shit up around Billy," Savage cautioned. "He can get a little sensitive sometimes about that racial heritage shit."

"Oh?" Mark replied. "You mean I shouldn't say anything like, 'Fuck, are you some kinda half breed?' I mean, Indians don't have much facial hair, and how come—"

Savage shook his head. The smile on his face was close to breaking into outright laughter.

"No, you demented asshole. I advise you most definitely not to bring any of that shit up around Laughing Dog. Not at all."

"Thanks for the tip, pal," Mark replied earnestly, "'cause here comes Geronimo now."

Savage spun back around and jumped off his scooter to face the man who walked toward them. He raised his open hand over his head, and the big Indian mirrored his motion.

Their palms slapped together as both men shouted simultaneously, "Fuck me naked! Rangers lead the way!"

The two men hugged one another for a moment, and Mark observed once again just how big the Indian really was.

A clever remark passed through Mark's mind, but some instinct told him to keep it to himself.

"Free at last, pal!" Savage declared.

Billy Laughing Dog replied with simple sincerity.

"Thanks."

"So, what say we score us a few brews now," Savage suggested. "Maybe at that place over by Messilia?"

"We won't have time for that now, brother. We'll get something to eat, though." The Indian then walked over to Mark and stared directly into his eyes.

Mark stared back into the big Indian's face, feeling more than a little uneasy.

"He's got to come, too," Billy declared.

"Come where, man?" Savage asked with bewilderment.

"Chedeski Point," the Indian replied. "We need to all be there before the full moon rises tomorrow night."

"Jesus Christ! I mean, let me guess. Chedeski Point, that's somewhere on the reservation, huh?" Savage's deduction did nothing to relieve his bewilderment.

"Yeah," Laughing Dog responded.

The big Indian glanced back at the steel door of the jail. "And maybe Jesus does have a part in it, too."

"Why we got to go there, man? And why by tomorrow night?" Savage asked politely but directly.

"Nothing happens without a reason, brother. There's a purpose to everything that happens. Your coming here now," Billy Laughing Dog said as he turned to face Mark once again, "and your friend here, his being here is no accident either."

"How you figure?" Mark asked the Indian.

"Because it's what all of us need right now, all three of us. We're now part of the same sacred hoop. If we break it, evil is free over each of us, and then at least one of us will enter the spirit world."

Savage reached into the coin pocket of his jeans and extracted the blank rune. Though he could not fathom Laughing Dog's mysticism, he went with his gut, and at that moment his gut was telling him very clearly that this was not the time to separate himself from this warrior, his former comrade-in-arms.

"OK, pal, we've come this fucking far. I'm ready to run with it." He handed the blank rune to the Indian. "And when you know the time's right, you return it to me. Then I'll know it's time to head back."

Mark's voice made his sense of exasperation painfully clear as he turned to the big Indian and raised his palms before him. "No offense, man. I mean, I don't know what you're into, but I gotta get back to Denver. I got a job and—"

"What you got now is a choice, pal!" Savage pointed his finger directly into the pledge's face. "You ride out now and you're telling me you ain't got the heart to wear my colors. I seen you got the juice, but you gotta have the heart too, 'cause it takes both. Now, what's it gonna be, pledge?"

Mark rolled his eyes over a vacant Arizona sky, then looked both men in the face and raised his hands as if in a gesture of surrender.

"I guess we're headed for this Chedeski ass Point, wherever the fuck that is."

Dog Soldiers: Chapter 19

Just as every cop is a criminal and all the sinners saints, if you meet me have some courtesy, some sympathy and restraint, for with all your well-born politics, I can lay your soul to waste! Please to meet you hope you guess my name.

Mick Jager: Sympathy For the Devil

Tom Brown counted the money into Detective Sloan's hand, one crisp $100 bill at a time.

". . . nine hundred, one thousand," Brown declared as he crossed the black cop's palm with the last bill.

"I was expecting 12," Sloan said coldly.

"You said to unload it fast," Brown replied, "and there's some new shit in town now, real smooth and real good. So I had to drop the price on the stuff you laid on me to move it out quick."

"Now, you'd know better than to hold out on me, wouldn't ya, nigger?"

"I ain't stupid," Brown responded flatly.

Tom Brown didn't like Detective Sloan, and he didn't like being called nigger, even by another black man.

"So tell me about this 'new shit' in town," Sloan asked.

"Nothing to tell yet, 'cept it ain't nothing I ever seen around Denver before. Price ain't bad either. Could be some out of towners. Maybe they made a rip-off somewhere outta state, dumping it here fast and cheap maybe. If that's it, then they'll be here and gone and things will be back to normal for us real soon."

"Maybe, but I'm not so sure," the cop said.

The two men sat in Detective Sloan's car parked under the elevated highway next to the railroad tracks. A few blocks away was a black and Hispanic bar called The Boiler Room where

Brown had parked his Dodge Charger before walking to the rendezvous to meet Sloan. The drop points varied, but otherwise it was all just like he'd done a dozen times or more over the last two years.

The two men's conversation was suddenly abated by two long pulls on an air horn that pierced the evening darkness signaling a train coming out of the switching yard. The train was just getting up to rolling speed, but the sound of the clacking tracks exploded through the car as it passed by overhead. A deafening roar made speech impossible for a moment as Brown studied the brilliance of the arc of white light that issued from the locomotive and illuminated the tracks ahead.

After the train had passed, Detective Sloan was the first to speak.

"You were careful coming here? You made sure you weren't spotted or tailed?"

"Always do," Brown replied. "You got some special reason to be worried about that right now?"

"What's your business with that white boy over in Mountain View?" Sloan asked.

The question hit Brown like a lighting bolt, but his poker face betrayed nothing.

"Who you mean?" he asked.

"You know damn fucking well who I mean, nigger. Savage, Pete Savage. Now, what are you two cooking up?"

Brown attempted to inflect his voice with a tone of moderate irritation over the cop's question as if it had no relevance to their current business.

"Him? Yeah, we talk from time to time. He's Road Captain for the Dog Soldiers. The Soul's got sort of a peace treaty with them. Got nothing to do with our business."

Sloan remained silent as he stared out the windshield into the darkness.

Brown didn't like this, not a bit, but the cards were falling out on the table now, and since Sloan had brought the subject up for the first time, the opportunity presented itself to probe the cop's knowledge of Savage and the Dog Soldiers.

"You got some reason I should stay clear of that boy? If you do, why not just tell me. Ain't gonna help neither one of us if he's scheduled for some sorta bust and I'm there cracking beers or snorting lines with him."

"You don't have to worry about that," Sloan replied.

"Well how you figure that?" Brown responded quickly.

"He's been asking about things, hasn't he?" Sloan continued.

Brown knew he had to respond immediately and naturally or this experienced street detective would see right through him.

Reluctant as he was to give any information about Savage to this cop, there seemed no way out. In for a penny, in for a pound, he thought.

"Well fuck, alright. Now that you bring the shit up, he was asking about Captain Shields in Mountain View. Seems Shields was grilling him over some killing. He asked me if I knew anything about it."

"And what did Shields know about this killing?" Sloan asked.

"Well, I guess you'd know a whole fucking lot more about that than me."

Brown saw the cop's face stiffen with impatience at this last remark, but he continued.

"Shit, he said Shields showed him some pictures, pictures of him and some of the club members at a party, shit like that."

"Who else?"

Brown was becoming increasingly uncomfortable at the cop's unusual line of questioning, but he decided to push his luck.

"Look, I sell the damn blow and crank that you rip off from some fuckers, then I give you the damn cash money right in your hand. Now you gonna third degree me? Shit, how about you tell me something?"

The black biker had calculated and even hoped that the cop would explode at this bold demand for information. Maybe

Sloan would order him out of the car or at least give him the chance to bolt in a conspicuous and "authentic" show of anger.

But there was no such luck for Mr. Brown. The detective's voice was as calm as it was repetitive.

"Who else was in the pictures?" Sloan repeated.

"Some Mexican guy," Brown replied.

"And what kind of car did this Mexican have?" Sloan pressed.

Brown rolled down the window of the car and spit through the large space between his front teeth to buy himself a moment to consider before responding.

"Yeah, I think he did say something about them showing him a picture of some big white car. A Mercedes, I think. So what the fuck does that mean?"

Detective Sloan rubbed his index finger over the bridge of his nose as if considering some weighty matter, but he said nothing.

Brown pushed the cop further. "So fucking tell me: What's the story? Who the fuck was wasted, and what you got on this white boy?"

"The guy who was murdered was a cop," Sloan replied.

"Shit! I fucking knew it. A cop. Shit!"

Brown was surprised that Sloan had given him this key information, and it encouraged him to probe further.

"So what kinda cop?"

"He was an undercover detective. Out of Los Angeles, on assignment with the DEA to investigate speed manufacture and distribution among the bike clubs here in Colorado."

The cop's matter-of-fact tone seemed more than strange to Brown. It sounded like the cop was responding to some cross examination in some courtroom by a prosecuting attorney . . . or maybe like he was rehearsing for same.

The black biker wet his lips with tension. This was getting all too strange now. Sloan was telling him all this and acting weirder than he'd ever seen him before even when Sloan had been buzzed on blow or meth.

Maybe the cop was high, Brown thought. But no, it just did-n't seem that way.

"This guy Savage—you got him pegged for the killing?" Brown asked.

Sloan did not respond.

"Yo, man! You gonna talk to me or what? You got some-thing on this dude, Savage?"

Brown knew he was now pressing his luck rock hard with the cop.

"What I got," Sloan replied, "is his gun."

As Detective Sloan drew the heavy-frame revolver from un-der his coat, Brown realized in an instant that he wasn't just go-ing to show him the piece.

Brown turned instantly to push the barrel away, but when his hand reached the cold steel of this instrument for killing, it became the last thing in this world he would ever touch or feel.

The first shot from the .357 blasted through Brown's ster-num, ripping apart the left ventricle of his heart.

The first shot had killed the black biker instantly. But the de-tective quickly fired a second, a third, a fourth, until all six rounds of the 125 grain jacketed hollow points were expended into the man's corpse.

Sloan reached across the dead man and opened the passen-ger's side door. Grasping the steering wheel with both hands to anchor himself, he used his right foot to push the body onto the asphalt.

He slid over into the passenger seat of the sedan and leaned his head out the open side door and used a small flashlight to examine the body and the blacktop around it for any potential evidence. He saw none.

All Detective Sloan saw was the dark blood pooling beneath the corpse and then flowing crazily in between the mosaic of cracks in the asphalt. The whites of the dead man's eyes were still open, and he noticed that they reflected in the light of his small flashlight.

Glancing about briefly but carefully, he satisfied himself of the absence of any witnesses and that the only material evidence left behind were the six slugs in Brown's body.

Those six .357 Magnum slugs in the body had come from Pete Savage's Smith & Wesson Model 586 revolver.

Dog Soldiers: Chapter 20

Billy Laughing Dog turned off the big chrome switch on the gas tank of his Indian motorcycle, and the engine's roar came to a halt.

The metallic sign attached to the wire gate in front of him read:

RESERVATION BOUNDARY

No admittance without permission of the Mescalero Tribal Council.

The big Apache pulled the slip wire off the post and dragged the gate open. Turning to his two companions, he pointed to their motorcycles and drew his finger across his throat to signal them to shut off their motors as well.

Savage and Mark complied, and silence returned to the juniper and grassland plain that lies before the foothills of Chedeski Mountain.

"Either of you got any alcohol packed with you?" Billy asked.

"I got a little whiskey left," Mark answered.

"Get rid of it now. We're not bringing any alcohol onto the reservation," the Indian declared.

Mark withdrew the remaining half pint of bourbon from his saddlebag and held it up against the blue Arizona sky. He saw that only a few ounces remained.

"Not too much of a sacrifice I guess, chief," Mark replied. He took a pull on the bottle and passed it to Savage.

"A little early in the day," Savage protested, "but waste not want not."

Savage grimaced at the whiskey in the bottle for a moment and shuddered before tossing the remainder of its contents down his throat.

"Oshh! Breakfast of champions!"

Savage smiled at the big Indian as he slipped the empty bottle into the leather jacket strapped to the handlebars of his bike.

"We're pretty, our bikes are pretty, and we don't litter." he declared.

Mark gestured toward the sign that marked the entrance to the Mescalero Reservation. "What's the story on that? We won't be staked out to an anthill or burnt alive or anything if we're caught in there, will we?"

"Not if you act right," Billy Laughing Dog replied.

"Swell," Savage responded.

"We got about 20 miles or so to go on the bikes; then the trail gets too rough, so we'll have to leave the scooters behind.

"Leave my fucking Pan behind? Not damn likely," Mark objected.

Savage interrupted him. "Stop your whining, prospect."

"OK, Billy," Savage continued. "Tell me, where we going to leave our bikes and how do we get from there to this Chedeski Point place?"

"We'll leave the scooters at my cousin's."

Billy Laughing Dog saw the true reluctance in Mark's face, so he turned to look the man directly in the eyes before he spoke.

"Nobody will bother your bike there, man, cause there ain't nobody there—nobody but my cousin and his woman."

Billy Laughing Dog began rolling his bike through the gate onto his reservation. His two companions followed.

After closing the gate behind them, Billy remounted his scooter and kicked the engine to life. He shouted over its roar to his companions.

"Two big tough guys!" he jeered. "Afraid you might have to do some walking, huh?"

The big Indian then let out a yell mimicking an Apache war whoop he'd seen in a black-and-white western movie as a kid. He hit the foot clutch on his bike and pulled away. The cloud of dust raised by his slipping rear wheel scattered Savage and Mark with Mescalero Reservation dust.

Mark turned to Savage. "You gotta know your pal is a full-on nut case." Mark then kicked over his Pan for the third time in an attempt to start the machine.

"Guess he could be considered a bit of a section eight case," Savage replied.

The "section eight" that Savage referred to was section number eight of the U.S. Uniform Military Code of Justice. It was the section that described psycho cases, and thus a "section eight case" became the tag for any soldier judged so mentally unstable that it forced his release from service.

"A section eight," Savage repeated. "So what's that make us for following him?"

Savage followed his question with a single leisurely drop of his foot on the Silver Serpent's kicker, which started the beast.

"Try not to get scalped, pal," Savage cautioned as he let out his hand clutch on first gear and departed.

Mark turned his face away from the dust kicked up by Savage's scooter and decided to rest a moment and let his motor cool down before continuing his efforts to get the mill running. He wasn't concerned about falling behind. There was only the one dirt road, and Savage and the crazy Indian would have to be on it somewhere.

The dirt road followed a stream that wandered across the valley floor causing Savage to temporarily lose sight of the Indian. He then caught a glimpse of the road ahead and a bit of dust settling out of the air on the far side of a curve.

A strong desert sun had illuminated the particles like gold dust, and Savage knew that Billy Laughing Dog had made that turn just a second before. His speedometer told him that 20 miles an hour or maybe a bit less was about all the velocity road conditions allowed.

Secretly, he admired the way Billy was able to throw his big rigid-frame Indian around those turns. But then again, he thought, Billy had likely been running a bike down this road since he was a teenager.

He suspected that Laughing Dog was opening distance on him at a pretty good clip now, a thought which concerned him not at all.

As the Silver Serpent bounced down the earthen road, Savage drew in a deep breath of Arizona desert valley air and felt the warmth of the sun on his face. "There are no destinations, only the journey," he said to himself silently.

He and the bike were one. His mind was clear and free of all concerns at that moment—either concerns for things in the past or concerns for what may lie ahead. His total consciousness was absorbed by an appreciation of the present moment. Riding the Serpent had a way of transporting his consciousness, but the current setting seemed to amplify that familiar experience.

He tapped his left foot on the shifter and dropped back into first gear as the road left the desert canyon floor and began to climb the hillside to the mesa above. The switchbacks were tight and had to be taken at a prudent pace. Still, everything required to negotiate his bike even through these somewhat dangerous turns occurred nearly without conscious thought from Savage.

As he gained altitude over the canyon floor, he glanced momentarily over his right shoulder and gained a broad view of the flats below. The dirt road that he had just traversed traced itself clearly across the valley floor. Looking ahead and higher, he thought he caught a momentary glimpse of sunlight flashing off chrome before the next switchback obscured his view.

Coming around that turn, Savage saw that the road became a long, straight run, and a quarter mile or so ahead there was an overlook pullout.

Billy Laughing Dog was parked at that turnout. He sat on his scooter admiring the view as he watched Savage climb the road below. The sound of the Serpent's motor was delayed and distorted by the distance and terrain, giving Billy a somewhat surreal image of his friend's progress.

A minute later, Savage glided into the pullout alongside Billy Laughing Dog's bike.

"A magnificent view," Savage remarked as he dropped his kickstand out and dismounted his bike.

"Yeah, you can see most everything below from here," Billy replied.

"Heh! I wouldn't worry about your pal just yet. Slow going like this probably overheats that old Panhead a bit. He likely flooded it real good when he tried to get it running back at the gate. He'll be along," Laughing Dog assured.

Savage realized that this was the first opportunity he'd had since he and Mark had arrived in Arizona to talk to Billy alone.

"You feel like telling me what this trip's all about, Billy?"

"It's about keeping things in balance," Laughing Dog replied.

"Yeah," Savage chuckled, "but like, could you expand on that a bit?"

"Tonight's the full moon. Santos—he's an old man. People respect him. He told me to meet him up there some time ago." Billy pointed to the top of the mountain before them.

"This man Santos—he's some kind of Apache medicine man?"

"He's half Navajo. Got some Sioux blood too. It don't matter. He's an old guy and he knows a lot. He's close to the spirit world, cause he'll cross over soon. Santos has always been close to this land. A long time ago, Navajos and Apaches were one people, you know."

"No, I didn't know that."

"Apaches broke away, chose the path of warriors and raiders. Navajos are a society ruled by women. The women own everything; make all the important decisions for the people. It's still a lot like that now with the Navajo."

"Ha! So you're telling me that the Apaches were one of the first men's movements?" Savage laughed. "Hunters and raiders. Yeah, they are sure famous for that. So what's going to happen when we get where we're headed and meet this holy man?"

"It's a purification ceremony. It prepares me to see my true path. Sometimes . . . well, sometimes people have their vision then."

Laughing Dog turned and faced Savage.

"You think all that's a bunch of crap, don't you?"

"Fuck, man, I don't claim to know," Savage said sincerely. "If it works for you, then why the fuck not? I mean, well, shit. I can sure deal with that better than if you told me you'd become a Jesus freak," Savage confessed.

"That deputy, Martinez back in that jail, he prayed to Jesus for me. He prayed to Jesus to help me get out here now. I think it came from the heart, too."

Billy opened both his hands to the sky. "I prayed too, man, so I could get out of that cell and be here tonight, so I could meet old man Santos for this ceremony. And you know what happened?"

"What?" Savage asked.

"You showed up with your pal and bailed me out. That's when I knew; that's when I knew for sure."

"And what was it that you knew for sure, Billy?" Savage inquired.

"That you and your buddy, Mark, we are all part of the same sacred hoop. This is exactly what's supposed to happen right now. It's a circle, the three of us all being here in this place at this time we so we can close the hoop."

Billy's hands made two fists. Bringing them together, he continued. "All of us being here now, it's to make the circle of power complete."

"And so what's all this for, man? I mean our being here, bailing you out and all that. What's it all mean?" Savage's tone was without a hint of judgment or challenge.

"We can't know that now. Maybe because we're supposed to do something important here, or maybe it's so we aren't somewhere else. Maybe it's to put us beyond the reach of some evil, or maybe we are the ones who have to go and destroy that evil."

"Evil, huh?" Savage reflected.

"You believe in good and evil, man, I know you do. At Ben Lai, you stopped them from killing that old woman and boy. They was both VC, you knew that they were VC, but they were unarmed prisoners and you wouldn't let 'em shoot them down. You believe in good and evil, man," the Indian repeated.

"Yeah, I guess I do, Billy," he admitted flatly, "but you gotta know all this stuff's a little . . . well . . . out of the ordinary. Besides, stopping some semi-literate, battle-shocked grunts from greasing an unarmed old woman and boy—well, that hardly makes me a saint, pal."

"Maybe not, but if saints knew who they were, then they wouldn't be saints, would they?

"People don't see their part in things. They're separated even from their own power. But everyone has a path that's theirs because the Great Spirit puts everybody here for a reason. They have to find that reason themselves and then live their true best destiny, a destiny that's interwoven with everyone else's. It puts things in balance. When a person's path is correct, then they're in harmony with everything, and their power is strong, because it's part of the infinite power. It's part of the scared circle."

"Well, buddy, it all sounds a little wild. But I'm standing with you, and whatever happens, happens."

Billy Laughing Dog stretched his arm out before him with his palm turned toward the valley floor below. Then, turning his hands to the sky, he brought them to his face as if smelling a scent on his hands.

"Your buddy, he's coming on now," the Indian declared.

Savage studied the terrain below and saw no sign of Mark. But a moment later he thought he caught the sound of his motor.

"You gotta be an Indian to tell things like that!" Billy Laughing Dog joked.

A minute later, Mark's bike became visible as he ascended Chedeski Mountain to join his companions. Savage watched as Mark struggled with the old Panhead up to the turnout. When he pulled in, he seemed a bit out of breath. Apparently, that old rigid frame on his Pan had beat him up a bit on this rough terrain.

"I didn't build this scooter for this kinda run, dudes. I gotta take it slow; otherwise she'll overheat for sure."

"Yes, you're right about that," Billy replied, "but we won't be traveling too much further on these iron horses, my friend."

Dog Soldiers: Chapter 21

Shortly after breaking camp that morning and getting their bikes warmed up, Billy Laughing Dog brought Savage and Mark across a wide, flat plane at the base of Chedeski Point.

To avoid eating the trail dust that the Indian's machine raised, Savage was forced to take a position on the dirt trail just to the right of Billy's bike. This in turn forced Mark to drop back and take a position just to the left of Savage's bike to stay out of his dust.

As this staggered formation of rumbling scooters approached the corral, the horses began to gallop around nervously in the confinement of their coral.

Savage surveyed the area from his slowly rolling scooter.

There wasn't much there except the horses, their water trough, the corral, a hay shed and small cabin. The cabin was even smaller than the shed.

He assumed that from time to time someone lived in the cabin. The horse trough was full of water, and there were several bails of pea-green hay in the shed, but there didn't seem to be anybody there now.

Despite the protection of the shed from the hot Arizona sun, the pea-green color of the hay meant that it had been harvested and placed there recently. It seemed Billy Laughing Dog had some help out here and that he'd clearly planned ahead.

"OK, palefaces. Do either of you know how to ride a horse?" Billy asked his companions.

Mark returned a mocking, almost contemptuous smile to the large Indian and proceeded directly into the cabin. He quickly exited with a saddle and tack and threw them over the rail of the wooden fence.

"Which mount is going to be mine?" he asked the Indian flatly.

"Heh, heh!" Billy replied as he dismounted his bike, walked over, and looked into the shed. "Good then. We got six horses in the remuda, but it's even luckier that we got three sets of saddles and tack too."

"Luck, Billy boy?' Savage returned somewhat mockingly. "I thought you said that all this was happening like the Great Spirit wants?"

"Yeah," Billy said reflectively, "I guess you're right, 'cause I sure didn't figure I'd be with you two white eyes when I asked Uncle Yahata to set things up for me here."

"You just take any mount that suits you," Billy told Mark.

Savage looked the horses over himself.

"They all look healthy enough. Why don't you pick one out for me and I'll get the rest of the tack from the cabin," Savage said.

"Fine," Billy replied.

The three men removed the leather saddlebags slung over the rear seats of their motorcycles and slapped them onto the rumps of the horses. Their sleeping bags and rain gear were quickly lashed down behind their saddles. The gear looked just as natural on the horses as it had on their bikes.

Shaking their heads, the horses tried to avoid the bits being placed in their mouths. Only Billy's horse remained still as he easily slipped the bit into the animal's mouth without any protest from the beast. He then swung himself up into the saddle and watched his companions mount their animals. He saw that both Savage and Mark did so in a surprisingly natural manner.

"Good. You dudes should have no problem on this trail," Billy declared.

"How far we gotta go?" Mark asked.

"Not far. We'll be there before dark."

Mark glanced at his watch. It was 8:20 in the morning.

Dog Soldiers: Chapter 22

When I was a child I caught a fleeting glimpse out of the corner of my eye. I turned to look but it was gone. I cannot put my finger on it now the child is grown the dream is gone. I have become, comfortably numb.

Pink Floyd

It seemed to Savage that Santos was somewhere between a character out of an old western movie and what city cops would call an EDP—an Emotionally Disturbed Person.

His lizard-like skin looked a bit like the stuffed iguana that he'd bought Sharon when they were on vacation in Mexico. His hair was shocking white, and his teeth suggested he'd never spent a moment in a dentist's chair.

The Indian rambled on incomprehensibly in what Savage assumed was Navajo or Apache.

He occasionally would cast some material from a beaded leather pouch into the campfire, which made the fire flair up, momentarily illuminating the faces of all four men present.

After each casting of the powder, Santo's eyes would close for a time, sometimes for a few minutes, sometimes it seemed like a lot longer. He would remain mute during these intervals, as if he were in a trance or in communication with another world. During these periods, Billy Laughing Dog would translate what the old man had previously said for Pete Savage and his Dog Soldier pledge, Mark.

Most of the old Indian's talk concerned the spirits of the dead, how they could be angered, and the ways they could be placated. In the Navajo's cosmology, it seemed there were three types of spirits.

First, there were the spirits of people who were born and died before you were born. Second, there were the spirits of people who lived at the same time you did but whom you never met. Finally, there were the spirits of the dead who you knew personally in life.

The first group was the most powerful and could cause the greatest harm. But they were also the ones most difficult to offend.

The second group was not quite so powerful. These were the people who had lived in your time but whom you had never met. Their power to disturb the living was more limited, but then they were also more easily disturbed or offended than the first class of spirits.

The most easily offended of all spirits were also the least powerful. These were the ones you knew in life personally. But their power was the weakest of all in directly intruding into the lives of the living. For the most part, they could communicate only with those they actually knew well in life.

However, if their personal sprits were powerful in life, so were they powerful in death. While they might be unable to affect the living in any material way, they could sometimes communicate through signs or visions, and most particularly if they had a great grievance to communicate to the one they knew in life.

When the old man's eyes opened, he began to chant again.

"What's happening now?" Mark asked Laughing Dog.

"It's a song, a prayer."

"What do the words mean?"

Laughing Dog remained undisturbed by Mark's questions as the old Indian chanted and rocked.

"He sings, 'Come grassland dancers. We are making a circle, a circle that is powerful. Come grassland dancers.'"

With that, Billy Laughing Dog raised himself up and danced about the fire, joining the older Indian in his chant. Their voices mingled in an unearthly fashion as the two white men sat and listened in silent wonder.

Savage observed what appeared to be a smile on the old Indian's face as Billy Laughing Dog's dance raised some dust that settled on all present. It was the first discernable emotion that he had seen on Santos' face. He then noticed a small ceramic object that looked like a teakettle on the stones next to the old man. The earthen vessel was set just outside of the fire but still near enough to it that a fine white vapor could be seen exiting its spout.

As abruptly as it had begun, the chanting stopped. Billy Laughing Dog sat directly before Santos, and the two spoke in their native tongue. While Savage could not understand a word of the language, the rhythm of their speech communicated something of its own: Laughing Dog was asking Santos questions, and the old man was responding.

Santos then raised his palm before Billy Laughing Dog, and the two pressed their hands together for a moment and smiled. The old man said something to Savage and Mark before raising himself up to disappear behind the blanket that hung inside his hogan.

"What did he say?" Savage asked.

"It was a blessing. He thinks you're good men, but that you are now separated from your true power, but good men."

"You guys talked more than that," Mark probed.

"The old man says for you to be watchful and careful. You must do what you have to do, but it's a time of danger for you both, but it seems that the spirits are with you—maybe Jesus, too."

With this, Billy Laughing Dog raised the small kettle of tea that had been set on a rock near the fire and next to Santos during the ceremony. He poured some of the liquid into three shot glass size ceramic cups that had clearly been made by hand and matched the color and symbols on the kettle.

Steam rose from the three cups as he filled them with the tea and offered them to his companions.

"What is this, man?" Mark asked Billy. "What's in this?"

Billy Laughing Dog replied, "You call it peyote. It has some sacred mushrooms in it, too.

"It's a high honor that old Santos has given it to you. We call it the 'flesh of the gods.' It helps people find their vision sometimes. It can sometimes help them to discover who they really are. It can remove a man's mask so he can see himself, but truly as he is, or he may see what he's forgotten or lost and what he should do about it. Sometimes the tea will open up a path for the spirits to speak to you."

Mark was more than apprehensive. "Thanks, but I think I'll have to pass. I got no idea what that stuff is, what it might do to me."

"Nobody ever does," Billy Laughing Dog replied indifferently.

"Jesus Christ on a bicycle, don't be such a wimp, dude. Think it's going to turn you into horny toad or something?" Savage chided the pledge.

"No, but then that's the whole deal, too. I don't know what it's gonna do to me," Mark repeated.

With that, Savage smiled at Billy and picked up his own cup.

"If you are with us, then you are with us, and if not, then not. Nobody's making you do anything here. You wanted to make the run, and like I said, what happens, happens. But you have to decide for yourself."

Mark hesitated, then reluctantly picked up his cup.

Billy Laughing Dog returned Savage's smile, and then all three men downed the contents of their small earthen cups at once.

"Now what?" Mark asked.

"Now you wait," Billy Laughing Dog replied. "You wait to see what the spirits will show you."

Dog Soldiers: Chapter 23

. . . and the traffic lights turn blue tomorrow.
Jimi Hendrix

Savage stumbled out of the hogan and looked up to see an infinite sea of sparkling stars.

He could see one star behind another since much greater depth was now imparted to the heavens. The larger ones changed colors from green to blue to white and then red as the cycle of color transformations randomly repeated itself. Yet, the moonlight was still strong enough to gently illuminate the ground at his feet. Looking down, he saw his own moon shadow moving with him. He waved at his shadow and laughed as it waved back.

A prickly pear cactus caught his attention, and though it seemed to grow at an astonishing rate right before his eyes, at the same time it never seemed to get any larger or taller.

In what seemed the far distance, he heard Billy Laughing Dog's muted chanting, but then the chanting became the sound of helicopter blades beating against an Asian sky saturated with humidity. For a moment he heard the thumping blades of the choppers, but when he tried to determine their direction, the sound simply disappeared.

Savage made a conscious effort to relax his mind completely through the force of his own will as he breathed deeply upon the cool night air.

"It's all just an illusion," he said to himself silently. "All illusion," he repeated. When he realized he was hearing his own words aloud, he laughed out loud.

Savage seemed to see halos of yellow and purple light around everything and everywhere he looked. He could see a shimmering halo surrounding Mark, who was now sitting with his back to a tree rocking back and forth and moaning. Incomprehensibly, his rocking movements echoed the rhythm of the Indian's chanting perfectly.

The color of the halo around Mark changed from green to blue. When Savage looked at Mark's face, it seemed to be making these same color shifts as well.

Suddenly, as if a bolt of lighting was blinding his sight, he saw a vision of an entirely different place. It was an asphalt street lightly covered with rain. He heard the light rain falling, and he saw the street lights reflected off the wet pavement.

A large black man walked on that street. Savage saw a revolver in another black man's hand. The muzzle flash of the pistol firing illuminated a dark area, and in it he saw a face he recognized as the gun fired repeatedly.

The flash of that gun then became an overpowering light as he saw a small black girl turn and smile at him as she ran away into that light.

Savage shook his head in an attempt to escape from this dark vision and regain himself. He walked slowly to his horse, retrieved the canteen of water, and gulped down the precious fluid.

Damn, he thought, that old man Santos sure cooked up some good old-fashioned psychedelic tea for sure.

It wasn't Savage's first trip, of course, but it was the first one in many years. He knew his brain would be humming for a few hours or more at least.

Dog Soldiers: Chapter 24

... none of us gets out of this world alive.

Van Morrison

Billy Laughing Dog held a large forked juniper limb in his hand as he sharpened it with his Bowie knife. After completing this task, he rolled the long stick over in his hands and examined it carefully. He then flexed the limb he'd cut to ensure its strength under weight. The juniper stand down by the creek was almost a half-mile walk back to the hogan.

When Billy arrived at the hogan, he saw that Savage and Mark had followed his instructions and had finished digging the six small holes in the ground. He walked over to inspect the holes closely and was pleased to see that they had been dug down to a workable depth and that they had the proper spacing. It had all been done just as he had marked out for them earlier that morning. That was good.

"Don't we need some kind of permit for this?" Mark asked. "I mean, is this really legal?"

Mark's voice reflected some small concern for the law, but also the fact that his head was still aching and humming a bit from the psychedelic trip the previous night. He'd not had enough sleep. Peyote and mushroom tea can do that to you.

"You're on the rez now. It's our law that counts here—Indian law."

"Besides," Billy continued, "Santos didn't need any white man's law anyway, not then and not now."

Savage and Billy Laughing Dog carefully forced the final stake that Billy had brought back with him into the last of the six holes. Small stones were dropped into the space between the hole and the stake before filling the rest of the hole with dirt and sand. Billy then tamped down the earth around each of the juniper poles with the butt of his knife as he chanted for a while.

In a short time he had all six stakes set up as firmly as the earth and stones would allow. The Juniper poles stood straight up in the ground, each with the forked end of their limbs at the top.

"OK, let's do it," Billy said.

With that, the three men entered the hogan and put the earthly body of old man Santos onto the travois that Billy had made earlier.

"OK, let's do it slow and right, guys," Billy cautioned his companions.

They carried the platform of the travois outside of the hogan and carefully raised it up onto the vertical stakes in the ground. To achieve this, each corner of the platform was placed into the fork of the juniper poles. This demanded pushing each of the corners of the travois up just a bit further than any of the three men could reach. Billy had anticipated and solved this problem by using another juniper limb that he'd cut especially for this purpose.

Billy used the extra limb to raise each of the four corners up into its forked notch. He then made sure that the two middle poles also held the platform securely.

This put the body of the shaman Santos about six and half feet off the ground.

Billy shook the entire burial assembly lightly. Savage thought he'd seen on his companion's face that it wobbled a bit more than Billy would have liked.

The Apache went to the saddlebags on his horse and retrieved a spool of nylon parachute cord and began to lash down each of the six points where the travois rested on the poles. His hands showed both experience and skill at making knots with this material.

"Hey, he had a radio, you know," Billy said.

Savage perceived that this information was offered as if to excuse Laughing Dog's use of this nontraditional nylon material to secure Santo's burial platform.

"He listened to the tribal station sometimes. Twenty-four hours a day, seven days a week they broadcast healing chants all over the rez. Sometimes he'd tune into it. I brought that radio to him. He didn't have any objection when I showed him how it worked. He was happy to have it."

Billy then knelt before the platform and again began to chant as he threw bits of dust and earth into the air.

Mark was feeling a bit under the weather. He took the liberty to walk into the shade outside the old hogan and sit down for a while. Seeing this, Savage followed.

"How long do you think this part will go on?" Mark asked Savage.

"Got no idea, pal, but we gotta show a little class here, you understand?"

"Yeah, OK. I don't feel 100 percent, man. What was that shit we drank last night?"

"A mixture of peyote and mescalito 'shrooms I think. Got you buzzing right proper, I suspect."

"Yeah, your pal was right. It made me think about a lot of things. Some of it was kinda scary."

"Yeah, my trip had some pretty dark shit in it too. Can't exactly remember it all very well. Like a dream, you know?" Savage replied.

Billy Laughing Dog's chant suddenly grew louder.

"Hey yah, hey ya, hey yeh hey, yah ta hey ya hey!" he shouted. Then he stood up to face his companions.

"You two still have a dangerous road to travel now. But it is a road of your own choosing. Still, Santos feels you are both decent men, and so do I." He spoke as if Santos was still with them.

"You guys think you can find your way back to the corral and your bikes from here?" Billy asked.

"Seemed like there was only one road back to me, Billy," Savage replied. "I think we can manage that. Why?"

"There is always more than one road, my friend," Billy said.

"This means you're not coming with us then? You're gonna stay here?" This was not a question on Savage's part; it was more of a conclusion.

"It's my place to stay here now, for a while anyway. You see, I was his apprentice," Billy replied.

Billy came closer to Savage. Without further speech, he reached into his medicine bag and slapped a small object into Savage's palm. Savage's hand closed involuntarily at this contact. He opened it and saw that the object that Billy had put there was his own blank rune.

Savage had not even remembered giving it to Billy, but that was easily explainable since that previous evening had been his first heavy 'shroom trip in about 12 years.

"Keep it with you, my friend," Billy said. "We will see each other again."

Mark was still sitting in the shade of the hogan when Savage approached him.

"What's up now?" Mark asked.

Savage opened his hand showing Mark the blank rune.

"It's time for us to leave," he said.

Dog Soldiers: Chapter 25

Same as it ever was, same as it ever was.

The Talking Heads

Mark glanced at the evening sky for a moment and studied the dark clouds and occasional lightning flashes that illuminated the northwest. He attached one end of his poncho to his bike using a few bungee cords, then staked the other end into the ground to make a shelter against what he saw was a fast approaching thunderstorm.

The lightning grew fierce and the clouds dark over the mountains, but Mark observed that Savage had simply spread his tarp on the ground and tossed his sleeping bag out upon it.

Savage pulled his leather saddlebags from his bike, propped them up for a headrest, and uncorked a bottle of white zinfandel with his Swiss army knife. This would be their last camp before they would get up in the morning and ride the remaining 250 or so miles back home.

Mark observed Savage on his sleeping bag. "Looks like it's going to rain to me, pal. Like a cow peeing on a flat rock, too."

Savage looked to the northwest for a moment. "That's Hesperus Mountain, man, over 13,000 feet. This time a year, mostly around sunset, you'll have this. But the storm's moving east. Might get a sprinkle here, but maybe not even that."

"You're going to get plenty wet if not."

Savage took a pull from the wine bottle before responding. "Not too familiar with this part of the country, are you?"

"I grew up in LA, but I like it out here. Not so many people, you know?"

"Indeed I do," Savage replied sincerely. Then he laughed out loud.

"What is it?" Mark asked curiously.

"Oh, shit, I don't know what put it in my mind just now, but I remember this woman at the unemployment office. This has got to be, shit, 29 years ago now, just after 'Nam. She smiled and asked me, 'Do you like people, Mr. Savage?'"

"Like fuck, man, what kind of question is that? 'Do you like people?' What fucking people was she talking about? I mean, some people I like and some people I don't. What kinda question was that to ask? 'Do you like people?'"

"So where'd it go from there?" Mark asked.

"Nowhere, I guess. At that time all I could do was just sit and look at her with a blank expression on my face. I guess there was a lot of shit I wanted to say, too much shit, cause it just seemed like this woman was from another planet, you know? The way she smiled . . . fuck!"

Savage pulled on the wine bottle a second time and was quiet for a moment.

"You know, man, I couldn't say anything. I tried, but then I just had to turn and walk out of that place . . . like immediately, you know?"

Mark extended his hand for the wine bottle as Savage passed it to him.

"Yeah, man, I think I do know," he replied.

Savage felt his mind traveling down that dark road to the past. But it was a road that he'd long ago decided was, most often, best left in the past. He quickly changed the subject.

"So what did you think of Laughing Dog and old Santos, our little funeral service for the old man this morning?" Savage asked.

"Definitely some of the weirdest shit I've seen," Mark declared flatly. "But what do you think about his seeing into the future and Billy saying it was a time of danger for us and all that stuff?"

"I just think we'd better be careful, think about what we're doing before we do it, that's all. Which really makes it pretty much the same as it ever was, doesn't it?" Savage responded.

Mark passed the wine bottle back to his companion.

"You don't really believe that old man could see into the future, do you? I mean, well, I sorta liked both of 'em, but they're out there, really out there on some weird Indian religious deal of their own, man. Nobody knows what's going to happen in the future. Like how could they?"

"I knew it wasn't going to rain here, didn't I?" Savage responded as he held his palm to the sky. "And it doesn't seem to be raining now, does it?"

Mark smiled back at Savage. "OK, I'm impressed. So you know the country better than I do. I mean, you've been here before, like probably plenty of times, so you know the country and I don't, but that's all it is."

"I know the country, huh?" Savage asked. "But that's just the physical country you're talking about. Did you ever think maybe that old Indian knows the spiritual country?"

Savage took a long pull on the wine before continuing.

"Maybe he can look at us—you remember how he looked right into our eyes back there? Maybe he can see into our spirits. Maybe even our thoughts. Maybe he's just looked at that 'spiritual sky' for so long and seen what's already gone down so many times before that he has an idea of what might happen next. Just like I knew it wasn't likely to rain here."

"That's a real reach, pal, a real reach," Mark repeated. "I don't think there's anything controlling my destiny, and I don't believe anybody can see into the future, either."

Savage set down the wine bottle within Mark's reach.

"Then you must think everything that happens is completely random, no cause and effect, just a random chaotic universe with no order or rules or anything. If it's like that, then nothing can really be predicted," Savage challenged.

"No, man. Some things can be predicted, but some things can't." Mark seemed vaguely frustrated.

"Then you're saying that certain causes do have certain effects. So tell me then—where does that chain of causality start to break down?" Savage inquired.

"Well, like how do you mean?" Mark asked.

"If every cause has an effect and if there are no effects without some cause, then everything is absolutely pre-determined, right? Our being here, our meeting the old man, everything—all of it was predestined from the beginning of time, whenever the fuck that was.

"Some things are predictable from their causes, like physical stuff," said Mark, "but not people and what they're going to do. Man, it's impossible to really predict what people are going to do. I mean, to predict it for sure. We can guess, but we can't really know before they do it. People can change their minds at any time."

"Can they really?" Savage asked earnestly. "That assumes there is such a thing as free will, pal, which is causes without effects, effects without causes, things—that is decisions—decisions we make that just happen totally by themselves with no reason, or cause. Well, if something can happen with no cause like that, it's the same as magic, isn't it?" Savage replied.

"Some things are predictable—like I said, physical things—but people aren't predictable."

"Then what you are saying is if we can't predict something, then it has to be unpredictable—that is, it happens for no reason, and not because of anything that happened before. It's just a random event.

"But a lot of stuff can be predicted because people figured it out over time by just watching and observing what goes down around them. So why does it seem so impossible to you that that old Indian Santos figured out some stuff about people too? So maybe he really does have a better idea what might happen in the future than we do."

"You can't really believe that, can you? That everything could be fucking predestined like that?" Mark asked seriously.

"I really don't know, man. Doesn't really matter either. What I do believe is that it's got to be one way or the other, and even so, believing that everything's predestined just isn't a practical philosophy for living your life, is it?"

"If we leave early enough in the morning, we should be back just a few hours after dark, and we won't have to push the sleds too hard," Mark declared. "It's been a hell of trip, though," he finished.

"Yeah, that's one of the things I like about the road. You never know what's going to come up. Goodnight, man."

Savage rolled over onto his side in his sleeping bag to find sleep.

Dog Soldiers: Chapter 26

Savage was more than a bit tired when he reached his home. He leaned over the handlebars of his bike to enter the code into the keypad of the electronic lock to his shop gate. It had been dark for about two hours, and although he could not actually make out the digits on the keypad visually, his fingers knew where they were. He tapped out the four-digit sequence, and the iron gate slid open.

As per the program, the gate closed itself after he drove his bike through.

He drove the bike briskly up the driveway very much looking forward to Sharon, a hot shower and a warm bed.

Halfway to his destination he observed lights coming on inside the house on the ground floor. Sharon had heard his motor and was coming downstairs to meet him.

The garage doors to the shop began to open, and Savage was even a little surprised by just how much he'd missed the woman. As the doors stopped in the full open position, he saw her smiling at him from inside. He cut his engine and coasted silently into the shop to park the Serpent.

Reflexively, he shut off his gas and sat for a moment on his scooter, and then returned the smile of his woman. He kicked his leg over the bike and dismounted to embrace her.

"I missed you," Savage declared as the two lovers held each other tightly.

"I'm glad you're back," Sharon replied, feeling a little stupid and almost embarrassed at the intensity of her own emotions.

Savage's finger gently lifted moisture from her eye as she playfully slapped his hand away.

"Salty tears, huh honey? I'm glad to see it. I missed me too," Savage told her.

"You are basically a true asshole, you know?" Sharon responded, trying to compose herself.

"I guess," Savage returned as he kissed her with a strong but gentle passion. In his own mind he wondered what cosmically benevolent deed he might have done in some past life to have found such a woman as he had.

"Let's go upstairs—" Sharon started, but her words were cut short by the commanding shout of a stranger.

"Police officers! Freeze!" the voice commanded.

Savage instinctively shielded Sharon with his own body as he turned to face the open doors of the garage and saw half a dozen uniformed police officers. Two of them nervously leveled 12 gauge shotguns at them.

"OK cops," Savage shouted out in a calm voice as he slowly raised both his open hands over his head. "Let's see some fire control discipline here, people. We're unarmed and whatever it is, I surrender."

The police advanced and began to handcuff Savage.

"You bastards, let him go!" Sharon spit out spontaneously.

Savage's head was snapped back violently when one of the cops struck him rudely with a blow from his open hand. Almost instantly, Savage stood and raised his hands above his head again.

He looked directly into the eyes of the cop who had struck him and spoke with a slow and deliberate calmness.

"Is that all you got, pig?"

As Savage's wrists were handcuffed behind his back, one of the policemen began the familiar drone of his Miranda rights.

Then Savage observed a large black detective approaching him. "What we got, punk," the detective declared, "is your ass on murder one."

"Fine, cop," Savage responded. "Then she's got nothing to do with this." Savage tossed his head toward Sharon, who was now handcuffed as well. "So you let her go. We'll go down to the station, and I'll tell you everything I know about anything."

"Let the woman go," the detective ordered.

"Call my lawyer, honey. Bosworth. You got the number up-stairs, but it's in the book anyway. Tell him what's gone down here, and tell him I want him down at the station tonight."

Savage gave these instructions quickly to Sharon as the offi-cers were pulling him out of the garage and toward the squad car.

As the cops manhandled Savage toward the car, something inside him decided to pause a moment. Employing an Aikido technique called the "immovable body," he assumed that pos-ture and mindset.

For an instant the cops pulling the handcuffed prisoner along lost their balance, and two of them fell down.

It was like the cuffs they were pulling Savage by were sud-denly attached to a telephone poll. The cops recovered quickly, and for another moment they pushed ineffectively on the biker as Savage stood all but motionless.

Savage then turned to the black detective.

"And who is it that I am supposed to have killed?" Savage asked with calm defiance.

"Thomas R. Brown," the detective replied without emotion.

The words struck Savage like a sledgehammer, and he invol-untarily sank to his knees.

"No! Oh, Jesus God, no," he uttered to himself.

Dog Soldiers: Chapter 27

And sometimes it's not so easy, especially when your only friend walks talks does exactly like you and you do just the same as him.

Jimmy Hendrix

It had become Pete Savage's nature to try to find the bright side of any difficult situation. His life experience had provided him with a very profound understanding of the importance of maintaining a positive survivor's attitude when faced with any type of adversity.

One of the mental techniques he would use when things were looking particularly nasty was to try to think back to a time when things were much worse. That wasn't too hard for the man, either.

He applied this positive mental strategy while sitting in his jail cell in the recently constructed Mountain View Criminal Justice Center.

Savage's thoughts drifted back to September of 1969 and an open rice paddy about 20 clicks north of Ben Wah when his platoon was ambushed and bracketed in by Viet Cong mortars.

The fact that the rice paddy was mined accounted for about half a dozen guys being cut down as they ran to the cover of the dikes to escape the mortar barrage. Judging by the accuracy of that heavy machine gun fire, this escape route had already been anticipated and was well covered.

Charlie had, no doubt, already zeroed their RPK machine guns for this ambush long before Savage's platoon had even arrived.

The survivors were left with the choice of getting up and running, thus risking the mines and machine guns, or to remain lying in the mud and water praying that the next mortar round didn't blow them to pieces. They also prayed that they didn't stop a stray AK round such as were zapping into the water of the rice paddy all around them.

Savage had chosen the second option, to stay put. Suddenly, a guy they called "Peanuts" ran past him screaming and firing his M16 full auto at the tree line. A spray of AK-47 rounds hit him across the chest, and the soldier splashed stone dead in front of him. Savage crawled up to the body and saw that the man was finished. He then pulled the corpse on top of himself for limited protection against mortar fragments.

He began to remove the dead man's flak jacket. They would not stop an AK bullet, but they could help a lot against the flying shrapnel from a mortar, and so would the corpse he was holding on top of him.

He placed the blood-splattered flak vest over his lower body and tried to draw his legs up under it too as best he could.

As he was lying on his back looking toward the sky, for the first time in his life Savage had seriously considered that there may indeed exist a deity to pray to, and if so, that *now* was certainly the time to do so.

He held that warm but lifeless body on top of him for what seemed like a very long time before he saw and then heard three F-4 Phantom jets roar overhead.

The fighter planes screamed over so low that he could see the white helmet of one of the pilots. That pilot's head turned, and it seemed to Savage that the man was actually looking right at him.

"Snake n' nap," thank you Jesus, Savage said to himself, and a few seconds later he felt the awesome concussion of the ordinance exploding into the tree line. The napalm created an instant inferno of roaring orange flame. Even from almost 300 meters away Savage felt the heat of the blast.

But it took a moment for the actual sound of the explosion to reach him. When it did, he rolled over and watched the napalm do the devil's work.

He saw several VC soldiers running out of the flames and splashing into the water of the rice paddy. They were ablaze like human torches. The napalm was stuck to their black uniforms and to their naked skins. Still, a number of Savage's surviving comrades sprayed at them with M16 fire.

What a hellish way to die, Savage thought.

He recalled that one soldier held his fire and simply watched the spectacle as he stupidly stood up and screamed out maniacally, "Burn you fucking gook scum. Burn, burn you devils!"

Savage's mind then returned from this nightmarish image of war to the reality of his current circumstances in his jail cell. He stretched out on the bed and pushed the memory of Ben Wah from his mind. Resurrecting that past horror had now served its objective. Being in jail and facing a charge of murder and the death of a very good friend was no picnic, yet things could be worse. The jail cell he was now confined in definitely beat that deal in the rice paddy outside Ben Wah.

The Mountain View jail was a high-tech marvel of modern penology. It was all quite in keeping with the town's image of itself as a progressive, pace-setting, humanistic community.

There weren't even bars in Savage's cell. There was just a steel door with a small shatterproof plastic and wire window. Sometime during the middle of the night, an officer had shined a light through that small window to check up on the prisoner. Savage figured that must have been to see if he'd hung himself or something, because he sure wasn't going anywhere.

In fact, it would have been tough to find anything to hang himself. Especially since they'd strip-searched him and shined a light up his ass before giving him his bright orange jail clothes.

On the far wall of his cell another clear plastic slit of a window provided Savage with a view of the interior courtyard. Shortly after dawn he had observed other prisoners walking about in the yard below, and he noticed that they were all wearing green jail clothes.

Apparently there was some kind of color-coding for prisoner types, Savage reasoned. The orange suits like his were no doubt reserved for the really dangerous, homicidal psychos such as himself.

When the cops had brought him in the previous evening, his lawyer, Bosworth, was already there. It quickly become clear that until his first court appearance, scheduled for Monday afternoon, he wouldn't even have a chance to plea for bail. Consequently, Savage resigned himself to spending at least a few days right where he was and at the expense of the city of Mountain View.

Savage had been in a few jails before, and as jails went, he figured this one was pretty plush, even if it was a bit sterile. Most times in a jail you could find a paperback novel left behind by some previous tenant. That novel would have the first three or four pages, both the beginning and the end, worn away from countless previous handlings by past prisoners of the cell.

No such luck in this sterile cage, though. There wasn't even any graffiti on the walls.

But, always looking for the positive side of things, Savage was thankful that he had a cell all to himself. No doubt one of the benefits of being in the orange jump suit—that is, being held for the big one: murder One.

As this thought passed through Savage's mind, he was startled to hear a voice.

"Please stand back from the door."

The voice sounded like the one in some of those new cars that tells you "Please fasten your seatbelt."

Savage then realized it was indeed a computer-generated voice as the door to his cell opened. Outside the cell door he saw a black-and-white TV monitor suspended in a bracket high on the wall. On that monitor he could see the face of a woman sitting at an electronic control desk equipped with a gooseneck microphone. She leaned forward to speak into the device.

"Mr. Savage, this is your shower period. If you will follow the yellow line on the floor to the door marked 3, I can let you into the shower room now."

The woman on the TV screen sounded reasonably pleasant. She actually seemed to be making a conscious and deliberate effort to be nice.

"Follow the yellow brick road," Savage said to himself.

"You have to speak louder," the woman on the monitor said.

"No, it was nothing. Let's get that shower," Savage replied loudly as he stepped from the cell and followed the yellow line on the floor. It brought him to another stainless steel door with the numeral 3 painted on it in the same bright yellow color.

"You have 12 minutes to complete your shower."

Savage heard the woman's voice but saw no TV monitor as the door slid open and he stepped into the shower facility.

He quickly glanced about the room and observed a row of steel sinks. Above each sink was a polished steel mirror. Savage looked a moment at his somewhat distorted and foggy image in one of the metal mirrors. He then hung his clothes on the wall pegs and stepped though the open portal to the shower room.

There were six shower heads, but Savage was alone in the facility.

He punched the liquid soap dispenser a few times, and a greenish, hospital-smelling liquid was deposited in his hands. Turning the hot water up high, he let the water pound his face as he quickly worked up a lather on his chest and under his arms.

For a short while he closed his eyes and let the water play directly over his face. He pretended that he was somewhere besides the Mountain View County Justice Center. He tried to imagine that he was in some other shower at some other time and that he'd soon be ready to put on his jeans and go wherever he pleased.

Savage realized that no matter how pleasant they might try to make the jail, there was simply no substitute for freedom. This thought passed through his mind in a disturbingly profound way as he shut off the water and stepped out of the shower. He grabbed the single gray towel off the wall peg and stepped back through the portal to the changing room.

As he rummaged the towel through his hair, the first warning that caught his eye was the reflection in the steel mirror of the color orange.

Savage jumped back on impulse, and as he turned his head, he saw the black man smile for just a fraction of an instant before the knife struck him hard in the back.

As the shank glanced off Savage's sixth rib, he was simultaneously turning to face his assailant. In the next instant he saw the next strike coming and drew his left elbow over his chest. The blade hit the outside of his left arm.

Savage's left hand slapped down immediately onto the knifer's wrist while his right hand struck a powerful palm heel blow that rose upward and impacted with tremendous force under the attacker's chin.

The knifer was knocked forcefully off balance. Savage struck a second identical blow with fluidity, power, and without hesitation. Savage could not risk releasing the knife hand of his would-be killer, nor could he afford this man even a fleeting instant in which to regain his balance and renew his attack.

Savage's right hand struck another open-handed blow to the knifer's throat that impacted into the man's esophagus. Savage felt the solid force of his strike on the man's throat between the webbing of his thumb and index finger. He kept his hand on the man's throat as he drove the man across the floor using his full body weight and the power that terror gives a man when he knows his life could be shut off in the next instant.

But the black man had killed with the blade before and knew the ways of steel. As he crashed into the far wall that Savage drove him into, the black man used part of the impact to liberate his knife hand and plunged it into Savage's left side.

However, he was denied a follow-up strike with his blade. Savage yelled out an animalistic guttural shout as his right thumb forcefully blasted through the knifer's left eye and into the orbital socket. An unearthly scream of pain erupted from the black man.

The blow had taken the man's left eye and had knocked him unconscious. But before he could fall, Savage used the grip that his thumb had inside the orbital socket of the man's skull to throw his head forcefully to the porcelain floor.

Staggering back, Savage realized that his left hand was now holding the blade that protruded from his side. He drew the knife from his body and was determined to finish off his enemy with it.

The spirit was willing but the flesh was failing. Savage's vision grayed, and his knees buckled beneath him. Trying to raise himself from the floor, his eyes fixated on his fallen assailant.

At least I'll take this bastard with me, a voice from somewhere in his mind said as he passed the blade to his right hand and began a crimson-trailed crawl toward his assailant.

Savage then felt a strange warmth flow through his body as his vision blackened. As he collapsed into unconsciousness he heard the metallic sound of the knife hitting the shower room floor.

The sound seemed strangely muted as if it were coming from a long way off.

Dog Soldiers: Chapter 28

The nurse thumped on the IV bag with her finger a few times to make sure that the needle was still properly secured in Savage's arm.

"You're doing just fine, honey," the nurse declared as she attached the oximeter probe to Savage's earlobe. She then removed it and began recording his blood oxygen level.

"Just fine," she repeated as she completed the information on the chart.

The woman looked about 56 years old and a bit on the heavy side. But despite her routine and her rather banal mannerisms, somehow Savage perceived her to be genuinely decent.

"Yeah? Great. So when do I get out of here?"

Savage observed the nurse turn to look at the two bikers sitting in the room. Both were dressed in their full scooter trash regalia.

For the last four days and nights, Speed and Shotgun had taken shifts guarding him, staying in his room all the time. The nurse smiled at Shotgun and Speed before she turned to reply to Savage.

"Honey, believe me, we are all doing just everything possible to get you out of here just as soon as we can."

"I can sure believe that," Savage replied as the nurse went out the door. This woman had a good sense of humor as well, and Savage imagined how that would be a real asset in her profession.

After she was gone, Savage turned toward his fellow Dog Soldiers. "Shotgun, would you crank this thing up for me a bit?"

Shotgun turned the ratchet on Savage's hospital bed, bringing him up nearly to a sitting position.

At the same moment Speed suddenly rose from his chair and moved quickly against the wall behind the door. An instant later the door opened and the club's attorney, Dan Bosworth, stepped in. He hesitated a moment, being slightly startled when he became aware of Shotgun's smiling face behind him. The lawyer then directed his attention to Savage.

"Well, you certainly look a lot better than the last time I was here, Pete."

"Glad to hear it, " Savage replied. " I mean, considering the last time we talked I still had fucking chest tubes stuck in me, a perforated lung, and I probably looked and sounded like something out of a damn zombie movie. Yeah, I'm glad I look better than that now, Boz."

Speed and Shotgun laughed in appreciation at the blunt and direct manner with which Savage spoke to the club's lawyer.

Savage looked both bikers in the eyes before he spoke.

"OK, bros, I got some heavy shit to go over with our law dog here, and I don't want to expose you guys to any kind of accessory charge or any other legal bullshit like that. So I'm asking you to stand outside the door while I talk with Boz."

Speed and Shotgun nodded their understanding and took their stations outside the hospital room door.

"OK, Boz, what gives now?" Savage asked.

"Well, I think you most definitely have a good negligence suit against the city of Mountain View and maybe Evergreen County, too. They are responsible for allowing the conditions to exist that permitted this attack, a near fatal attack," the lawyer emphasized.

"You were in the custody of the Evergreen sheriff's office, and they were responsible for your safety. It's clear they were grossly negligent here. I think what we should do now is file a—"

"Hold on, man," Savage interrupted. "I don't want you to file any claim like that, not just yet anyway."

"And why the hell not?" Bosworth replied, almost as irritated as he was surprised.

Savage had worked with the Boz for years, and it just wasn't like the him to use any sort of profanity. Savage now found it a little touching.

"You're a good law dog, Boz, but there's more going on here than negligence. That guy didn't get in that shower room by accident. No way in hell that could have happened. Somebody put him up to it. They arranged for the doors to be unlocked for him, and they knew when I'd be alone in the shower room. That means it's gotta be a cop, or at least somebody real close to a cop, pulling all the strings now."

"If that's true, then all the more reason to get this thing into court," Bosworth protested. "That's what the law is for, Pete, to get everything out in the open, to discover the real facts of the case. And I'll tell you something else: The fact that the DA had already dropped all charges against you before the attack even occurred, well that's likely to carry some real weight with an awards jury. That is, if you will just give me a chance to take the city and county to court over this thing."

"Well, Boz, I'm not quite ready to do that just yet—that is, like you say, get everything out in the open right now," Savage replied.

"You had better confide in me, Pete," Bosworth cautioned. "Otherwise you are just crippling my ability to help you."

"I'll confide this much, Boz. I know the guy who attacked me is dead. Now why do you think?"

Bosworth paused a moment, clearly puzzled as to the relevance of Savage's question.

"Well, as I understand it he apparently died of complications from the drugs he had in his system and the injuries he sustained while you were defending your life against his armed attack."

"I don't think so, Boz," Savage replied flatly." Somebody got to him before the paramedics did. Somewhere between the justice center lock-up and this hospital, somebody made sure he didn't make it."

"Well, they should be making the autopsy report available soon. It might be available now. I don't know . . . ."

"You find out for me, Boz," Savage requested.

"OK, I'll do that. Now, give me one substantive reason why you won't file a civil suit against them for your injuries," Bosworth demanded.

"Because I got some plans of my own, and it's going to be a few weeks, maybe more, before I can get around like I want. In the meantime I'd rather not stir things up."

Bosworth glanced toward the closed door to the hospital room and turned back to Savage. His face reflected the new thought that had just entered his mind.

"That's why you've got Steve and Grissom out there now. They're guards."

"Go to the head of the class, Boz."

Steve and Grisom, Savage chuckled under his breath. He couldn't remember the last time he'd heard anyone refer to Speed and Shotgun by their "real" names.

"Who are they guarding you from, Pete?" Bosworth asked earnestly.

"That's the big question right now, isn't it?" Savage replied.

Savage tried to relax his mind. He was clearly aware that coming from Bosworth's world, it would be easy for the attorney to imagine that his client had turned paranoid on him.

"On the other hand, I could just be having paranoid delusions, like post-traumatic stress syndrome and all," Savage chided.

Bosworth's face was as serious as his tone of voice when he responded.

"No, I don't think you're paranoid. I think you've probably thought this thing through very logically. What's more, Pete, I think you know, or at least suspect, a great deal more than what you are willing to tell me now, and as your attorney, I'm telling you that's a real mistake."

"Could be, Boz, but if so it's going to be my mistake to make right now."

"Well, you're telling me not to file against the city or county. OK, but I do want to draw up the complaint, and I expect that sometime in the near future you'll tell me to file it. And so there is no misunderstanding on this, I'm strongly recommending that we make that filing right now," Bosworth reiterated.

"Drawing up the complaint is a good idea, pal. Go ahead with that part. Maybe we might have a use for it soon."

"Very well," the attorney replied with significant satisfaction.

"I talked to Dr. Nyuen on the way in here. He suggested that they might be letting you go on Monday or Tuesday as long as you continue to improve as you've been doing. I assume you'll be going home then." Bosworth's tone made the remark more of a question than an expectation.

"Just as soon as they release me. I'll be trying to get my strength back. Speed and Shotgun will be staying out at the shop for a while too. You can reach me there. I'll be staying pretty close to home until I'm feeling right."

"That's a good idea, Pete, so stay with it," Bosworth declared. "I'll find out what I can about the details regarding Mr. Johnson's cause of death."

Johnson. It was the first time Savage was aware of the name of the man who had attacked him in the shower.

"What was his first name?" Savage asked.

"Matt. Mathew, I think. It will be on the autopsy report."

"Good," Savage replied. "Did the DA tell you why they dropped the murder charge against me?"

"I haven't seen the District Attorney to ask. I assume they discovered new evidence or another suspect. Having dropped a charge as serious as the one you faced, I just wasn't immediately disposed to quiz them on it. At that moment my concern was just obtaining your writ of release and getting you out of jail. Besides, well, frankly, sometimes the best thing to do legally is just to let things be."

"Yeah, I understand, Boz," Savage replied. "I heard the DA was holding Brown's body down at the city morgue for evidence."

"Yes, they are. I expect they will hold it there for sometime too."

Sometimes the best thing to do was to simply let sleeping dogs lie, Savage thought. Only there was a bastard out there who had murdered his friend and who had come damn close to killing him, too. Pete Savage wasn't about to just "let things be" on that score.

Not so long as he was still breathing anyway.

Dog Soldiers: Chapter 29

His mother had named him Thomas Benjamin Brown, but the 67 black bikers who made up the Wheels of Soul Motorcycle Club in the funeral procession knew him as Ali Jamal.

Five weeks had passed since Brown's murder, but the DA had not allowed the release of the body from the coroner's office. It was considered material evidence in a continuing homicide investigation, so his funeral had to wait until now.

The new president of the Wheels of Soul, Mohamed Jamal, surveyed the faces of the Marine honor guard.

They were all spit and polish, decked out in their dress blue uniforms, their rifles ready to fire a final salute. He saw a soldier with a horn ready to blow Taps.

Had some of the Souls had their way, that honor guard wouldn't have been there at all. Only the brothers, the members of the club, would have been allowed, and no whites.

But Mohamed, the new president, figured that it wasn't their call. It was Brown's call, because it was his party.

Brown had that Marine Corps banner hung up in his crib. All those photos of him and his pals in Vietnam surrounded it. Next to that were his medals. Most of the guys in those old photos with him were white. Nobody ever said anything about that, but they all knew that his fellow Marines meant a lot to Brown.

During that war Mohamed was just getting out of elementary school. To him, it was just another example of "whitee sending the nigger to fight a white man's war." That was all Vietnam meant to him.

The Marine honor guard seemed a little corny, but all this was what Brown would have wanted. Mohamed knew that, and Brown had been a man to respect. Mohamed Jamal had told the members of the Souls beforehand that the guard was going to be there.

The club meeting to plan Brown's funeral had turned out kind of weird for Mohamed, too. Some of the members had spoken out, and real loud, too, saying that only the Souls should be at the funeral. A few others conceded that Brown would have wanted a Marine honor guard, so maybe they could come, but only if they were all "brothers"—that is, all black. Mohamed found himself shouting them all down and damn near having to call some of them out physically.

He told them straight out that they weren't thinking of Brown or the Souls but only of themselves and their own little beefs and hang-ups. Brown had been the president and it was up to the Souls to give him the full righteous send-off that he would have wanted and that he deserved. That meant the Marine Honor Guard and all no matter what color some of those jarheads might turn out to be.

Mohamed knew that the Marine Reserve unit in Lakewood would never agree to any "blacks only" deal, anyway. Besides, he'd never ask them to.

The funeral arrangements for Brown had been Mohamed's first real test as the new president. He had made the members see it his way and understand that he was in charge now. And it felt good.

That's how Brown would have handled it, and that's what made Mohamed proud of himself.

He wished he'd talked more with Brown when he was still alive. Maybe talked about being pres and how to keep the few hotheads from bringing the heat down on the whole club, and a lot of other stuff, too. But as vice president, at least he had seen Brown's example of how to handle the club.

The patch on his colors now said "Pres," and that was some real serious weight. It was all on him now, and Mohamed found himself thinking in new ways—larger ways that he'd never really considered before.

"Yo, Pres!" the sergeant at arms shouted. Mohamed was pulled from his thoughts back into the here and now.

"There's some cracker at the gate. He wants us to let him in. Riding a real nice Shovelhead, too," the man added as he turned his head back toward the gate of the cemetery.

A second club member jogged up and blurted out breathlessly, "I seen him before, Pres."

"Calm down, man," Mohamed chided. "Are we getting all this worked up over one white man?"

"Don't know his name, but I seen him fly colors. He's a Dog Soldier," the member continued, now seeming a little embarrassed over his initial loss of composure.

"OK, Digger," Mohamed replied as he placed his hand on the club member's shoulder. "Let's you and I just mount up and ride down there and see what's up."

A Dog Soldier? Mohamed tried not to show any of the bewilderment that he felt at this surprising turn of events. Why would a Dog Soldier show up at Brown's funeral? What did he want? And besides that, where the fuck did this white dude get the stainless steel balls to ride in here alone?

Dog Soldiers: Chapter 30

Stranger in a strange land.

Savage stood at the gate of the cemetery. Two large black men wearing black berets, dark glasses, and hip-long black leather coats flanked the gate entrance. Their coats bore the colors of the Souls.

There was no doubt in Savage's mind that beneath those coats both men were packing iron, too.

In his mind's eye Savage could easily imagine seeing these guys on a black-and-white TV set in 1965 on some national news story about the rise of the Black Panther Party.

Well, Savage thought, if you live long enough, you will see every fashion style come around again at least once and maybe twice.

The two men on the Harleys approaching him from the other side of the gate were dressed more like any other hog rider who was flying colors. The taller of the two was wearing the "Pres" patch in the traditional spot over the left pocket of his cutoffs. The man stepped off his scooter and removed his sunglasses before looking Savage straight in the eye.

"What do you want?" he asked very clearly and calmly.

"Brown was a friend," Savage replied. "I want to attend these services for him. I don't want to make any trouble for anybody. I don't want to offend anybody. I'm here asking you to please let me go up there and pay my respects before he goes under."

Mohamed studied the white man's face before speaking.

"You a Marine? With him in 'Nam maybe?"

"No," Savage replied. "I was regular army in 'Nam. I met Brown afterwards. I ride with the Dog Soldiers but I'm just here as me now, just as a civilian." Savage's voice underscored that last word, "civilian."

Mohamed paused. Being club president meant being more prudent, so he thought before he spoke. What possible motive could this man have in coming to this funeral if not simply the one he'd just expressed? More importantly, what danger could this man's attending Brown's funeral possibly have for any of the Souls?

Mohamed knew that if he allowed this white man to attend the service, then later there would definitely be some flak with some the brothers, some real heated words . . . but maybe that was OK, too.

He was the president now. That meant he'd have to call the shots and make his decisions stick. So maybe it was just as well that he found out who the real hot heads were going to be early on. Allowing this white man, a Dog Soldier no less, to ride in and attend the service for Brown would sure accomplish that in a hurry.

Mohamed was confident that the majority of the members would stand behind him, certainly not for any concern over "whitey," but because they had made him pres, and they knew the club had to stick together under one leader. They could bitch as much as they wanted—that was their right—but in the end, as long as he was president and ran things right, his decisions would stand.

"OK, white boy. You got the balls to show up here—" Mohamed glanced around at the faces of his people standing around him before he continued "—and you seem to know how to act right. Besides, my gut tells me Brown would have wanted you here. You packing?"

"No, I got no gun on me," Savage quickly replied.

"You bring something to put in the box? Some mojo, something to send with him?"

Savage was taken back a moment by Mohamed's question.

So, these black dudes had the same custom as the Dog Soldiers, tossing some small item into the casket of the departed. Something symbolic, like maybe something the deceased had

175

Dog Soldiers

given them, a small part of a scooter, or a wine bottle that they had shared. Sometimes it was a small bindle of blow or some smoke for the afterlife, sometimes a weapon. It would be something that they had both shared in life, something that now connected the living with the dead.

And sometimes along with that "mojo" there was also a short eulogy and sometimes even a promise made to the dead.

"Yeah," Savage replied. "I did bring something, thanks." He found himself bewildered by a sudden flood of emotion that left him momentarily unable to speak.

Mohamed looked at the white man in embarrassed amazement. He'd seen the biker quickly flip a hand to his eye to catch the start of a tear, and he also saw that the man hoped that nobody would see this. Mohamed had heard Savage's voice quiver a bit when he spoke.

The new President of the Souls laughed silently to himself. He had seen it all displayed so clearly on Savage's face. This white guy's effort to "play it off" like it hadn't happened was truly a futile one.

"You wait til it's time, when the brothers line up to drop their stuff in the box. You find the end of line, understand?" Mohamed instructed Savage.

"I understand," Savage responded.

"OK then." Mohamed motioned toward Savage's bike. "You kick over that Shovel and follow behind us." He then glanced into the faces of his brother Souls and added, "And try not to get too weepy eyed on us, boy. Brown wouldn't go for that." This comment brought a subdued flurry of short, mocking laughs and some smiles to the faces of the nearby Souls.

A mojo, Savage thought as he plopped his ass down on his bike. Wasn't sure he'd ever heard it called that before.

As this thought passed through his mind, he reached into his jacket pocket and clutched the "mojo" he'd brought to place inside Brown's coffin—six .357 Magnum cartridges and the blank rune.

"It took six rounds to put you under, man," Savage said silently to himself.

"I'll find 'em, bro. And when I do, I'll take it out of their fucking skulls."

Dog Soldiers: Chapter 31

Cry havoc, and let slip the Dogs of War.
William Shakespeare

A few hours' drive south of Mountain View, the pine forests became only foothills as the two-lane blacktop spilled out onto the plains. Savage glanced at the gas gauge in his jeep and figured that he could bypass gassing up in Colorado Springs. He'd take the cutoff that ran across the western perimeter of Fort Carson.

The wind buffeted him in the seat of the open-air vehicle. He felt like he could actually inhale the strong Colorado sunshine that now bathed down upon him. He'd been out of the hospital for three and half weeks now and was just beginning to feel pretty good again.

The radio was turned up full blast, and Jimmy Hendrix cranked out "All Along the Watchtower."

It was always necessary to crank up the radio volume just to hear over the wind noise in the open-air Jeep. But then again, full blast was just the way Savage liked it anyway. As usual, there was hardly another car on the road, and Savage liked that, too. For the next hour and a half, a few antelope and some cattle watering themselves at stock tanks were about all he would see.

After he turned off the pavement, he traveled down about 17 bumpy miles of dirt road until that crude road ended and brought him to the flat, treeless portion of the alkali plains. He was headed to Benny's place.

He glanced at his watch. Just under three hours' drive, he thought. Not bad time. He hoped Benny would be there, but since Benny didn't have a telephone, there was no way to know in advance.

Benny didn't have a phone because the phone lines didn't go this far out, and neither did the electricity. Benny figured he didn't need any such luxuries anyway. Moreover, not having those utilities out here also ensured that Benny wouldn't have to deal with any neighbors.

He had installed two photovoltaic solar panels and a bank of marine batteries to store the juice so he could run a radio, stereo, and even a small TV if he wanted.

The meat he got from hunting he smoked cured and hung in his root cellar. The temperature in his root cellar would seldom rise over 43 degrees. He had drilled a well, and although it produced only three to five gallons a day, it allowed him to keep his water tank nearly full all the time.

Passive solar panels heated the water in the tanks, so even in winter he always had a hot shower on tap. A hot shower, at least every three or four days or so, was something Benny wasn't quite ready to leave behind.

Savage knew that even these few other creature comforts that Benny had were principally motivated by pressure from his ex-old lady.

Ultimately she had found Benny's retreat a bit too rustic for her tastes, so she had split about a year ago. Savage wondered if Benny had got himself a new woman by now.

The dirt road ran up a sandy wash and entered a short canyon before crossing a dry streambed. Once across the streambed, Savage's jeep made a short climb up a hillside, and the terrain began to turn into a sparse pine forest again.

As Savage crested the rise, he spotted the top of Benny's greenhouse. It was a simple but productive affair. Plastic sheeting stretched over an arched PVC frame. It provided Benny with a year-round source of fresh vegetables, and his rifle or shotgun put the venison, elk, rabbit, ptarmigan, and even an occasional pheasant on the table.

Benny was a hell of a shot and a very experienced tracker and hunter.

Benny was also a little crazy.

Savage stopped the jeep about 30 yards from the partially bermed Quonset hut that served as Benny's home. He then yelled out very loudly, "Yo Benny! It's me, Savage!"

Savage knew better then to get out of the Jeep and poke around Benny's place. Not only would that be impolite; it could also be downright dangerous.

"Benny! Benny! You here?" Savage shouted out again.

"I'm right here, Pete," came the response.

Savage spun around, but he saw no sign of Benny even though the voice had sounded as if he were right behind him. Benny's unmistakable laughter caused Savage to look up. He saw the man squatting above him on the water tank platform with a CETME assault rifle in his hands.

"Nice piece of iron, buddy. Don't see too many of those," Savage commented.

"You recognize it?" Benny asked.

"What?" Savage joked. "You think I'm some sort of uneducated scooter trash that doesn't recognize quality iron when he sees it? It's a Spanish CETME. Uses the roller block, delayed-breach locking system like the HK. What's yours chambered for—5.56mm?"

"No, it's a 308," Benny corrected.

Savage jumped out of his jeep, and the grizzled biker climbed down from the water tower. The two men laughed and smiled as they embraced briefly.

"You're getting some more fat on your ass, city boy," Benny offered.

"Shit, man, I was in the fucking hospital for three weeks. I'm just getting back together. Besides, you don't look like you're exactly starving—or getting any younger, either."

"Plenty to eat in these hills, and I can still hunt 'em all day and all night long, too," Benny said. "How come you were in the hospital?"

"Got into a little legal jam, and this dude tried to shank me when I was in the jailhouse."

Benny looked Savage in the eye. "So maybe you need to settle a score. That why you here?"

"Well, man, it ain't exactly like that. The guy who stuck me is dead now anyway, so there's no score left to settle there." Savage didn't like to mislead Benny, but he'd been taken off guard by such an abrupt question.

It was also more than a little disturbing to Savage that Benny had immediately determined the true objective of his mission in coming before he'd even been there for more than four minutes.

But since that was clearly the case, he decided that he might as well get directly to the point.

"Well, since you asked, buddy, fact is I was looking for some special parts."

Savage was one of the few people who knew Benny was still around, and one of the fewer still who knew he had a stash of weapons and gun parts that might be the envy of the most well-financed paranoid survivalist or small militia group almost anywhere in the country.

During Benny's 17 years of military service, he had been in depot-level small arms maintenance, and during that time a lot of parts and ordinance had found their way into his hands. He was also quite a gunsmith and had worked for a Class III firearms dealer in Dallas who specialized in importing surplus military firearms and parts as well as in rebuilding and selling automatic weapons. As a licensed Class III dealer, it had all been quite legal, but ultimately the BATF harassment and paperwork drove Benny's employer out of the trade and Benny out of a job.

But not before Benny had collected a lot of "special" gun parts.

"What kinda parts we talking about?" Benny asked.

"Nothing you'd likely miss, pal. I was hoping you'd let me go through some of the stuff by myself. Might be better for both of us like that," Savage replied.

"Ha!" Benny barked. "Look, man, maybe you're thinking you're helping me out, like protecting me or something by my not knowing what you're putting together, or trying to get working right, or whatever. But I'm way past all that now. Anyone comes here to take me in for whatever, well, they're just going to have to come up that canyon shooting. It's going to come to that for a lot of us sometime, you know? Government wants all the guns, and they know there's only way they'll ever get 'em. Constitution don't mean crap to them."

Savage figured it might go like this with Benny. The old vet had some pretty strong opinions on freedom and the rightful limits that the Constitution placed on the central government.

He'd hoped he could work it so he'd get the parts he needed without Benny ever knowing exactly what parts he'd taken, but clearly that wasn't going to happen.

Hence, Savage figured he might just as well avail himself to Benny's considerable technical expertise on iron and his ability to quickly locate the parts he was looking for.

"OK, man, that's straight enough. I got to tell you that I hope it isn't going to be like that with the feds. I don't think the politicos are really that stupid, anyway. Nobody wants a civil war, and they know that's what it would come down to if they try to disarm the people."

"I wouldn't count on that," Benny replied as he led Savage toward the house and shop.

"Shit," Savage continued, "even a lot of cops wouldn't go along with any house-to-house search mission for peoples' guns—some cause they know it couldn't be legal, others cause they just don't want to be shot dead over some political dickhead's bullshit."

The tone of Benny's reply told Savage he was prepared for this argument and that in Benny's mind the federal government's plan to disarm the people was now all quite clear to him.

"They will need some incident," Benny said flatly. "Something to get the media stirred up so they can declare some sort of temporary state of emergency, martial law, or some new anti-terrorist shit of some sort. You think that guy in Oklahoma was working on his own?"

Benny continued, "Well, maybe he was, or maybe it was a probe. The feds could have put him up to it, maybe even without his even knowing it. That gives 'em the big media incident so they can cram through some new anti-terrorist laws. Tell me, man: Who were the real fucking terrorists there in Waco? OK, some people got to think that some weirdo's God. Does that mean the feds have to go down there and burn 'em all up alive? Women, kids, everything? Your church gotta be 'BATF approved' now to be safe from an attack by the feds? That ain't how I read the Constitution." Benny turned and stopped a moment to face Savage on the way into the house.

"The Constitution," Benny repeated. "I took an oath to defend it from all enemies both foreign and domestic same as you."

Savage was trying to figure out some way to get Benny's mind off this vitriolic political diatribe. Although he liked him and knew the man to be absolutely trustworthy, he was now close to having some second thoughts about doing business with him.

"What you need, Pete?" Benny asked directly.

"Well, I was thinking about a Smith & Wesson Model 76," Savage responded, "with a suppressor if you can give me one," he finished.

Benny's eyes widened and a big smile broke across his bearded, sunburned face.

The Smith & Wesson Model 76 was a 9 mm submachine gun. A U.S. Navy SEAL had introduced Savage to the weapon in Vietnam.

"I don't think you want one of those, Pete," Benny responded.

"And why not?" Savage asked in surprise.

"'Cause they only made about 36 hundred of them back in '66, and that makes 'em kind of a collector's item. Maybe sorta easier to trace, too, you know? Special extraction marks on the brass, the twist on the slugs—maybe you need to think about stuff like that."

Savage had not considered that. He didn't realize the gun was that rare, either. He just liked that particular submachine gun a lot. It was real controllable in full-auto fire and a reliable, natural pointer. The folding wire stock made it real compact as well. Still, he figured Benny knew best regarding the choice of weapons.

"So what do you think I need, Benny?"

Benny simply motioned Savage to follow him into his shop.

He picked up a huge vise off a wooden workbench and set the weight down on the shop's earthen floor.

"Put this little beauty together awhile back. Hell, don't exactly know why. Guess I was bored or something," Benny said as he raised the top of the workbench and withdrew an olive-drab, zippered M-60 extra barrel bag from within.

Savage watched intently as Benny unzipped the bag and began assembling the weapon. After screwing on the barrel, Benny paused a moment before slipping the metal butt stock on the gun.

"Now listen to this," Benny said. As he slipped the stock on, a single, solid metallic 'click' was heard. This seemed to give Benny immense satisfaction.

"All hand-fitted, pal," he declared proudly. "The original parts were probably made after the war. Not much wear on 'em. The original gun these parts came from may had not have even fired more than one full magazine, maybe two, before being scrapped in '47," Benny continued as he tossed the weapon to Savage.

The war Benny referred to now was World War II, and the gun he handed Savage was a 9 mm submachine gun.

"The old STEN MKII submachine gun," Savage said as he drew back the open bolt to cock the gun and inspect the chamber. Making sure that the horizontal magazine was empty, he pulled the trigger to determine its pull and stiffness. A sharp metallic ping was heard as the heavy, open bolt slammed down on the empty chamber.

"None other than," Benny replied, confirming Savage's identification of the weapon.

He was glad Savage recognized the gun and smiled as he completed the loading of the 27th round into one of the gun's 32-round magazines.

"Damn simple weapon but a great design. Hell, everybody seems to have one these days, the parts kits are so dirt cheap now. Shit, all you need is a piece of muffler tube and welder to put one together. Bad magazines were the only real problem with the STEN," Benny declared, "but these magazines here have all been tested with this particular weapon."

Benny tapped his index finger on the gun in Savage's hand. "Another thing is the ejector has to be welded in just right spot inside the tube in relation to the magazine for proper loading and extraction. A lot of people don't realize that, you know? But I made this one, and it works just fine."

"Go ahead, try her out," Benny offered as he handed Savage the loaded magazine.

The two men stepped out of the shop and back into the harsh sunlight outside.

Savage snapped the magazine into the STEN gun's magazine well and placed his hand over the top of the horizontal magazine collar. He shouldered the weapon and got his sight picture with both eyes open and the barrel at the bottom of his peripheral vision.

"OK to cut lose over there?" Savage asked.

"See that blue plastic antifreeze jug? Over past the prickly pears?" Benny replied.

"Yeah."

"Try not to hit the cactus. It draws the javelina sometimes. Those little pigs can make a nice meal."

"Right," Savage acknowledged. He then cut loose with three short bursts of automatic fire.

Da! Da! Da! Dow! Da! Da! Da! Dow! Da! Da! Dow!

The submachine gun spit out the lead, and the blue antifreeze jug was tossed into the air.

An instant after it hit the ground, Savage hit it with another shorter burst of fire that sent it tumbling further across the alkali.

Da! Da! Da! Da! Dow!

Savage drew a long, deliberate breath then chuckled aloud as he slipped the bolt into the safety notch.

"Goddamn! Sweet!" he exclaimed with enthusiastic sincerity.

Benny picked up the bullet-riddled antifreeze jug and turned it over a few times examining it as if it were something more than just a plastic jug full of bullet holes.

"Yeah, I'd say you have the hang of the weapon," Benny declared. "Think it will do the job for ya?" Benny asked as he tossed the plastic jug back out onto the alkali.

Savage's reply was to drop the bolt out of the safety notch and cut loose with another burst of automatic fire. The hail of bullets skated the blue jug off the alkali and onto the sand.

Da! Da! Da! Da! Dow!

"Yeah, Benny," Savage replied. " I think this will do the job just fine."

Dog Soldiers: Chapter 32

Savage rested the metal cutter on the tool rest of his lathe as the lathe turned and the tool cut shards of glistening steel that spun out from his work.

It was an essential piece of equipment to have in his motorcycle repair shop. With his lathe and his vertical milling machine, he could manufacture almost any obsolete or custom part for any bikes made in the last 56 years.

But of course, he only worked on Harleys at his Hog Wild Bike Shop.

He blew the remaining pieces of steel splinters from the work with a blast of compressed air and cranked back the spindle wheels of the lathe to remove the finished product from the machine.

Savage removed his safety glasses and held the piece up against the shop light to examine his latest handiwork closely when he heard the telltale rumble of an early Blockhead motor arrive just outside his shop.

His guest had arrived. Savage set down the piece he had just made on the bench and tossed a shop rag over it.

The twin doors of Savage's garage and shop rolled up obediently when he pushed the remote control. Brilliant, almost blinding sunlight spilled into his workplace. He had to squint a moment against the light to see for sure that it was Ortega getting off the bike.

"*Que pasa, amigo mio,*" the big man asked in a jovial tone. The two Dog Soldiers embraced one another.

"*Es el mismo, hombre, y con tu ese?*" Savage replied.

Having lived most of his life in the southwest and Rocky Mountain area, Savage had picked up more than just a working knowledge of the Spanish language. Even so, that wasn't quite good enough to serve him for the very challenging translation job he had on his hands now. That's why he had enlisted Ortega's help. It was the Chicano's fourth visit to see Savage in the last three months.

"Yeah, it's the same old shit with me too, but you know my old lady's having a kid now?" Ortega said, though he knew Savage already knew this.

"Gotta work all the overtime I can get now at that fucking plant. Gotta get that overtime and make that cash. But you know, I don't think there will be any more overtime after this contract that we got now's finished. But then shit *ese!*" Ortega said with a beaming smile. "Then I'll have the time to make some of the longer runs with the bros again. I missed the shit out of that, *hermano*."

"Yeah, I'm sure you do. The other bros ask about you too man," Savage assured him.

The two men walked directly into the shop and down the stairs to the basement.

"It's cooler down here," Ortega noted.

"It never really gets hot down here," Savage replied as he slid back the cover of a large steel toolbox and removed a coaxial cable from a smaller box inside. With the coax cable freed, he lifted the smaller box out and placed it on the counter.

The two men sat on the white plastic shop chairs as Savage cued up the tape recorder.

"This is the part I can't get. I know he's talking about somewhere out on the plains, but damn they use so much weird-ass slang and shit. I must have listened to it 50 times now."

When Savage had arranged for Danny Mapes to place the cell phones into Gold Chains' hands, he figured the dealer would be speaking Spanish, of course, but he had hoped they would be speaking more freely knowing that they had the digital encryption working for them.

But they did not. After so many years in the drug-dealing business, it seemed that habit still had Gold Chains and his partner talking in their personal codes even on the encrypted phones.

"OK," Savage said as he hit the play button on the cassette recorder, "what's your call here?"

The voices on the tape chattered away, and Ortega had parts played back several times, listening intently.

"It's the same as before, man. It's some kinda code they got, The guy says like . . . "

A puzzled look suddenly came over Ortega's face as he gave up the idea of trying to directly translate it again, and his mind came upon a new line of thought.

"Well, we know they're setting up some sort of meeting, and the one guy's telling the other how much money something will be." Ortega laughed. "I mean I don't have to be a fucking Einstein to figure it's a dope deal, pal, but like when and where? They ain't making that easy for anyone to know. Maybe these dudes are like paranoid or something. You know, like maybe they're afraid somebody's tapping their phones."

Ortega then chuckled at his own joke.

"You think?" Savage replied wryly.

Savage knew they talked in a personal code on top of the L.A. Chicano street-gang dialect they used for certain words. But a very few times they didn't speak in the code. On three occasions, one of them—he thought the man's name was Julio—had spoken in straight Chicano Spanish. That was pretty easy for Savage to understand.

Whenever the other guy had repeated the date, time, and place back to Gold Chains in plain old Los Angeles Spanish, he'd been strongly chastised for it. But each one of these slipups had provided one more clue to help Savage and Ortega figure out another piece of the linguistic puzzle.

When Gold Chains set up a rendezvous, the time was the first thing given, then the weight of the drugs, then the place. They always seemed to be given in that sequence, and the men always appeared to be setting up the details of almost every deal "on the run," so to speak. Everything was set up at nearly the last minute.

Yet, they did have some routines that could be identified, too. Like Ortega said, you didn't have to be an Einstein to figure out they were setting up a dope deal. Actually, some of it didn't even seem that cryptic anymore.

For example, Savage figured out that the words that translated as "ten spotting somebody" was their Chicano slang for "dropping a dime" on somebody. At first he though this meant rating somebody out. But that wasn't it.

That "dime" meant $10,000 as far as Savage had been able to figure. The time was also always given in half-hour increments, and so he'd ultimately figured out how to translate the time of the meetings from their gibberish on the audiotape.

The amount of the drugs was always expressed in an even numbers of kilos, too. Gold Chains apparently would not split up a standard kilo block of his speed. The amount of kilos was also always expressed as a multiple of some minimum amount of purchase weight. Savage guessed that the minimum purchase from Gold Chains was one kilo.

If not, then this guy, Gold Chains, was a much bigger speed cooker and dealer than he'd ever figured; if it did not mean one kilo, then the code words could only mean 10 kilos. If so, then that was big-time drug dealing.

Unfortunately, Savage had never been able to check out the accuracy of his translations because he had no idea where the meetings were to take place. Hence, thus far, knowing the time or the amount of drugs to be sold and for how much money was of little use to him.

If he could only translate the cipher they used that told them where the meetings were to be held; then he could risk a little covert surveillance and go to that place. If they showed up at the right time, then he'd know he had the codes figured out.

He also knew that they had a list of predetermined places where they would meet for a deal, and on the cell phones they used some sort of alternating series of code words to identify those places. But the words they used made no sense to Savage or Ortega in identifying a specific place for the meeting.

"You know what I think, man?" Ortega asked as he punched the stop button on the tape machine. "He was talking about Highway 24. Remember? He just said it pretty much straight out 'cause he said he would be losing his cell signal until he got to the Divide."

"Yeah," Savage asked. "And?"

"Well, you put it all together. He could mean the town of Divide. Highway 24 is about the only road to get there, and he would lose his signal in that canyon just before he got there."

Ortega continued with this reasoning.

"We know the times the deals are going down, but no meeting has ever been set up for more than an hour and a half from when they set it up over the phones. Some of the deals were set up just a half hour before they happened, so you have to figure that wherever these guys are when they talk, they are talking about a place to meet that can't be much more than, say, 60 miles apart, probably a lot less than that most times."

Savage had already figured that out for himself. He also realized that he'd just been fooling himself to have ever thought that Ortega would not have figured out what he was up to from square one. Ortega had never come directly out and said it before like he had today, but that was just because he was trying to be polite. Savage also realized that, for Ortega, it was now all becoming an interesting linguistic mystery that he was taking personally.

"These guys are dealing speed for sure, bro. Speed freaks," Ortega cautioned Savage. "Dangerous people, bro."

"That's a fact," Savage responded. "You think we've taken this as far as we can tonight?"

"Man, I'm here now, but I can come back anytime you got something new for me to listen to," Ortega replied.

Ortega was pensive for a moment.

"I just need to think about it some more. But I don't think any more translating of this shit tonight is going to help until I find the key to this whole deal, you know? Shit, maybe that key, when we finally figure it out, will seem so obvious, like we'll wonder why we didn't see it right off. I got a feeling that maybe I'm getting close to it."

Savage reached into his shirt pocket where he'd earlier placed two $100 bills. He handed them to Ortega.

"You don't got to pay me, man. This ain't no work for me, and besides, we're bros in the club, right? Shit, man, you don't got to pay me nothing. I told you that before."

Savage genuinely appreciated Ortega's attitude, because he knew it was sincere. He took the two hundred dollar bills and stuffed them into the pocket of Ortega's leather vest.

"Hey bro, you can't be so selfish anymore," Savage smiled. "You gotta think about that kid on the way now. And listen, man, if this works out, I mean, if I make it work out like I want, then I'll see to it that you and your family get something out of it too."

"Thanks for the thought, hermano," Ortega replied. "I think it's just a matter of time, really. Hell, it might just hit me when I'm scootering home. I think we're that close. You are a smart dude. Maybe you might figure this shit out before I do."

Savage stared at the translations he'd put to paper and tacked the notes up on the wall next to his map. Running his finger over a yellow highlighted part of the paper, he turned back to Ortega.

"Ya know, bro? With the help you've given me, I think we will figure it out."

"Hasta luego then, amigo mio!" Ortega said. The two clubers slapped palms before he departed.

Dog Soldiers: Chapter 33

The sound of Ortega's scooter leaving Pete's shop faded, and Savage returned to his metal lathe. He took the rag he'd thrown over the metal part that he had just finished before Ortega arrived and wiped his hands with it.

Taking the part out, he examined it by looking down the bore of the STEN gun barrel that he'd just cut threads into.

From a locked metal toolbox he removed the STEN gun itself. He slipped the barrel nut over the new threaded barrel and re-installed it on the gun. He then removed a cylindrical aluminum tube from the same lock box.

The aluminum tube was about two and a half inches in diameter and 14 inches long. He placed a few drops of oil on the barrel threads before screwing the long aluminum tube onto the end of the barrel.

The threads on the silencer he had made and those on the barrel mated up perfectly and locked down securely.

With the shop door closed again and the room darkened, Savage pressed the switch that turned on the laser sight he had installed on the gun. The red dot of the laser was projected onto the wall and could be seen quite clearly in the dimmed light of the shop.

He walked to the other side of the garage, pulled up a mattress that was lying on the floor, and propped it up against the wall. he then taped a standard police silhouette target onto the mattress. To put as much distance as the garage allowed between himself and the target, he walked away from the target along a diagonal path to the corner of the shop.

Savage cocked the bolt of the gun and slapped in a nearly full magazine of 9 mm soft point ammunition and raised the weapon to eye level.

In the movies submachine guns are most often seen being fired from the hip, but Savage knew better. Dramatic Hollywood imagery was no substitute for accuracy.

Savage placed the red beam of laser light on the head of the silhouette. He pushed the fire selector switch into the semiautomatic position. Then he fired a single shot that struck right where the laser dot was projected.

The shot sounded like someone was using a broom to beat out a rug on a clothesline, and Savage grinned in satisfaction at his new creation. He fired off two more quick rounds in semiautomatic mode. Both struck the target just where he'd placed the laser.

Pushing the fire selector to the fully automatic position, he fired a short burst of lead into the center of the target. *Da da da dow! Da da da dow!* the weapon barked out in a muted voice.

He then held back the trigger and fired the weapon fully automatic until the magazine was empty and spent brass littered the shop floor.

Looking at the target, Savage stared at the tiny shards of paper, dust, and mattress stuffing that now gently floated upon the air. In the ruby red light of the laser, these tiny floating particles seemed like fine crimson snowflakes.

Dog Soldiers: Chapter 34

And pay back can be a bitch.

Anonymous

It had now been six weeks since Savage had gotten out of the hospital. He'd been working out to rebuild his strength and had done some running to get back his wind and endurance.

Savage still felt some pain in his lower intestine when he pumped heavy weight and occasionally just when lying in bed after a large meal. He had thus learned not to eat large meals.

He reminded himself of this prudent dietary prohibition as he downshifted the Serpent and rode into the large group of Dog Soldiers partying in an open meadow in the Pike National Forest.

Savage saw from their numbers that most everybody in the club was there. That was good to see, too, especially since he was the guest of honor at this little get-together.

The shock absorbers on the Serpent had been cut down in length by an inch and a half to make the bike sit lower and thus lower its center of gravity.

On a two-lane blacktop this gave Savage just the ride he wanted when accelerating out of the pocket of a sharp turn at high speed, but he paid a small price for the cut-down shocks when he went off the pavement. On the grassy meadow he was now rolling over, he crept along slowly. Even then it was a somewhat bumpy ride.

Looking ahead, he saw the club President and beside him Bulldog, the club's sergeant at arms. He gave the Serpent a bit of throttle and bounced over to where the men stood.

Bulldog heard Savage's motor and turned around to see him ride in.

"Recalled to fucking life, Pete Savage, the man that would not die," he shouted loudly enough in his gruff voice that almost everyone could hear.

"I'm too damn pretty to die just yet, Bulldog," Savage yelled back over the noise of his motor.

A group of three club members drifted by as they passed a bottle of whiskey between them.

"Good to see you're still with us, bro," the taller of the three declared as Savage cut off his engine and parked his bike.

"Thanks, Razor. It's definitely good to be back, especially—" Savage looked around a moment.

"—Especially right now, with damn near everybody in the club. Feels good, bro, feels good."

Macahan moved closer to Savage to speak to him with some privacy. "I want you to have a good time here, pal. Just chill and party. We can talk about any other club shit at some other time."

Any other club shit, Savage thought.

Macahan was a sharp president, and he was very perceptive of people, too. Savage knew from his tone that Macahan was aware that something wasn't quite right with him at that moment—this despite his display of earnest pleasantries with the club members he'd just spoken with.

The Pres sensed something wasn't right with him all right . . . that is, besides his just having been recently arrested for murder one and then having been shanked in the county jail.

Well, Savage thought, Macahan was right as usual.

But, what was eating at Savage now he planned on attending to right there at the party. Only there had to be nobody else around when he did—just himself and his pledge, Mark O'Shey.

A tremendous whoop of joy suddenly arose from the pack, and Savage turned his head around to see a very fine looking young girl dancing topless on the hood of a 1954 Chevy pickup.

Two Dog Soldiers held a crudely scribbled sign made with magic marker and cardboard. It simply read, "Show us your tits."

This kind of stuff still cracked Savage up even after a full 33 years of doing it.

Not to be outdone, a second girl jumped into the bed of the pickup. She was leaning out over the side of the truck as a Dog Soldier sprayed her tight T-shirt with beer from a large aluminum keg.

Suddenly the spray of suds dropped off, and when it did a loud "Boo!" spontaneously arose from the multitude.

The large man holding the heavy keg was frantic at this disapproval from his bros, and yet somehow he managed to both hold the heavy keg while pumping the pressure up at the same time. The beer then sprayed out onto the girl's tight T-shirt with renewed vigor. A booming cheer arose from the crowd as they spontaneously expressed their admiration of the keg bro's feat.

Savage walked over to the pickup. The first girl looked to be 19 or 20. That was OK—she was legal. The club didn't need any legal hassles at an official club function. She was a damn fine looking girl too, Savage thought.

Not too many non-members ever got to attend a Dog Soldier's party, but girls like this found it pretty easy.

As Savage admired the girl's body, there were a few shouts from the crowd as they recognized his presence. The girl then realized who Savage was and that the whole party was for him, the road captain of the Dog Soldiers MC.

She looked in his face and leaned over smiling and shaking her stuff at him. Savage returned her smile as he tipped his beer can in admiration and acknowledgement.

The second girl's nipples were now clearly outlined under her wet T-shirt. She danced about wildly so as not to be outdone by her companion on the hood of the truck.

"Outstanding," one of the bikers shouted out. "Out fucking standing!"

But even his booming voice was almost drowned out when the girl crossed her arms to reach under the bottom of her beer soaked T-shirt.

She clearly enjoyed teasing this shameless crowd of bikers. Her tongue came out of her mouth and she swirled it around at the adoring and appreciative crowd as she pulled up on her T-shirt a little bit at a time.

Then, with a sudden jerk she lifted the shirt off completely allowing her apparently artificially augmented breasts to spill out. The crowd went wild with near deafening hoots and hollers.

She tossed her garment to her admirers, and the Dog Soldier who caught it brought it to his nose and began to sniff it in an exaggerated fashion as the pack exploded with still more hoots and jeers.

"Another fun-loving girl to entertain the troops," Savage said to Bulldog as he came beside him.

"That second set of teeters may not be all real, but you know, they'll do. They sure as fuck will do!" he exclaimed.

The first, slightly younger girl seemed to feel that the attention was now centering on the other woman, so she jumped off the truck bed and embraced Savage, giving him an exaggerated "movie-style" kiss.

This girl probably thought she was in some kind of a movie too, Savage thought.

When the girl jumped off the truck, a portion of the crowd surged and immediately swarmed around Savage.

He could hardly disappoint them. Besides, for the road captain of the Dog Soldiers to allow a beautiful, young, half nude girl to go totally unmolested at a club function, well, that might give the Dog Soldiers a bad name.

This party was for him anyway. His bros put it together to show that they were glad he was still alive. It was thus incumbent on him to demonstrate that he was very much alive, and at this moment he did not find that a difficult or onerous task, either.

Savage slipped his tongue down the girl's throat and felt its warmth. His hands fondled here young breasts as the thundering crowd simultaneously screamed out both its approval and envy. Slipping his head down to her chest, he ran the point of his tongue over a nipple as the bikers continued to howl.

When Savage raised his head from the girl's chest, he spotted Mark O'Shey. He could see that Mark was well amused by his antics.

But Savage immediately and deftly spun the girl around and slapped her perfect little ass to dismiss her. She turned around and gave him a shallow pretense at displeasure with such curt treatment, then jumped back up on the truck bed to continue to parade herself before the crowd.

Savage walked directly over to Mark, smiling all the time.

"Yo, Pledge! We got some talking to do."

"Sure thing, shoot," Mark responded.

"Kinda confidential, pal. Follow me."

A short walk brought the two down to Arapaho Creek and out of the sight of the others. The water in the creek flowed clear and very cold.

"OK, so what gives?" Mark asked as casually as he could manage.

In that next flash of an instant he saw purple lights explode against a black background, and he fell to the ground.

Mark was shocked both in mind and body by Savage's strike. Still, he began to try to clear his head at once and to get up.

Before he could do so, however, a kick to his rib cage knocked the breath completely from his body, and he fell sprawled out in the dirt once again.

Savage then searched the man that he had just knocked semi-conscious and retrieved a .38 Detective Special from an ankle holster strapped to Mark's leg.

After a minute or so Mark pulled himself together and was allowed to get up. He flopped his back up against a tree for support and just sat there trying to fully recover his breathing.

Savage was sitting on a log in front of him pointing the pistol directly at Mark's head.

"You broke my heart, man. I mean, I'm real sensitive, you know."

After the few moments to regain his breath, Mark responded.

"Yeah," Mark gasped, "you're a real sensitive guy, I can see that."

"Yeah, I'm just too damn sensitive, I guess. But I'm patient, too. Real mellow and forgiving, really," Savage returned.

"But you know what the one thing I just can't excuse is? I mean the thing that I really can't accept and move on and forget about? Well, I think you know what I mean. Maybe you can guess now what that is, huh, pal?"

"I don't think I can, but I suspect—" Mark had to catch his breath again before he could continue, and he now wondered if he'd cracked a rib. "—whatever it is I guess I must have done it."

Savage motioned to Mark's side. "Hurts, don't it?" he asked. "Because I'm such a sensitive guy, it hurt me too."

Mark was bewildered.

"Then again, maybe I should be a little more appreciative of you, huh? I mean, what do you think?" Savage spoke as if he were making small talk over lunch.

"After all, you did get me out of jail, didn't you," Savage declared. "I wished they'd processed that paperwork a little faster, though. Got myself shanked before it got through, you know?"

"What are you saying?" Mark returned, now catching both his wits and his breathing.

"Don't lie to me," Savage cautioned as he drew back the hammer of the pistol and pointed it at Mark's head. "Might piss me off if you lied to me again. Then I just might have to shoot you."

"I wouldn't want to see that," Mark said earnestly.

"No, I imagine you wouldn't," Savage replied calmly.

Savage stared at Mark a moment. It was clear to him that Mark felt that he might really be thinking about pulling the trigger, and that's just what Savage wanted to see.

Mark wondered if he had totally misjudged Savage's character all along.

"What you got against me then?" Mark asked with all the calmness in tone that he could possibly muster.

"Well, I got to say this for you, Mark. You got some style, buddy. I mean, some people might be—well, you know—like be real scared and shaky at this point, you know, maybe begging for their lives and stuff."

"Would that help?" Mark asked.

"No, I don't think so. It'd be a bad idea actually," Savage responded flatly. "You see, the thing I really liked about you is that you really did have a sense of style, a sense of adventure, and a pretty good brain, too. But maybe most of all, you had a sense a humor that I could really get off on."

Savage's tone then became more earnest. "You surfed it all like a champ, pal. Fooled us all, didn't you? You see, that's why with my being so sensitive and all, well, I'm real upset with you now, you know."

"I hope you can try to control yourself," Mark replied, "and do what's best for you, the club, and everybody else," he added.

"Poor salesmanship, pal. Not really a smart thing to say right now."

Savage pause briefly to stare into Mark's face, then continued. "I mean, to me that might mean shooting you dead right now, you see? Yep, I might see blasting your brains out as really being the best thing for the club and me too. Hey, maybe it's just that I'm just so damn sensitive that I can't just get right to it. What'ya think?"

Savage still had the pistol pointed at Mark's head. His finger was on the trigger and the hammer was drawn. The slightest pressure on the carefully hand-tuned pistol would instantly fire the shot.

"Then let me rephrase that then," Mark said.

Savage let out a guttural laugh. To Mark it seemed close to being demonic.

"Yeah, you got style all right," Savage acknowledged.

Savage let down the hammer with his thumb in fast and fluid manner, but he kept the gun pointed right at Mark's head.

Mark spontaneously released his breath in relief at this action. He knew that the slightest slip on that drawn trigger would have sent his brains scattering from his skull.

"Not the OSHA-approved way to de-cock the pistol is it?" Savage asked. "My thumb could of slipped, and it might go off accidentally."

Savage kept the gun pointed at Mark as he looked up into the sky as if bewildered at some deep mystery. He then sighed and looked back at Mark.

"I know you're not stupid, pal. Couldn't have gotten this far if you were. But I still just gotta ask you—how *did* you figure you could possibly get away with it?"

"I think I was doing real good for awhile, wasn't I?" Mark asked.

"That you were," Savage admitted. "You couldn't know things would go down like that on our run down to New Mexico. It was all pretty inexplicable for you, wasn't it? You can't plan for weird shit like that, us being sent out to the reservation, being held up another day with my pal Laughing Dog, then getting back here just when we did. No way you could have planned for that shit."

Maybe old Santo's spirit was looking after yours truly after all, Savage thought smilingly.

Mark knew he was far from out of danger, but he had already decided on his best survival strategy.

"It was only when they cut me loose from the slammer in Mountain View that I figured it all out. Maybe if we hadn't gone down to New Mexico like that and I'd stayed here, maybe I'd still be facing that murder charge right now, wouldn't I?"

"Yes, I think you certainly would be," Mark replied.

"There is only one reason I could come up with for why they'd just cut me loose so fast like that, only one," he repeated.

"That would be if I had some sort of totally ironclad alibi—somebody to establish exactly when and where I was when that murder took place."

'That murder'—but Savage wasn't going to say the man's name—Brown—because he did not want Mark to gather the slightest scrap of intelligence from him. Not even that he knew who Brown was.

Savage looked at Mark innocently but with the gun still in his hand.

"Now who would they believe about something like that? I mean, who would they just *have to believe* if they provided an alibi like that for me? Not a Dog Soldier pledge, that's for sure. No, couldn't be that. Pledges all take an oath when they pledge up to support and protect their brother members in the club. So, like they wouldn't even listen to what a Dog Soldier pledge might have to say, would they?"

"No, I don't think they would." Mark had his eyes on the gun in Savage's hand.

"You're sure right there," Savage replied at once. "They couldn't accept a pledge's word for something like that. For the cops to believe it, then it would have to come from somebody who they really knew well and trusted, too, wouldn't it? And that could only be another cop, right Mark?"

Savage paused a moment. "And that's exactly what you are, isn't it? A fucking cop!"

"Well," Mark replied, "you said if I lied to you that you might have to shoot me. Doesn't seem to be much point in denying it now anyway. Yes, I'm a detective. Now why don't you tell me what you intend to do about it, and then let's just get on with it."

Savage was struck at how Mark's diction and choice of words had changed instantly from that of the pledge he had previously known. He even sounded like a cop now.

"I'm not going to shoot you," Savage replied. "Never really intended to. Like you said, that just wouldn't be best for the club or for me either, badge boy. I'm not going to let anybody else here know that you're a cop, either. Otherwise, some hot head here might just grease you himself and bring all kinds of heat down on the club."

Savage shook his head before continuing.

"Fact is, if some of those people over there knew who you really were, I'm not too sure you'd have one fucking chance in hell of leaving here alive."

"Good decision, Pete," Mark declared. "But I'll tell you right now that the heat's already on the club, and big time, too. Why do you think they would take a chance on sending somebody like me in here? You think they don't know how dangerous that is? You think I didn't realize I could get myself killed here?"

Savage was further surprised with Mark's candor. He wasn't going to give Mark any information, but he was quite willing to obtain some from him.

"OK, I figure you knew you might get your ass greased with a fucking stunt like this. So tell me: why did you do it?"

"I shouldn't tell you anything, so if it ever comes up, remember, I never did tell you anything," Mark replied.

"Well so far, sport, you haven't," Savage responded.

"I see how you have your friends here, what it means to be a member of the club and—" Mark said this with a tone of grudging acknowledgment, but Savage interrupted.

"No, I don't think you see that at all. I don't think you understand the first goddamn thing about what it means to belong to this club."

"OK, maybe I don't. But listen to me, Pete. I'm a member of a club too. It's called the Gang in Blue, and when one of our guys gets killed, we do something about it. We have to do something about it no matter what, and we do."

"The guy who was killed, the one Captain Shields was so hot and bothered about," Savage replied, "that's who it is, isn't it? So he was a undercover cop and he got greased, it figures."

"That's right," Mark said, "and Shields figured that you and your little band of merry men up there were also involved in the production and distribution of methamphetamines."

Savage probed further. "So that's what the cop was looking into? He was trying to find some speed lab?"

"I'm not at liberty to say," Mark responded.

"You don't have to," Savage replied flatly. "So why you telling me this all shit now?"

As soon as the words left his mouth, Savage regretted them, because he really did need to know more about what this cop knew.

"I'll tell you this," Mark said. "I know the Dog Soldiers aren't cooking meth. If you were, I'd have found out about it by now."

"Against the club by-laws," Savage reminded him.

"Shit, man," Mark almost laughed. "You fuckers really do live in a different world, don't you?"

Savage waved a hand toward the 60 or so Dog Soldiers partying in the distance.

"Yeah, that's the basic idea—to get out of the world of the 'citizens' and make one of our own. I'd say we're doing a pretty fucking good job of it too."

"Pete, if you can tell me anything about this murder, then you should do it now," Mark declared.

"Well I don't know anything about the fucking murder," Savage protested. "Shields yammered away at me in his office, and that is the sum total of what I know about it."

"You don't know the guy whose picture Captain Shields showed you, then?"

"No, I don't know the fucker. I can tell you I have seen him before, but that's it. I don't even know who the fucker is."

"Why do I have trouble believing that?" Mark asked.

"Don't know and certainly don't give a shit, cop. Now let me tell you what I do know. I know that you came here and you lied to us. You pretended to be somebody else, and you set out to gain our trust so you could whack us down. That's some of the lowest shit a man can ever do, as far as I'm concerned," Savage challenged.

"I tell you straight. It wasn't long before I felt, well, a little bad about some of that. I didn't think I'd ever think or feel that way, either," Mark confessed.

"I feel your pain, cop," Savage mocked.

Mark continued as if he hadn't even heard Pete. "You were just a gang to me, a criminal association, and my job was to get inside. It's the only way something like this can be successfully prosecuted, with a man on the inside."

Savage's tone was still a mocking one. "And what big criminal conspiracy did you find? A few guys popping some pills here and there or smoking some weed? Maybe some guy driving a scooter without proper insurance?"

"No, I didn't find any criminal conspiracy, but that doesn't mean there isn't any, does it? You can't know what every member is doing outside the club. A police officer was killed, goddamn it. I came here to do a job. OK, you are right, it is a fucking dirty job, but I'm still going to get it done, and if one of your members is involved, his head's just gonna have to roll."

Savage grudgingly admired the man's pluck and his dedication. For him to utter these words while he stood before a Dog Soldier like himself with a gun in his hand took a pair of stainless steel balls, because this cop sure wasn't stupid.

"I think that's going to be real dangerous for you, Mark, or is that your real name? Somebody's already put two men in the ground over this shit. They damn near got me, too."

"What do you mean by that? You were attacked in the jail by a rival gang member. He probably was with the Wheels of Soul and heard that you were in there for killing their leader, so he went for some jail house pay back."

Savage's expression changed to one of wonderment at this remark.

"Maybe you are a little stupid," he said. "Think about it. How did my gun get to be the murder weapon? Why would the Souls send somebody to kill me in the joint when all they had to do was wait til' I made bail and then handle it nice and neat on the outside and without their gang's name all over it? How come the guy who attacked me never got a chance to be interrogated by anyone on account of he was dead? And who said he was really with the Souls in the first place? Connect the dots, pig," Savage barked. "Who could have arranged all that shit? *Only another fucking cop.* So yeah, I figure it's going to be real dangerous for you alright!"

Savage abated his rant a moment and composed himself. He then reached into the pocket of his jeans and removed a small object.

"This is the rune we drew that night in my kitchen." Savage had put the actual rune in Brown's coffin, but the one he held in his hand was identical, and he had brought it with him quite deliberately.

Savage had brought it with him because he had come to believe that the blank rune was now a symbolic part of the "great circle" that Laughing Dog had spoken of.

"It was just before we came over to your place to ask if you wanted to make your pledge run that I cast the runes. The same night we left for New Mexico. It's the blank rune, remember? It represents the void, the unknowable. But I think I neglected to mention to you that it can also mean death."

Savage ran his thumb over the blank stone.

"But before whatever is going to happen to you does happen, you're going to go up there and give the Pres your pledge colors. You're going to tell him that you decided you were not cut out for the club after all. That's all you're going to tell him too, understand? Then you just get your pig ass on your bike and get out of here now," Savage ordered.

Mark said nothing and just started his way up the hill alone.

Savage was going to tell the President who Mark really was, of course. The situation demanded it. But Pres was the only person he would tell.

It would be better if the cop did not know that, though. If he did, it might later expose Macahan to some sort of accessory charge.

Dog Soldiers: Chapter 35

Law and Order

The man's temporary security badge read "Detective Matthew O'Hare," but the face belonged to the man Pete Savage had known as Mark O'Shey.

The detective walked down the carpeted hallway on the fourth floor of the Federal building in Denver. When he came to the security station marked "D.E.A.," he turned and presented his credentials to the man at the desk.

"Good morning. I am here to meet with Special Agent Rhodes and Captain Shields."

"Go ahead, Detective. You will find them in Room 223. Take a left at the end of the corridor."

When he got to room 223, O'Hare rapped twice on the door before he entered. He recognized Captain Shields and the large black man, Detective Sloan. But he'd never met the DEA agent behind the desk.

The DEA agent smiled and got up to extend his hand. "Good morning, detective O'Hare. I'm Special Agent Rhodes."

"Sir," O'Hare responded as he briefly shook the man's hand.

Agent Rhodes dropped a folder on his desk, then drew a long breath as he shook his graying head.

"Well, I have read your report, detective, and . . . " The agent stumbled for the right words. ". . . and, well, to be frank, I just have to ask myself what we are all supposed to be doing here this morning. Your cover with this motorcycle gang is clearly lost. You're totally exposed now, and in my view you're quite vulnerable. I don't immediately see any way you can continue with this case, not with any measure of security."

Detective O'Hare replied slowly and with measured deliberation.

"I have a great deal of my time and of myself invested in this case, sir, more than I ever expected I would, actually. And I also have a meeting with Gutierrez this Thursday evening. I am sure he's got to be tied into Agent Parker's murder somehow. The photographs Captain Shields turned up make that all but certain."

The detective then pulled out the photo. It showed the man with the gold chains around his neck stepping out of a white Mercedes. He examined it a moment before tossing it down on the table.

Mark pressed his argument.

"If I make that meeting, then he's going to have to show me the drugs. It's as simple as that. I've convinced him I needed to see the weight and the quality before I can get my people to front me that kind of cash. So he knows that I won't be bringing any cash with me this time. We won't need any buy money for this, either. Once I see the drugs, then we can get a warrant and bring him in. Then you can sweat him out, and I think he's going to want to talk."

Detective Mark O'Hare then looked directly at Special Agent Rhodes.

"I imagine he's going to be pretty anxious to make a deal with a DEA man at that point."

Make a deal with a DEA man, O'Hare thought. He knew how the DEA operated, and despite his courtesies, he was never much of a fan of the agency.

He figured that they'd make a deal with Gold Chains, all right, and of course they'd get what information they could on their agent's murder.

But assuming Gold Chains wasn't the killer, and Detective O'Hare didn't think he was, then likely as not they would set Gold Chains up in some other city with drugs and money and a new ID. Then he'd have carte blanche to sell whatever drugs to whoever he could round up. He'd buy and sell to any dealer in that city.

Then after a year or so of this, the DEA would have enough evidence collected to bust each and every one of those dealers. Meanwhile, Gold Chains would skate when the big bust went down.

The local newspapers would report a sensational story: *"An ongoing investigation carried out for more than a year by local, State, and Federal law enforcement agencies resulted in a raid this morning at 17 different locations. An undisclosed amount of drugs, weapons, and more than $300,000 in cash were recovered."*

It was a sure bet that the TV news would announce "film at 11" too. It all made for good press for the DEA. It made their budget appropriations for another year a bit easier, and it was a career builder for men like Rhodes.

Sometimes guys like Gold Chains did not live too long in their "new" line of work. But it also seemed that sometimes they became even richer than before the DEA busted them. Others were even put into the Federal Witness Protection Program and given a monthly living expense.

These were a "last out" that the drug dealers at Gold Chains' level hoped to swing if busted by the Feds.

Detective O'Hare had seen it all before and more than once.

Most of the DEA guys seemed to honestly think that they were waging a "War on Drugs" this way. But O'Hare wondered just how many people first got into the business of drug trafficking mainly because the DEA brought the cheapest and best drugs to town with their "bust proof" distributor.

He also wondered just how many thousands of people originally got strung out on DEA-supplied drugs.

The Los Angeles detective often felt that the real objective of the War on Drugs was simply to keep law enforcement, especially Federal law enforcement, as a growth industry.

Still, he restrained himself from dwelling on that aspect of reality for the moment. He had his own job to finish now, and he had to convince the men in that room to give him the chance do it.

"No, I definitely don't think so," Detective Sloan announced loudly and with conviction. "It's just far too dangerous. You are out of it now, Detective O'Hare."

The black detective's tone then became a bit softer and more empathetic to Mark's situation.

"I can continue with this investigation myself, and *we will* get this man. We will get him in time. We always do. Maybe we'll have to find another deep cover agent like you. If so, then that's what we will do."

Sloan's tone then slipped into one of dignified and earnest conviction as he continued. "Detective, you have already shown tremendous courage here, and for the first time you've proved that it is possible to penetrate these local outlaw motorcycle gangs."

Captain Shields rubbed his hand beneath his chin a moment before he spoke.

"We have to make every effort we can to put a cop killer where he belongs, and that's what we have here: a cop killer. I think Detective O'Hare is right about this Gutierrez guy as well. We know he's a major player, so at some point down the line we are going to have to go after him anyway. Why not now and make it really count? Why not use it to get us some leverage and get some hard information here? I'll remind you that despite Detective's O'Hare's courage, we are still not one bit closer to solving this case than when we started."

Captain Shields walked over to the water cooler and filled a small conical cup with cold water. He immediately tossed this refreshment down his throat and dropped the crumpled paper cone into the wastebasket.

" What we do know is that these guys almost always roll over on each other when they are busted. And if we bust this Gutierrez guy in conjunction with the murder of a federal officer, then I'm sure he will start singing for us very quickly. So why not let the detective go through with the meeting and bring this Gutierrez in?"

Captain Shields picked up the photograph from the desk and looked at it briefly.

"This guy will know that O'Hare won't be bringing any money with him. And even if he knows the detective is a cop, which is something we can't really be sure of, then I don't think he's going to be there to meet with a cop anyway. This guy hasn't been in this business for 20 or more years without a single drug conviction by being stupid. I'm inclined to think the rewards might outweigh the risks here. I also think it should be Detective O'Hare's call. He's already put his life on the line on this case, so it's his choice now as far as I'm concerned," Shields declared.

Detective Sloan immediately protested loudly and strongly.

"I don't get this, Captain. This Gutierrez has already been involved in the murder of one officer, so why not another?"

DEA agent Rhodes fumbled through the file and then looked up at O'Hare.

"How is this meeting going to be set up? Where and when is it supposed to go down?"

"It will be like the last time, I figure," O'Hare replied. "When I first set up this deal, I met with his driver in a public place. It was a bar in Boulder. We sat there until the guy's cell phone rang. That's when he gets the details about where and when to meet, and then he tells me. Last time I had to drive out to Left Hand Canyon and turn down a dirt road. I don't think the road even had a name. He's no fool. There is no way I could have carried a tail on me; they would spot it right away, and I figure it will be the same thing on Thursday."

Agent Rhodes looked at Detective O'Hare a moment as if he was trying to imagine or visualize what might happen if the detective made that Thursday appointment. He then asked, "What do you have on these motorcyclists? What about this man Savage?"

"I don't have anything on any of them really—nothing that's worth our pursuing anyway. Certainly not anything worth compromising this investigation over."

"I don't see it that way at all," Detective Sloan injected. His tone betrayed his growing impatience with O'Hare.

"You have a clear charge of assault on a law enforcement officer here! You have a felony menacing charge on this man Savage. He pointed that gun at you, didn't he?"

"Yes he did, but I just won't testify for any Mickey Mouse charges like that. I can't do it and I won't do it. That would blow any chance I have to finish the real assignment, the one I came here for: to nail a cop killer."

Sloan rose to his feet to respond, but Agent Rhodes held up his hand and restrained him.

"Detective O'Hare, I think you were quite right when you said you have more invested in this case than you thought you would have."

DEA Agent Rhodes interrupted. "That concerns me, too, because I've seen this sort of thing before when a deep cover agent makes the mistake of getting too close to the principals of his investigation. It's a tough tightrope to walk. I even had one agent go native on me."

Rhodes paused a moment and looked down at the folder on his desk. "But I'll be straight out with all of you. It was my man that was killed, and that puts me pretty damn close to this thing too. So if you think you can go to this rendezvous Thursday and come back in one piece, then it's your call, Detective."

"I want to put in my two cents again," Sloan interjected. "I *know* that it's just too dangerous. His cover's been cracked, we know that. He's got an outlaw motorcycle gang that's probably gunning for him right now, and those bikers are tied up with this Gutierrez guy. Anything these bikers know then this fuck wearing the gold neck chains knows too. I'd think that should be obvious as hell right now."

Things weren't going at all like Detective Sloan had expected or wanted, so he vigorously returned to his original argument. "I can get this guy, I know I can. Maybe it will take another few months, or it could take a year, but what it doesn't have to take is another officer's life. I know this city, and in time I will get this guy. It's just foolish for this detective to go back in now. Why can't you all see that?"

Sloan then appeared to hold himself in check as he lowered his tone and intensity and faced Agent Rhodes and then to Captain Shields.

" With respect, sir, what are you people possibly thinking?"

Sloan turned to Detective O'Hare. "How can you even consider sending this man back in?"

O'Hare looked straight ahead and replied calmly.

"What I am thinking about, Detective Sloan, is catching a cop killer, and I am going back in."

Dog Soldiers: Chapter 36

A life of leisure and a pirate's treasure don't make much for tragedy, but it's sad my friend whose living in his skin and can't stand the company!

Bruce Springstein

Gold Chains poured premium tequila into a glass of freshly squeezed orange juice and picked up some ice cubes from a crystal carafe.

"You know, I been thinking. Maybe it's time to get out of this business. I got some real money now. Maybe take my money and start something totally legitimate, you know?"

It didn't take more than two or three drinks for Gutierrez's thick Chicano accent to reassert itself, and he had already had a bit more than that.

"Maybe a real fine Mexican restaurant in Boulder, man. They all like that kinda shit there. The rich yuppies, you know."

Detective Sloan replied dryly, "Yeah, I think they're called something else now. To me they're all just more white people."

"Heh!" Gold Chains laughed. "I know you don't like them too much either *ese!*"

"Yeah, a fine Mexican restaurant," Gold Chains continued to babble.

"You know, everything top of the line where you don't get out of there for less than a hundred bucks, maybe more. I'd have a whole cellar of fine wines. Yeah, that's it man, everything top class." He looked into his glass a moment as he swirled the drink around the sides and pictured this fantasy in his mind.

"Course I'll have to hire some nice waitresses, yeah, maybe a lot of them too. You know, I'm going to have to see to it personally that they can—" He searched for the right words. "All serve properly."

With this vision of these women "serving properly" in his mind, Gold Chains let out a deep belly laugh and tossed the reminder of his fourth Tequila Sunrise down his throat.

"Yeah, *ese*, any woman works in my place, she's got to have a fine ass and nice tits, you know?" he continued.

Sloan chose not to show his growing impatience with his drunken associate. Gold Chains was drunk, but he still perceived a bit of the detective's impatience with him.

"I think you're still pissed over that last deal, man. OK, I fucked up, but not this time. I did like you said, *ese*. I told you about this meeting from the first, and then you tell me that fucker's a cop too! I mean, like, I owe you, man," he added earnestly.

"Yeah, you do," Sloan replied. "You got through to your driver—what's his name—Julio? You told him it's off and not to meet with that guy in the bar, that he's a cop?" Sloan asked.

"I will, *ese*. He must be with his woman. His phone is turned off maybe, or he's in the canyon, but there is plenty of time to get ahold of him anyways, man. The meeting was not going to happen till tomorrow night. I'll get Julio on the line long before that."

"Would he have to contact you before going to meet with this cop? I mean, have you already told him where the meeting would be? We can't take any chances on this shit. I been trying to get that through your head," Sloan said pointedly.

"OK, man, cool it down. Nothing's going to happen now," Gold Chains replied while mixing another drink.

"That isn't what I asked you, is it?" Sloan said.

"No, he don't have to contact me, mano. I knew I can't get through to Boulder on my cell from here cuz of them mountains, so I told Julio the place Wednesday when I saw him at La Souza. It's no problem now, man."

"Where was the meeting supposed to be then?" Sloan pressed.

Gutierrez had to finish swallowing the tequila before he could reply.

"Well OK, man, but shit, what fucking difference does it make now? It was going to be right here. This is a nice spot to do business; no chance for a tail, and it's nice here in the day-time. You got the shade of the trees, and I like that stream down there. But I'm gonna be getting outa here real early to-morrow. I'm be getting my ass on that road in the morning."

"That's a real good idea for you," Sloan replied.

Gold Chains took a moment to concentrate and appear more sober before he replied to Detective Sloan.

"Something is bothering you, man. I mean, what is it? What's the problem, *ese*? Nobody's been able to get a step ahead of us yet, man. You always got a line on the heat out there, you know what they're doing. It's business as usual man, right?"

"Maybe business as usual has been going on too long." Sloan replied as he reached for the tequila bottle and poured himself a short drink into a salted shot glass. He immediately tossed it down, and his face winced at the taste. "I'm thinking of closing up shop too. I can't do this forever any more than you can, and there's more heat than ever going down now."

"Hey man, you was the one that blew that cop away," Gold Chains replied quickly, and then realized that the alcohol had suppressed his better judgment.

"OK, OK, you wouldn't have done it—it wouldn't have been necessary if I hadn't fucked up, man. I was the one that fucked up by letting him come without hearing from you first," he fin-ished.

"That's right. I just do what's necessary," Sloan said.

Detective Sloan pulled an envelope of money from his in-side jacket pocket.

"Look, partner. I picked up a drop today, a pretty big one, too. I can't be carrying it with me when I go back to the sta-tion."

Sloan tossed the stack of hundred dollar bills secured with a rubber band onto the table next to Gold Chains' drink. "I know I can trust you," he said wryly.

Gold Chains picked up the money and instantly had it counted with the speed of someone very experienced at such a task.

"Ten grand, *ese*. Shit, you know, I think maybe you're smarter than me, huh? I have been working at cooking up this shit for years to earn what I got. And besides the risk of the law, I mean fuck, the chemicals I gotta use could blow me straight to hell if I didn't know my business. You know that, man." Gold Chains' last remark was a statement to the detective rather than a question.

Gold Chains pointed a somewhat wobbling finger at Detective Sloan and continued. "Yeah, you're smarter than me, man. All you gotta do is just make your rounds and pick up your money, eh?"

Gold Chains pulled out a well-concealed pin on the ornately hand-carved wooden cabinet beneath the table. This allowed a panel to slide to the side revealing a safe.

When he slid off his chair to get down into a position where he could work the combination of the safe, his ass hit the floor harder than he expected.

"Chinga tu madre!" he exclaimed in surprise at how hard he'd hit the floor.

Gold Chains spun the combination on the safe concealed inside the cabinet.

"We'll keep your money here, man. It's safe here. Yeah, you're smarter than me," he repeated jovially.

While Gold Chains had his back turned to open the safe, the detective reached into his jacket pocket to remove two soft earplugs, which he inserted into his ears.

Sloan's Glock pistol was chambered for the .40 Smith & Wesson cartridge, and the shock wave and concussion of the two shots he fired into the back of Gold Chain's head rocked the interior of the motor home.

The detective winced slightly as he examined the man's brain tissue splattered all over the wall like some colorful, crazy *Rorschach* inkblot. He then removed his earplugs and put them back into his jacket pocket.

He pushed the near headless corpse aside and began to remove the money from the safe. Sloan was surprised to see that the bills were all in neat packets with paper bank wrappers on them. Some of the wrappers read "Five Thousand" and some "Ten thousand."

He wet his lips reflexively and smiled broadly. He figured there had to be at least three hundred and fifty grand there, maybe more. It was a lot more money than he'd expected.

"Yeah, you're right." he said to the dead man. "I am smarter than you."

Dog Soldiers: Chapter 37

What goes around, comes around.

Anonymous

Detective O'Hare studied the dirt road turnoff and looked for some confirmation that it was the right road to take for his rendezvous with Gold Chains.

He had met with Gold Chains' driver earlier that morning. Julio had given him verbal directions, but he had refused to let him write anything down.

The green cattle guard he saw was at the right mileage point according to his odometer. But that fact inspired less than full confidence since nearly every side road he had passed in the last 45 minutes had one of those green cattle guards. Reluctantly, he decided to turn down the road and see if he could find the next marker.

After two miles he saw it—the rusted-out 55-gallon drum that marked the second turn. In the soft dirt of the unimproved road, he could clearly see the distinctive tracks made by dual rear wheels—the kind of dual wheels he knew were on Gold Chains' motor home.

He knew he was on the right path now. He also noted that the road was more than a bit narrow for the typical motor home vacationer. The tracks were pretty fresh too.

O'Hare reached into his jacket and pulled up on his pistol and then dropped it back into his shoulder holster to make sure it would draw smoothly and without any snagging. He took a deep breath and reminded himself to relax and just flow with things.

As a veteran undercover cop, he knew that if he showed any apprehension at such a meeting, an experienced dealer like Gutierrez would smell the fear on him.

If that happened, Gold Chains wouldn't produce the drugs. No drugs meant that there would be no basis for a warrant. Gold Chains would be back on the road again, and even worse, he'd know he'd been under surveillance.

The dual-wheel tracks led him to the third marker—a red handkerchief tied to a juniper bush. He knew that the next left turn would lead him to the meeting place.

This "road" was even narrower than the first, and he saw where the motor home had uprooted some bushes as it barely scraped by.

He cleared a short hill and saw the white motor home under the trees. He couldn't see other cars around as he pulled up in front of Gold Chains' vehicle. The detective had placed the safety of his pistol in the "off" position before he got out of the car.

"Yo, man! I'm here!" he shouted out. There was no reply, so he took a few steps toward the trailer and shouted out again.

"Come on man!" Mark shouted as he glanced about the area. "It's getting dark and I gotta find my way outta here. Let's get this shit done!"

At that same instant the metallic door of the motor home crashed open violently and a large black man sprang partially out.

The quiet of the desert afternoon was shattered as the man blasted away at Mark with three rapidly aimed shots.

O'Hare had drawn his gun on reflex the instant he heard the sound of the door bust open. Both men had fired almost at the same instant. Mark's second shot crashed into a lamp on the outside of the motor home that sprayed his assailant's face with shards of flying glass.

Then Mark's body collapsed to the ground.

"Motherfucker!" Sloan screamed. "Motherfucker!" he shouted again as he carefully brushed the glass from his face and saw his own blood on his hands.

He glanced at the lifeless body on the ground and then hurriedly went back inside the trailer to the bathroom.

Running water from the sink over his cupped hands, he splashed it into his face and examined in the mirror the slight lacerations he'd sustained.

He looked down and saw his blood dripping in red splatters onto the white porcelain sink.

"Motherfucker!" he repeated as he held a wet towel to his face.

Still holding the towel, Sloan left the bathroom. With his free hand, he picked up the green military body bag and the collapsible shovel he had previously placed inside it. He was still cursing as he went back outside to deal with the body.

What he saw when he stuck his head out the door made his blood freeze. He instantly ducked back into the limited safety of the motor home. Sloan thought nervously for a moment, dropped the towel, and yanked the earplugs from his ears. He could not grasp how it was possible.

O'Hare's body was gone!

Dog Soldiers: Chapter 38

Wounded and bleeding, Detective O'Hare had crawled through the dirt and sand to find himself under a scrub juniper bush. As his consciousness returned, he wasn't sure how he had even gotten there.

He knew he was hit bad, but only then did he realize just how bad. The bullet had collapsed a lung, and he found himself desperately but ineffectually and loudly sucking for air. Blood was running from his mouth, and he felt that he did not have much time to live.

Mark then realized that he'd lost his pistol in his semiconscious effort to crawl away.

He had seen that it was Detective Sloan who had fired on him, and he prayed he could remain alive long enough to kill the man. If he could just hold on just a bit longer, he knew Sloan would be showing up any second to finish the job. He hoped Sloan would come close, because Mark knew that would be his only chance to put a slug into him.

His backup gun was in his ankle holster, but when he bent over to reach for it, a lightning bolt of pain shot through his body, and his vision went to flashing purple lights against a jet black background. He involuntarily jerked his body back up.

O'Hare's vision was darkening as he became shockingly aware that Sloan was now standing directly above him with a gun in his hand.

"What did I tell you, boy?" Sloan asked almost quietly. "Didn't I tell you to drop the case and let me handle it? Didn't I try to get you to do that? It didn't have to be like this, boy, but nah, you just weren't going to let it go, were ya? No, you were the fucking super cop who just had to stay with it."

Sloan leveled the gun at O'Hare's head as the wounded detective's face involuntarily winced and his vision grayed further. But in the haze of that graying vision O'Hare seemed to see an unearthly red light dancing on the black man's chest.

Sloan noticed it, too, and the whites of eyes grew wide against a black face.

The black man heard the muffled, staccato sound of five slugs that spit full-auto from the 9 mm STEN gun. His body then fell like a stone into the dirt.

Mark couldn't understand exactly what had happened, but he smiled as if in a trance before he slipped into the darkness.

Sloan had brought a zippered duffle bag filled with the drug dealer's cash with him when he had come to search for Mark and finish off the wounded cop. He hadn't been willing to leave that kind of money out of his sight for even a moment. Now, while gurgling and dying on the ground, he still incomprehensibly clutched at that canvas bag.

"Here, let me help you with that," Savage's voice said calmly as his boot pushed Sloan's corpse away.

Dog Soldiers: Chapter 39

"All cops are pigs," Savage said aloud as he looked down at Detective Sloan's body, "but some are real swine."

He raised the submachine gun and fired another half-dozen suppressed rounds into the lifeless body of the man he now knew had murdered his friend Luther Brown.

Raising the gun above his head and looking up into a clear, star-filled desert sky, he shouted out to the infinite.

"I told you, man! I'd take it outta their fucking skulls!"

Savage pulled himself together, but he still spoke aloud.

"I told you I would. I know you aren't in that box they planted you in, either, bro. I know you're somewhere out there."

His previous combat experience allowed him to compose himself further from the stark adrenal pump he felt after having to kill another human being. It had been 30-odd years now since he'd had to do that.

"Your daughter, she's going to be taken care of, too. She's going to be somebody just like you said!" Savage again shouted his promise only to the infinite sky.

It surprised him to discover that his lips were trembling and that he was actually feeling moisture run down his face as he made this declaration.

Savage heard a faint gasp come from somewhere! He kicked Sloan's body, but he was a clearly a corpse now. Then he spotted the dying Mark O'Hare beneath a juniper bush. He reflexively spun around in shock and leveled his weapon ready to fire.

"Fuck, man, you're still alive?" Savage said quietly.

He moved over to the bush and bent down to examine O'Hare's injuries. He'd seen enough bullet wounds to know that this guy was pretty much finished. That is, unless a chopper suddenly appeared from nowhere to fly him out to a hospital and a good trauma surgeon. But at this point even such a miracle as that would have to happen real fast.

Fuck, he thought to himself. He could be out of there now, clean and free and with all the cash, if he just left now. Mark was likely as good as dead anyway.

Maybe if Sloan or Mark had a police radio on them he could call in a slick to chopper Mark out. Then the cop might—and only might—have a chance to live.

The money was right there in his hands, and he knew he'd be home free if he just split right then. But he also knew that Mark would die for sure if he did.

Savage unzipped the bag and extracted two bundles of bills in bank wrappers. It was 20 grand. There was a hell of a lot more money in the bag than he expected. But how much?

Dog Soldiers: Chapter 40

Now did you ever have to make up your mind and to let one ride and leave the other behind. Now did you ever have to make up your mind?

John Sebastian

When Savage entered the trailer, he had the STEN submachine gun in his hands at eye level ready to fire. He could not know what to expect once inside.

He saw the body of Gold Chains on the floor with most of his brains sprayed out on the nearby wall. It took only a few moments to search the motor home to assure him that there was no one else inside.

In those few moments he also discovered one of the encrypted cell phones that he had indirectly arranged to come into Gold Chains' hands through Danny Mapes.

It had been Savage's final decoding of the cell phone chatter that allowed him to know that a deal of some sort was going to go down there that night.

But he had only planned to put the meeting under surveillance to confirm that his decryption was correct. He had sure not planned on killing a cop! Even a crooked cop like Sloan being killed was likely to mean some real heat. Paybacks are a bitch, he thought.

Savage could never have dreamt that this night would end up like it had. He couldn't have possibly imagined that Mark would be lying out there in the bushes bleeding to death while he had all that cash money right in his hands. And the black canvas bag full of cash was surprisingly heavy.

Savage knew he had to keep his head and think straight and fast. Everything was on the line at this moment.

What did he owe Mark, anyway? He was a cop and he'd infiltrated and betrayed the club. He really owed this cop nothing.

Yet Savage knew that he was only trying to convince himself of something that he couldn't really accept in his own heart.

But how could he do it? How could he call in help for Mark without seriously risking spending the next 25 years in prison? What were the odds of Mark making it even if he could get him help?

An idea suddenly burst upon him. It was a long shot, he thought, but he'd stay just long enough to give it try.

Savage ran from the motor home and rifled through the clothes of the cop he'd just killed . . . and there it was.

Somehow, Sloan's two-way police radio had miraculously escaped being hit by Savage's gratuitous spray of 9 mm rounds into his corpse.

Returning to the RV, he picked up the cell phone and frantically began yanking drawers out of the kitchen of the motor home. As their contents went spilling and crashing to the floor, he saw what he needed—a roll of electrical tape.

In just a few moments Savage had the speaker of the cell phone taped to the microphone of Sloan's police radio.

The cell phone could only call one number, but the voice-scrambling feature that Horowitz had put into the system could still be activated independently. Savage's scrambled voice would be heard over the cell phone's own speaker as he spoke.

Savage hesitated. The moment he turned on Detective Sloan's radio, he knew some police dispatcher would come on the other end, and there might no turning back if it didn't work. Moreover, if they got there fast enough to save Mark, then they'd have a good chance of getting there fast enough to catch him, too.

He rubbed his sweating palms over the sides of his pants. It was then that Savage felt the slight bulge of the GPS in his front pants pocket. He'd forgotten that he'd had it with him.

Savage wasn't sure what had made him bring the device that night. He didn't need this satellite-based navigational tool since knew this particular area of the Colorado backcountry better than the cops did, maybe better than almost anyone else, for that matter.

But the fact was that he had brought the GPS with him. Now it would allow him to keep his radio communication very brief and yet provide the police dispatcher with the exact location they needed for the helicopter to find Mark quickly.

Any lengthy directions that he might try to give the cops on that radio might fail to get them there soon enough to save Mark. But just as important to Savage was that the cops would be recording the radio communication, and that might give them some evidence later on despite the voice-scrambling feature.

Hell, Savage worried, maybe the cops even had their radios set up to broadcast their locations as soon as they were turned on. The GPS readout that he was now looking at solved most of these problems for him. He pushed the call button on Sloan's radio, and a female voice answered at once.

"Mountain View Police, Unit 67, come back," the voice said in a routine manner.

"Listen carefully," Savage commanded. "You have a detective shot and bleeding to death at these coordinates: 39 degrees and 4 minutes and 19 seconds North, 105 degrees and 24 minutes and 24 seconds West. He has not got much time. Send a medical evacuation helicopter at once."

As he spoke Savage heard his mechanically altered voice at the same time. He hoped that it would not make the cops think that his call was a prank.

"Please identify yourself and the officer at once!" the dispatcher demanded.

"I can't. This radio's batteries won't last. Repeat the coordinates to me *now* and then get moving or he's dead for sure, lady. I'll be staying right here with him."

The dispatcher repeated the coordinates correctly. But when she asked again for the caller's name, his radio was no longer transmitting.

Dog Soldiers: Chapter 41

But please don't throw me into the briar patch.
Briar Rabbit

Savage knew that a rescue helicopter would be zoning in for a landing on his basic coordinates in 10 minutes or so, maybe even less if the air medics were real pros and right on station.

If they didn't get there that fast, Mark's medical records would soon be closed.

Carrying the heavy canvas bag full of cash, Savage found himself nearly out of breath when he arrived at the rented Jeep. He had hidden the Jeep beneath a military surplus desert camouflage netting. Military surplus was always a pretty good bargain. That included the bargain he'd gotten on the Russian first generation night vision equipment he now withdrew from the vehicle.

He tossed the bag of cash into the seat of the Jeep along with the STEN gun. He quickly made sure that the vehicle was still well camouflaged both with the camo netting and some surrounding juniper branches.

He then headed back to the top of the dunes overlooking the motor home.

A low crawl for the last 20 meters brought him to the edge of the dunes. He then heard the chopper blades and held himself perfectly still.

It wasn't likely that the chopper crew would spot him. They had the exact coordinates, and most of the lights of the motor home were still on. That's where their attention would be focused during the landing.

It would be standard operating procedure for the old Huey's landing lights to illuminate the LZ below it.

Just as Savage had anticipated, the brilliant white landing lights of the helicopter came on and illuminated everything around the motor home for about 35 meters.

He had forgotten just how bright those lights were. It seemed almost as if daylight had returned to the entire area around the motor home.

Savage put the daylight filter caps over his night vision equipment and observed the helicopter land amidst a blinding swirl of flying sand and other debris. Three men jumped from the helicopter immediately after it touched the ground.

Without the landing light for illumination, Savage had to remove the daylight filters from the night vision. He studied the grainy green-and-black image that this older Russian-made surplus equipment provided him.

Savage saw that Sloan's body was found first, but after a cursory check, the medic moved on.

As the second man from the chopper entered the motor home, the medic who had checked Sloan's body shined his light toward the juniper bush where Mark had made his last stand. The medic ran to the Mark's body and began working on him.

Good, Savage thought. That man was on the job. Perhaps he had made use of the strong illumination of the helicopter's landing light to survey what was below and had spotted Mark beneath the bush.

The other medic jogged over to his partner's position while a third man from the slick exited with a stretcher. They seemed to work for some time on Mark before they placed him on the stretcher to bring him back to the chopper.

Savage could just make out the line of an IV bag swinging on a stick attached to the stretcher. Well, he thought, maybe Mark was still alive. But then again, Savage had seen more than one medic plunge an IV tube into what was, or would shortly become, just another corpse.

Immediately after Mark's body was placed inside, the chopper took off. Nobody in the landing party stayed behind, and Savage was left alone beneath the stars and the silence of the desert night.

After a few minutes of jogging, Savage reached the Jeep, pulled off the camo netting, and quickly rolled it up, tossing it into the back of the Jeep. He started the motor and then stopped to consider his situation.

The helicopter would have already radioed back that they were coming in with a wounded officer. They would also have reported that they had found another officer dead at the scene and yet a third unidentified body in the motor home. The police would be looking real hard for a cop killer now.

He considered his tactical position. He was in a vehicle with at least a few hundred thousand dollars in cash. He also had in his possession an illegal 9 mm silenced submachine gun that he had used to kill the cop Sloan.

On the plus side, he knew the country here quite well, and he had the night vision to drive away without any lights.

Things could be worse, Savage thought. There were any number of places close by to both bury the cash and dispose of the gun, places where they would never be found.

He knew that he'd better get moving before an entire fleet of police helicopters was buzzing overhead and lighting up the whole countryside looking for him. Savage reasoned that once he'd gotten rid of the money and the gun and had traveled another 20 miles or so on the dirt desert road, there wouldn't be any real evidence with him even if the cops did find him out there.

He also knew that once he'd gotten several miles from the area where he planned on ditching all of the evidence, the best way to "get the hell out of there" would actually be to stay still and dig in right where he was.

Dog Soldiers: Chapter 42

Oh the sisters of mercy they were not departed, not gone. They came to me when I felt that I just could not go on.

Michael Cohen

The vibration of the old Huey Iroquois helicopter and the return of body fluid through the IV in his arm brought Detective Mark O'Hare momentarily back to consciousness.

The next thing he was aware of was being placed on a gurney and wheeled down a hall and seeing the bright white lights on the ceiling. He felt something dangling over his face, and with some reflex that was still left in his body or mind, he grasped at it.

His eyes opened again and he saw that it was a purple string of cloth. He realized a Catholic priest was giving him the last rites. Mark's right hand reached up to the priest and pulled his ear down to his mouth.

"Not dead yet," Mark said in a zombie-like voice.

"My son, you should make your confession to our lord Jesus Christ now," the priest replied.

Dog Soldiers: Chapter 43

Outside in the distance hear the siren's wail. Somebody going to emergency and somebody going to jail...if you find someone who loves you, you better hang on tooth and nail. Because the wolf is always at the door.

G. Fry

The man behind the teller's cage looked out among the swarm of gamblers at the Paradise Casino.

This was something he had done in one casino or another for almost 35 years. How much the town of Las Vegas had changed, he thought.

In the mid-sixties it was run by the mob. It was a "cash cow" for them, and that helped supply their other business interests with cash capital.

Back then, a body would occasionally be found buried out in the desert, but he also knew that back then most of those bodies were never found.

In those days entertainers like Frank Sinatra, Dean Martin, Sammy Davis Jr., and Joey Bishop had their names plastered all over the marquis in front of the Sands, the Flamingo, and the Dunes casinos. The town of Las Vegas had developed a wild and wicked reputation back then, and it was quite happy with that reputation, too.

Once, but long ago, the old man thought.

The last of the mob had left more than 15 years ago. Now the casinos were run on a totally legitimate basis. There was often an IRS man on the premises, and the casinos themselves were now corporations, complete with boards of directors.

This new breed of casino owner had carefully crafted the image of the "new" Las Vegas. Now, Las Vegas was an experience for the whole family, sort of like a giant amusement park.

Mercifully, however, the teller did not have to deal with kids in the casinos, because the law barred them from entering. But he saw them everywhere on the streets. The families would walk down the Strip, whole broods of them, the father dressed in Bermuda shorts with his overweight wife and a digital camera dangling from his neck.

The old man tried to take it all as philosophically as he could, but he still missed the old days. Things just seemed more alive, more dangerous, and a whole lot more exciting back then.

A beautiful young woman approaching his cage brought his thoughts back to the here and now.

She was dressed in an expensive gown, and as young as she was, perhaps 33 or so, she still somehow reminded him of the glamourous old days. She carried herself with a relaxed confidence as she approached his cage. He noticed that she had a full stack of black, $100 chips in her hands, too.

"Cashing out please," she said pleasantly.

'Yes ma'am," he replied.

He began to count the chips. Seeing that they represented a little more than $5,000, he passed some of the chips under an ultraviolet light to make sure they bore the casino's special codes. This was all done routinely and discreetly under the teller's counter and thus out of view of the customer.

Satisfied that the chips were not counterfeit, the teller took out five bundles of hundred dollar bills, each containing one thousand dollars, and began to count them out on the counter.

"One thousand, two thousand, three thousand, four thousand, and five," he said. Then he picked up three hundred dollar bills from the drawer and counted them out in the same manner.

"Five thousand and three hundred dollars," the teller declared. "Would you like for me to call a security officer to escort you, ma'am?"

She returned his smile.

"Thank you, really, but no. I'm staying right here at the hotel."

The woman turned and walked toward the elevators. The elevator doors were already open, and she was thankful to be alone there.

There were 16 floors in the hotel, and she pressed the button for floor number 16.

When the elevator arrived there, she stepped out, walked to room number 1634, and tapped on the door. She saw the peephole in the door momentarily dim as the man behind it looked through.

The door unbolted, and Sharon entered the room to see that Pete Savage had already poured the champagne into two frosted flutes.

"A touch of the bubbly, my love?" Savage asked while smiling broadly. "You look great, sweetie."

Sharon smiled and shook her head as she dropped the money on the bed and on top of a rather sizeable stack of bills already there.

"So, what are we going to do now? I mean, what . . . what's your plan?" she asked Savage plaintively.

"Just like I always said, honey, just have a ball," he replied.

"I counted it again while you were gone," he continued. "Three hundred and sixty five grand all total. Now with your contribution, we have changed just over fifty thousand of it into nice, new bills."

Savage held up a $100 bill to the light and studied the picture of Benjamin Franklin.

"You know, sweetie? Now that we are people of property, we can think in different ways. And I think fifty grand is enough of the cash for us to change over for now. We can leave Vegas whenever we want, or we can stay a bit longer and take in some more of the shows if you like."

Sharon looked at him like a mother talking to a small child who naively believed that he had gotten away with something.

"We haven't stayed in the same casino for more than one night. You never let me buy more than five thousand in chips, and then I gamble with it for a few hours, and then you have me turn right around and cash it all in," she said mockingly.

"Surprising thing is, you're even a little bit ahead on your bets," Savage said cheerfully.

Sharon took Savage's face into her hands and looked him in the eyes. She needed to do that sometimes when she had something important to say.

"Your little Sharon wasn't born yesterday," she continued. "We seem to need to do some money laundering all of a sudden. I wonder why? Well, creepo?"

She gave Savage an exaggerated yet concerned smile as she interrogated him.

"All this beauty, umm, and brains too," he said. "I am a fortunate man indeed."

Sharon shook her head. "I can see that you are absurdly pleased with yourself, aren't you? And you're really not going to explain to me how all this money came into your hot, sweaty little hands, either, are you?"

Her tone made her statement more of an acknowledgement of fact than a question.

Savage tossed the last taste of the imported champagne in his glass down his throat.

"Well, baby, I didn't rob any bank for it, and I didn't kill anybody for it either . . . not for this money I didn't."

Sharon noticed that his last words were spoken with earnest reflection.

"But I did take it from someone who . . . um . . . well, someone who no longer needed it."

"And why do we have to launder the cash like this? " she countered sarcastically.

"Well, actually, baby, the more I think about it, the more I think we really don't. But I thought it best to be prudent."

Savage hadn't had much trouble figuring out what had happened when he found the dead body of Gold Chains next to an empty safe inside the motor home. Still, it was slightly possible that some of the money he'd taken off the late Detective Sloan was originally "buy money" provided by the DEA. If that were the case, then the serial numbers on the bills would have been recorded.

He held Sharon as they both looked out over the traffic and garish lights of the Las Vegas Strip below.

Savage reflected. He and Brown had set out together to make this score, and now Brown was dead and buried. But so was the man who killed him. The fact that he had done that killing did not bother Savage in the least.

He knew that it had be Detective Sloan who killed Gold Chains for the money and who had shot the undercover cop, Mark, a man who had falsely pledged his loyalty to the Dog Soldiers' colors. Savage wondered what that cop's name really was.

Sloan had killed Gold Chains for the cash and then Mark had somehow shown up, and Sloan ambushed him. Savage had seen that Sloan was about to finish Mark off when he decided to fire his weapon.

He also remembered his warning to Brown: "Never trust a cop."

The odds were pretty good that Detective Sloan had also stolen the pistol from his Jeep to kill Brown to set him up for the murder charge.

No, it didn't bother Savage a bit to have killed the man. Perhaps his only regret was that you could only kill a man once.

The security cameras in the casinos were always recording the action on the floor, but the odds were not likely that any such evidence would ever come to light.

Besides, what could the videotape really show except that Sharon had a good amount of cash and that they were together there, but that she was the one gambling. What would come up to motivate anyone to look over hours or days of videotape to find their faces anyway?

Videotape would not show the serial numbers on their bills, either. Once they had passed the money to the teller in the cage, that was that. There was no direct way to connect any previously marked bills with anyone once they were in the hands of the casino. Savage figured that the money he'd taken off Sloan probably was not marked anyway.

He looked at Sharon and sat her down on the bed for a moment.

"Listen, honey. The less you know about this, the better for you. What I can tell you is this: The money was going into a drug deal, and the deal went bad. I happened to be around, so I took it."

"But what about the people whose money it was? Won't they be looking for it? Won't the cops be looking for them too?" Sharon asked anxiously.

"Well, I read in the papers where the Hispanic dealer whose money it was had been shot and killed by the police. And as for the cops, I don't see how they have anything really solid to work with. If they did, I think they would have paid us a visit by now.

"Remember how quick they cut me loose before? It was immediately after arresting me for the killing of that other biker club's president. Before the cops try to hassle or harass me for anything again, I think they will be more careful. We can afford a lot better legal council now too," he joked.

"It was horrible that night they took you away. I just couldn't stand going through that again," Sharon cried.

"You won't have to either, honey, and neither will I," Savage responded sincerely.

"But what if the cops ask me questions? What am I going to say to them?"

"You won't be able to say anything more than you know right now, will you? That puts you out of it, baby. They wouldn't have any real legal basis to go after you for anything.

"Besides, I have a proposal to make, one that can ensure you can't be brought into this, and I sure hope you will go for it, because you know I love you."

Pete Savage reached into the pocket of his faded denim jacket, produced a small jewelry case, and handed it to Sharon. She saw it was a wedding ring.

"I want you to marry me, Sharon."

Sharon's face reflected her astonishment as well as her joy.

"Yes, you slobbering pig. I'll marry you, I'll marry you," she repeated tearfully.

"Great, honey. I know I am not too young of a man anymore, but we've gotten along this far. We've been real happy together. Maybe that's the best thing anyone can ever have—someone who truly loves them and who they love just as much.

"I know we can work it out. I know if we trust each other, love each other, and realize what a precious thing we have together, we can make it work.

"This money will help a lot too. But we won't be stupid, sweetie. We will just spend and invest it little by little, a bit at a time over a period of years."

Sharon and Savage embraced firmly. She continued to cry over the fulfillment of a dream she'd dared not let herself dream until now.

"And by the way, pretty girl, remember—the law cannot compel a wife to testify against her lawful husband."

Sharon pulled her face from his shoulder and looked him in the face, still smiling with joy.

"Well Crepo," she said, " seems you have that figured out."

"Yeah, baby. It's a simple plan alright—we live happily ever after," Savage replied.

Dog Soldier's: Epilogue

"If dogs run free? Then why not we?…or else what must be will be, …and that is all…If dogs run free."
Bob Dylan

Savage didn't like hospitals.

They made him feel a bit spooky, and he went into one only when medical necessity demanded it.

He wasn't bleeding or anything, but he thought he needed to go into this particular hospital just the same.

When Savage entered the room, he saw Mark lying on the hospital bed with a two and a half pound dumb bell in his right hand. He was forcing himself to do curls with the scant weight. It was about all he could do to manage twelve repetitions with it. He had been hospitalized for nearly two months, but he was getting stronger every day.

"Well, still breathing I see," Savage said coolly.

Mark's eyes dilated when he saw Savage enter the room.

"Damn, I didn't ever expect to see you here."

"Yeah, wasn't too sure I'd come myself."

"Why did you?" Mark asked.

The directness of Mark's question took Savage by surprise.

"Maybe . . . well, guess I had to come to say I told you so," Savage taunted.

"And how's that?"

"I read the papers, man," Savage replied innocently. "Seems you were shot by a bad cop, a really bad cop, a Mountain View detective too. I seem to forget his name. I guess you managed to get a few slugs into him, though, since now he's dead. Didn't I tell you some cop was behind this whole deal? Didn't I? I told you that you could end up on the wrong end of his gun, too."

Savage lifted the cover off Mark's hospital food tray. Finding a roll inside, he tore it apart and began to munch on it.

"Help yourself," Mark said as Savage munched on the roll and then took a pat of butter off the hospital food tray.

"Yeah, you warned me," Mark acknowledged.

"Terrible thing when a cop goes bad. Just terrible, now ain't it?" Savage asked.

"It was almost fatal for me, and it *was* fatal for some others," Mark said with a stone-cold seriousness.

"Well you don't look so bad. Shit, I was in this place myself sometime ago, you know."

"Yeah, I know."

Savage scratched his head a moment as he looked directly at Mark. "That detective, what's his name? He was a killer all right. Guess you must have been real lucky getting yourself out of that gunfight out there in the desert, huh?" Savage spoke with a tone of pleasantly mocking admiration.

"A real super cop," he added.

"Was I?" Mark asked.

"Well, you are still here, pal," Savage replied flatly.

"Yeah, I am. Kinda hard for me to figure just how that all came about, though."

"You must have had a guardian angel, I figure," Savage replied.

"Strange you should mention that—angels, I mean. They must have thought I wasn't going to make it, so they gave me the last rites and everything. Priest even took my confession," Mark taunted.

"And what did you confess, pal?"

Mark detected the subtle hint of concern that Savage's voice betrayed.

"Well you know, with a priest, that's like a talk between a lawyer and his client, a legally privileged conversation," Mark said.

"Yeah, I heard about that sort of thing," Savage declared. "I suppose that you are going to walk out of here and go back to wherever you came from and continue to be super cop some-where else?"

Savage's face assumed the exaggerated look of a perplexed child as he continued. "Now that detective—what was his name? I mean the one that shot you? He wanted to hang me out to dry for the murder of that black gang leader, Brown, but somehow he just failed to get that done, didn't he? But then, thanks to your providing me with that ironclad alibi, that bad cop's dead and in the ground himself now. Guess justice is served, huh?" Savage asked.

"Justice? I wonder about that. Maybe so and maybe not. Be-sides, justice . . . well, I figure that's for somebody higher up to judge. I'm just a cop. I'm just supposed to deal in the law."

"You know what I wonder about?" Savage asked.

"What's that?" Mark replied.

"Just how differently things could have all been. I mean sup-pose that weird turn of the runes in my kitchen that night came up with different stones and we never went to your crib to pledge you up? Or, what if you decided you couldn't go on your pledge run that very same night?"

"Oh, but then I forget. That was part of your job to go, was-n't it, cop?"

Savage walked closer to Mark's hospital bed as he contin-ued. "And what if we hadn't gotten into that little gun fracas down at the Torro De Oro and met that county sheriff? In that case I might never have found my old pal Billy Laughing Dog. Remember?"

Mark remained mute. He knew Savage wasn't done with this diatribe yet. Besides, he wanted to know where Savage would finally take him with it.

"Then things would have turned out a lot different for old Billy Laughing Dog too, huh? Then Billy sees us as part of, well, I guess you could call it part of his personal 'vision quest' or something like that. That's why he had to take us onto the reservation for that ceremony with Old Man Santos. Remem-ber what that old man and Billy told us back there, cop? Billy said that we were all there for a purpose—a sacred hoop he called it—and all three of us were part of it. Looks like he was right about that too."

Mark was becoming a bit impatient now. "OK, I remember all that. So what's your point?"

Savage continued as if Mark had not spoken.

"Then, if you think on it, that unscheduled two-day delay we spent on the reservation made all the difference for all three of us. It really upset that crooked detective's plans for both of us.

"No phones or two-way radios where we were on that res," Savage noted. "You didn't count on that. Just no way for you to phone home, huh cop? Just a different turn of the runes, and it all would have been so different for both of us. I might be in prison for murder one now. Hell, who knows? Maybe you would be dead too." Savage finally finished.

"I have my doubts about those runes," Mark commented, "but yeah, I have had time to give it some thought, especially why I am not dead and Detective Sloan is. You do a good job of pretending to have forgotten his name, by the way."

"Well," Savage said calmly, "it's all those years of drug and alcohol abuse. It affects my memory like that, cop."

Mark had now decided that Savage was not going to address him as anything but "cop."

"I guess you must have a guardian angel," Savage repeated just as he heard the door to the hospital room open.

He was quite surprised to see a Catholic priest enter.

The priest held out his hand to Savage, and Pete took it warmly, if a bit awkwardly, and he returned the priest's smile.

"You must be Mr. Savage. I am Father Harris. The doctors tell me your friend is going to be just fine."

Mark thought it was quite comical with the priest in the room. Savage appeared to be totally out of his element and more than a bit uncomfortable. This was definitely the most fun Mark had had since he'd been in the place.

"Yeah, I'll be damned. Looks like he is going to make it just fine. I'll be damned," Savage repeated to the priest.

"Perhaps not, Mr. Savage," the priest replied. "Perhaps not."

CPSIA information can be obtained at www.ICGtesting.com
Printed in the USA
LVOW072032171111

255364LV00001B/153/A